FUNNY FEELINGS

Tarah DeWitt

ST. MARTIN'S GRIFFIN
NEW YORK

First published in the United States by St. Martin's Griffin, an imprint of St. Martin's Publishing Group

FUNNY FEELINGS. Copyright © 2022 by Tarah DeWitt. All rights reserved. Printed in the United States of America. For information, address St. Martin's Publishing Group, 120 Broadway, New York, NY 10271.

www.stmartins.com

Designed by Gabriel Guma

Library of Congress Cataloging-in-Publication Data

Names: DeWitt, Tarah, author.
Title: Funny feelings / Tarah DeWitt.
Description: First St. Martin's Griffin edition. | New York: St. Martin's Griffin, 2023.
Identifiers: LCCN 2023024718 | ISBN 9781250329363 (trade paperback) | ISBN 9781250329370 (ebook)
Subjects: LCGFT: Romance fiction. | Novels.
Classification: LCC PS3604.E9236 F86 2023 | DDC 813/.6—dc23/ eng/20230526
LC record available at https://lccn.loc.gov/2023024718

Our books may be purchased in bulk for promotional, educational, or business use. Please contact your local bookseller or the Macmillan Corporate and Premium Sales Department at 1-800-221-7945, extension 5442, or by email at MacmillanSpecialMarkets@macmillan.com.

First Edition: 2023

10 9 8 7 6 5 4 3 2 1

FUNNY FEELINGS

Also by Tarah DeWitt

The Co-op
Rootbound

THIS BOOK IS DEDICATED TO ALL THE WOMEN WHO'VE EVER BEEN TOLD THAT THEY'RE TOO MUCH. Maybe you're too loud, too crass, too open, too bawdy. You overshare too often, say too many bad words, you're too weird, or too emotional.

To the women who, in their quiet moments, still think back on their social interactions and wonder if they really are too much, if they should feel embarrassed, or ashamed.

You are fucking incredible. You are my people. Don't you dare dilute yourselves to make yourselves more palatable. You are all heart and fire.

PLAYLIST

- "Could Have Been Me," The Struts
- "Shelter from the Storm," Bob Dylan
- "Song 6," George Ezra
- "It's Called: Freefall," Rainbow Kitten Surprise
- "100 Bad Days," AJR
- "Take a Chance on Me," ABBA
- "For Me, It's You," Lo Moon
- "Wait," JP Cooper
- "Fool's Gold," One Direction
- "Run" (Taylor's Version), Taylor Swift ft. Ed Sheeran
- "Stone," Alessia Cara ft. Sebastian Kole
- "Crowded Places," Banks
- "The Sound," The 1975
- "Home," Edward Sharpe & The Magnetic Zeros
- "There She Goes," The La's
- "Only Love Can Hurt Like This," Paloma Faith
- "Alone," Jessie Ware
- "Never Let You Go," Third Eye Blind
- "Simply the Best" (Acoustic), Ben Haynes
- "Rainbow," Kacey Musgraves
- "Stand by Me," Ben E. King
- "Don't Worry Baby," The Brook & The Bluff
- "Just a Cloud Away," Pharrell Williams

AUTHOR'S NOTE

This story felt like an important one for me to write. It was partially inspired by what it felt like to write my first book and have it be out in the world, what it feels like to create anything for anyone else's consumption.

When you put something into the world for others to judge, especially when you hope to entertain and elicit some kind of feeling from them, you know, logically, that it won't be "for" everyone. Creating something that *does* connect to someone, though, is an absolutely irreplaceable feeling. It's an addictive feeling. Writing somehow made me feel more *myself* than ever before, while simultaneously making me more deeply self-conscious than ever before. It was this rush of joy that was often swiftly followed by a dark downhill tumble into Imposter Syndrome.

So, in this particularly low period, I utilized one of my go-to mental health tools: I reached for a way to laugh. When I have blue periods (notice I said blue, not depressed) in life, one of my favorite things to do is to watch stand-up comedy. I put funny stuff in my face. I allow myself to sit in the feelings and acknowledge them, and then I do something good for me: I laugh. Don't get me wrong, I do the other, less sexy work to keep my mental health in check, too, but I partner it with finding a laugh. Because I can tell you this: The *last* thing I want to do when I am feeling low is a mental checklist of my blessings and telling myself that I'm being ungrateful, or that I'm wrong for feeling bad. It only leads to me feeling worse about myself. So instead, I have found that comedy can be a truly healthy coping mechanism for me.

Comedy has educated me, has helped me see a new perspective on many things in my life. Comedy can be so profound.

That being said, something touched me deeply one day when I realized that often the comedians in our lives, not just the comedians on stages, are the ones who are privately struggling the most. It really clicked for me that you should never dismiss a person who is willing to lay a piece of themselves before you, in any art form, even if it's just to make you laugh.

When I received a message on my personal Instagram from a random woman telling me that I should be ashamed to have written such trash, especially when I have two little girls who will undoubtedly grow up to be as foul as me, I knew I needed to write Farley. I set aside 30k+ words in another book and started to write this one.

I wanted to write a woman who has a "foul" mouth, who tells sex stories to the public, who is loud and obnoxious and willing to be self-deprecating and even makes a living out of it. I wanted to write a character that makes silly, stupid jokes, but is deceptively brilliant, driven, and feels deeply.

I wanted to show her softer side.

Because even the most sarcastic, irreverent people in your life have intensely sensitive sides, as well. Trust me on that.

I wanted to write a man who saw all of this and accepted every bit of her, who still struggled with his own mental health, but was deeply self-aware and just as loving.

While the characters in this book work in comedy for a living, I as a writer don't fool myself into thinking that I can write an entire stand-up set. So, this story is probably the least "done-for-laughs" that I've written so far, and a few of the stand-up-specific jokes told are inspired by certain comedians who helped me in some low periods. Of course, I made sure to still make the jokes my own, but I refuse to not at least acknowledge inspiration and give credit where it's due.

BUT, most importantly, the characters in this story have safe harbor in one another, so we see their sensitive sides more than anything else, and it is not entirely comedy focused.

Content warnings for this story:

- Death of a loved one is mentioned in two scenarios, with the deaths happening off page
- Strong language
- Sexually explicit content
- A toxic parent / absentee parent

Just like I won't claim to be a comedian, I'll also never claim to be an expert at mental health. I recognize that my blue periods are not the same as someone else's true medical depression, and I would never seek to advise anyone on how they should handle that, nor would I expect them to solve it with some funny Netflix specials. But this is my homage to a tool that happened to greatly help me.

Lastly, to anyone who decides to take time out of their day to create something for someone else . . . what you do matters. Even if it's silly memes or videos or dances or jokes, or pictures of books with reviews. Even if you don't see a dime from it, just know that it likely brightened someone's day.

FUNNY FEELINGS

ONE

You're only given a little spark of madness. You
mustn't lose it.

—ROBIN WILLIAMS

FARLEY

The diarrhea joke splatters.

The bit was a gamble; I knew this, as most comedians do.
Sometimes you are absolutely certain a bit is going to kill,
and instead it dies a slow, lackluster death: the equivalent of
a whoopee cushion blowing around the room. And then there
are some bits that you think are just fillers, setups for some epic
callback to come later, and *those* are the ones that deliver. I have
learned this from experience, but I still falter at the crowd's response, just slightly, before pressing on.

I suppose drawing an insightful comparison between the
fruits of a misguided dairy binge and the works of Jackson
Pollock was quite possibly Too Much. The only laughs I get

are generally uncomfortable ones. This is why I've prepared another self-deprecating piece to segue into, this one a little more
*"Oh, that poor funny girl, that's just sad. But look! She's joking
about it, so it's okay for me to laugh. Yes, I'm laughing because I can
laugh at her. This is what I paid for."* It is also one of those bits
that's based very closely on my personal truth, so . . . yeah, those
bits tend to murder.

The shitty (*haha*) joke is quickly forgotten, and I'm back
to being a conductor in my masterpiece. It's a symphony of
laughter that I stir and tickle and prod. I work one side of the
room with my sad, weird awkwardness. I spin a tale about
some delightfully aloof (nonexistent) men I've dated and the
ill-begotten adventures of my sex life before my yarn gives way
to an impression that has me lemur-walking to the other side
of the stage, coaxing the room into a legato of laughter.

It's beautiful, glorious, overwhelming; it's warm and it fills
me, fuels me. I feel like a spark that's been begging for tinder,
and this room is one of those old-timey blowers that puffs and
fans me until I'm ablaze.

With each crescendo I think, *I might really make it, I am
f-u-n-n-y.*

The applause is magnanimous. And then it's over.

It crashes.

I fizzle out.

Each step I take toward the side stage has me sliding down
from an adrenaline mountain, and it's jarring and dreadful.

The only thing that helps—my emergency pickax into the
side of that mountain—is Meyer's face. Everything around him
is in disarray. The sound techs are wiping tears from their eyes.
The MC is bent over with her legs crossed tightly around each
other, presumably so she doesn't piddle. Meyer, however, is

as solid and stoic as ever. His arms are crossed, hands tucked into his armpits with his thumbs out. He manages to lift those thumbs toward me in salute—roaring adulation coming from him. His mouth is an underscore across his face, his brow as furrowed as always.

Meyer's steadfast grumpiness is my tether. It lassos me, pulls me back into my own body and into the present rather than in my head where I'm always formulating a comeback or measuring and feeding a crowd. He's not my rock, he's my hammock. He holds and cocoons me in the shade on a summer day. Not that he's actually aware of this.

He's also my manager. My manager, who, incidentally, has also become my closest friend since he came into my life three years ago. Though he's been a figure in my life for a bit longer. Not sure if he's entirely aware of *that,* either, or how much he even truly likes me back, but that's neither here nor there.

He likes to pretend that I annoy him endlessly, but I've caught the corners of those lips turning up on occasion. I get him every single time I do the bit about that guy back in college. The one that slung my knees up to my temples like I was some sort of human sleeping bag he was trying to roll up—*insert enthusiastic charades display of this act*—and, after approximately sixty seconds of uninspired thrusting, yell-whispered in my ear, "I WANT YOU TO ORGASM," to which I responded, terrified, "OKAY?!" with a thumbs up. I then proceeded to do whatever the opposite is of orgasm, as well as prayed to the heavens that I would not let a fart out onto this man and risk this being turned into *his* funny story.

There are only a handful of occasions on which I've been able to get Meyer to crack his best, fullest smile, typically accompanied by a single-syllabled laugh. It's a smile and sound that Rocks. My. World. It has teeth and dimples and crinkled, jovial eyes. The first time I saw it, I audibly gasped before he zapped it away, practically vacuuming it off his face. The date was marked on my calendar and will live on in renown.

There's just something that feels elevated about making another comedian laugh—especially one who was as good and as sharp as Meyer was. As I suspect he still could be. He was big for a while there. He'd been featured on a TV special that showcased a great group of up-and-coming comedians and had even opened for some huge names. His comedy was the kind that cut deceptively deep. His delivery was just a degree away from monotone—almost bored, irreverent, but always surprising. The sort of comedy that hit right away, but the more you went over it in your head, the funnier it became. He didn't require animated facial expressions or anything in the way of physical comedy, and rarely uttered a curse, which only made them more effective when he did. Each bit always flowed seamlessly into the next, like he was telling you one long story.

It was quite the opposite of my brand, come to think of it.

"I told you that joke was shitty," he says with mirth in his icy blue eyes as I turn off my mic and earpiece.

"Did you just make a joke about a joke, Meyer?" His only response is an eye roll as he turns to keep walking with me.

"Where's Hazel?" I ask, searching around for his daughter.

"Marissa took her tonight. She was supposed to write an essay but didn't."

"An essay at ten years old? Jesus, what kind of school do you have her in? I'm on her side."

He sighs tiredly, rolling his eyes some more. "The kind with the best programs and teachers available for Deaf students. The very expensive kind. The kind that I'd like to be able to continue to afford, so let's perhaps avoid the fecal matters in the future."

"*Nice.* Also, you're saying I *should* include more of that '*Awful Offal*' in my set, so she can go back to hanging with us all the time?" I ask, including the headline from the last, most negative review I received. "And, as I've told you repeatedly, Meyer, hot girls have tummy troubles."

He ignores that last part. "I think I've reached my limit on the judgment I can take for having a child at a comedy show featuring you giving a QVC-worthy presentation on your sex toy collection, Jonesy."

"That bit is a long-winded public service announcement. I'm using my platform wisely."

"I've been threatened with CPS twice."

"Only *before* you explained that she couldn't actually *hear* anything I was saying." I hold my hands up in placation.

"Which, as you'll recall, only had them judging harder." And I can't help the genuine laugh that tumbles out of me when he says this, because Hazel *loves* it. She loves to be in a room of laughter despite the lack of sound. And I think that's why I fell in love with her, because she can feel it, can feel that energy around her and is just as addicted to it as I am.

She's also entirely oblivious to any of the complications it causes her father, and he intends to keep it that way, which is maybe why I'm a bit in love with him, too.

"You think me being judged is funny?" He smirks and quirks an eyebrow at me.

"Well, no, but when you get the hang of it. . . ." I shrug, and his expression deepens. We both know the judgment that comes with this line of work, the risks you take with certain material. And while I always strive to push the envelope on social commentary, I refuse to do it at the expense of someone else's humanity. I'd rather tell shitty fart jokes and make fun of myself than be an asshole in the name of being edgy.

But, while I feel like my career is gaining traction, I'm not quite big-time enough to avoid being sucked into the vortex of reading the comments online. This week's Imposter Syndrome is sponsored by one that said, *"I don't care if she is mildly hot when she actually speaks like a human being. I can't stand this obnoxious woman. She complains about the audacity of men, yet (if the shit she blithers on about is any indication) I'd bet money that she has a body count higher than her IQ. This bitch is a train wreck, and if she didn't dance around or scream like a banshee, nothing she said would even be remotely funny."*

Before you ask, yes, the commenter's name was Chad and yes, his profile was a photo menagerie of him in dudebro trucker hats—hiding what is undoubtedly a receding hairline—holding all the flavors of Monster energy drinks and wearing white Oakleys backward on his head. Obviously.

But did I look up what a body count was on Urban Dictionary thanks to Chad? Yes, yes, I did. I'd always assumed that the term was some weird new way of referencing weight. Not so, my dudes.

Then I spiraled into wondering if anyone had ever asked me what my body count was and how I'd answered. Meyer assured me I had not, at least not that he was aware of. And he's basically aware of everything when it comes to me.

I take in the hard lines of his profile now. How the man has time for the gym, I'll never know, but it's clear that he does. Along with whatever super soldier serum he's microdosing, he's also grown so much grayer since I first met him. The stubble around his jawline is peppered with it, and where it was lightly scattered in the hairline surrounding his ears before, it's now flowing throughout. He's thirty-five, so ten years my senior, but he's only just beginning to look it.

It occurs to me that maybe this is *because* of me. Because of this life I've dragged him back into. Being a single dad, with a Deaf daughter and one (adorable-slash-exhausting) comedic client to manage, combined with the hours and the travel that go along with it . . . Well, it must take a toll.

"Do you regret taking me on?" I ask before I can think twice about it.

He stops, head turning to me quickly with a confused pout—as opposed to his normal, simply-just-existing perma-frown. My brain backpedals immediately, and to my own horror, my hand reaches up and pokes him between the eyebrows, into the crease there with a *boop*.

"Because that's too bad if you do. You have all the TV sub-scriptions and know all of my passwords and I'm too attached at this point . . . *Hey, Bob!*" I beeline when I see Bob, my favor-ite security guard. "Looking good, man. Jesus, I swear you have less and less neck each time I see you." I give his bulging biceps a quick squeeze. "Pretty soon you'll only have your personality to blame when women reject you."

"You know your set's over, right?" Bob chuckles at me. "Be-sides, I'm only trying to keep up with Meyer here."

But before I can come up with a snarky response and engage in our standard back-and-forth, Meyer's hand grips my elbow, and I jolt. We spend a large percentage of our lives together, but I take care to avoid too much casual touching when it comes to him. Twice in one night might be a record.

"Farley." I look up at him and then follow his eyes . . . *Holy. Shit.*

Kara Wu is here.

At my show.

The show that just killed.

She's smiling in my direction.

My favorite comedienne, one of the most famous in the country—who has written for wildly successful shows and has hosted *Saturday Night Live*—is here and she is smiling in my direction.

So, naturally, I do the thing. The thing that no cool girl ever does.

I look around to see who she is smiling at.

I close my eyes and sigh through my nose when I realize what I've done, steel myself, and turn back to her with a shaky smile.

When she is in my immediate proximity, I glance back up to Meyer to check that I'm not hallucinating. He just tilts a close-lipped grin down at me, a mildly entertained look in his eyes.

I tear my eyes away and turn back to Kara Wu, still smiling expectantly. I also vaguely register Bob in my peripheral, silently laughing and pulling up his phone to snap a photo.

"Farley?" Kara Wu says.

"Kara Wu?" I squeak. It comes out like an accusation.

She laughs. "Just Kara is fine. Fucking great show." *Ohmygod,* I love her. A mom who doesn't pull her punches with the language in her set and obviously not in regular life, either. Gritty, real, raunchy, and naturally hilarious. I want her to be my friend. I would follow her around and slice grapes for her kids, I would talk on the phone to her, I would . . . I don't know, the talking on the phone thing short-circuited my brain.

Meyer elbows me but speaks on our behalf while I continue

my brain reboot. "Kara. It's been a few years, but I met you a while back." He reaches out to shake her hand.

"Oh, I remember you, alright. Back from when I was touring with Marshall. I wouldn't forget your face." She looks up at him through her lashes with an appreciative grin. Can't blame her; he is a sight worthy of the appreciation. Tall, muscular, perfectly weathered with that salty brown hair and beard. The boy-next-door turned into a devastating man. But, when she maintains her grip on his hand a little too long, a flare of possessiveness runs through me and forces me to reset.

"Thank you. I cannot believe you're here," I say, and punch out my own hand for her to take.

"Well, believe it. I've had you on my radar for some time now, which brings me to this." She gestures for someone to come over. "This is my manager, Clay. Clay, Meyer, you guys talk. I'm going to have a chat with Farley over here." *Oh, God. Okay. It's happening. This is happening.*

We walk a few paces away before she turns to me. "I'm just going to lay my cards on the table here. I want you to open for us on our tour."

Don't burst into violently happy tears, Fee. Don't. Not yet, at least. "Open. For you. For you, and—"

"For me and for Shauna Cooper. We love you, and while there are a few others in the running, you'd be our first pick. I just wanted to feel some things out with you first."

Steely determination crawls through me, my heart hammering in my ears. That's *my* spot. "What do I need to do?"

"Well, to be frank, there's nothing really that you can do in a work aspect. Your sets speak for themselves. You're our first pick because we want the sharpest comedy from start to finish. Not to mention on paper, you'd be the perfect addition to round us out. We have good representation between us in terms of age, sexuality, and ethnicity, and we're not afraid of being dirty. You bring the quirk, I bring the mom factor, Shauna brings the take on the political-social climate. But we're still an all-female comedy tour, and this is still a primarily male-led faction of the entertainment industry. And I want to blow this shit out of the water, Farley. I want all the hype for this. We need to have a killer PR run before this thing starts, which means we need to garner some media attention. Hence, this conversation."

"Okay. I'm okay with that. I'm totally on board." I love the sound of that. The number of Netflix specials featuring male versus female comedians is staggering. I am vibrating with excitement and motivation.

"It also means interviews, potentially, and unfortunately, people getting invested in your *personal* life—a definite. People tend to be more invested in female comedians when they feel like they know, or get, where the jokes are being developed."

Okay . . . I don't love the sound of that. . . .

"I'm not proud of it, but if it gains a bigger following for this and gets us the exposure we deserve, I'm not above a little healthy exploitation."

"I get it. I do," I say, but don't mask the wary tone to my voice.

"We have an idea. Well, *I* have an idea, at least."

"Okay. . . ."

"*Well,* you're young, cute, and nothing garners attention quite like other people's love lives."

I freeze in panic, my tongue swelling in my mouth as I grimace and huff out a laugh, suspecting the direction this is headed for.

"I would just prefer that part of my real life to stay some-what private," I lie. I don't need to explain that what I share on stage is different.

"Understandable. But, even if we don't stoke the flame of publicity beforehand, you do understand that it would be a natural byproduct of taking this on? I have *SNL* booked two months from now, plus Shauna has a movie coming out and will be photographed at every one of Tyson's games un-til the tour starts. . . ." Right. Shauna Cooper is dating Tyson Callahan, star something for the something-somethings of a sport. I don't care who she dates. I care deeply for her comedy, though. . . .

But that's just it, isn't it? I have an investment in her af-ter years of watching her and looking up to her. And even I still know that who she dates is newsworthy and has probably drawn more people to look her up.

"My . . . dating life. It's not actually existent," I admit.

She laughs quickly before smoothing it away. "Oh, believe me, I know. I figured that. Not that you seem undateable or anything. I just know how it is when you're starting out." She smiles warmly before blowing out a breath. "Would you object to being photographed with a celebrity faux-beau? Let some speculative gossip happen?"

"Oh my god, that's a thing? Celebrities really fake attach-ments for publicity?"

She curls an eyebrow my way. Oops, she did *not* like the judgment implied in that tone.

"They do. Most people are willing to do a lot of mildly un-comfortable things when it comes to furthering their ambi-tions."

Touché.

My eyes clash with Meyer's from across the room, and I'm

transported back to months ago when we were working through the material that's in my current set. We stayed up for hours, him helping me work through a bit about the bleakness of Tinder, about how being in stand-up always hinders dating. . . .

"Why do you think it is, though, Meyer? For real. Why do I get ghosted when men find out I'm in comedy?" I asked him, genuinely wondering. Hazel's head laid in my lap while she dozed softly.

"I'm not sure. It seems cliché, but I think men, especially the ones who want to think that they themselves are funny, are intimidated by funny women. Probably because they don't want to risk being source material."

"Well, how interesting. Men are afraid of women being funnier than them, and women are afraid of, oh, I don't know, being oppressed, beaten, raped, or killed by men. But look out! Funny chick here might follow you down an alley and make you chuckle without consent!"

"I think you just found your punch line." He smiled, a megawatt thing that deepened the creases around his eyes and brought my attention to the ones that bracketed his mouth. New ones that I'd never noticed before. A laugh escaped him.

"Oh my god," I said with unfiltered awe before I could even think to stop myself. And, immediately, the smile was gone. He didn't break eye contact, though. A muscle in his jaw rippled.

"Anyone who is pathetic enough to let you being funny—or your career—get in the way of being with you doesn't deserve you, Fee."

Kara's words pluck at my brain in the present, and I remember, "You said you had an idea?"

She looks at her manager and Meyer, waving them over. "I do."

TWO

38 MONTHS AGO

Before you judge a man, walk a mile in his shoes.
After that, who cares? He's a mile away, and you've
got his shoes.

—BILLY CONNOLLY

MEYER

I've stood alone on a stage, sweating under blinding lights, talking about genitalia, politicians, and "your mom" in front of a thousand people before, and I still don't think I've ever been this nervous.

I wipe my palms on my jeans as I look around at a table full of seven-year-old girls staring blankly back at me. It's the first birthday party I've ever thrown for Hazel, and so far, I am patently *not* crushing it. "I'm going to go call and check on the pizzas," I tell them, and I speak it as well as sign it, since her friend Olive is not Deaf.

I walk over to the bar where Lance is throwing me a sympathetic look. "I know, I know. I'm improvising here," I say.

"I seem to recall you being a bit more entertaining when it came to improv." He chuckles as I school my face into a baleful glare. "You're welcome to stay as long as you need. Which doesn't look like it'll be more than fifteen minutes anyway, but open mic doesn't start until eight," he says.

"Just like old times with the heckling, huh?" I sigh. "Thank you again. I didn't think I needed a contingency plan for rain in August."

All Hazel wanted to do was have a few of her new school friends join her at the water park for her birthday. Simple enough. She's at a new school; an excellent school with a bunch of other Deaf students like her, along with many other multilingual kids who know ASL.

She was so excited to have enough friends to warrant a real celebration, and I wanted to make this perfect for her. I did the necessary prep work with the other moms, ensuring they all felt comfortable with their girls under my watch, and I reserved a cabana thing with pizza, cake, ice cream. . . . Hazel wanted to make "favors" after attending another L.A. kid's birthday last year—*I know, I know, I am groaning at myself here, too.* So, after the fever dream that was a foray into the land of Pinterest, we made bags for the girls that contained sunscreen, goggles, mermaid-printed hair ties, and a plethora of snacks that "fit the theme": licorice pool noodles, shark gummies submerged in homemade blue Jell-O cups, seaweed chips. . . . Never did I think—back when I was in my early twenties and being passed a joint backstage at a Dave Chappelle show—that my life would one day involve squeezing melted chocolate onto a Nutter Butter to make it look like a flip-flop but alas, here we are. And most days I love it here.

But then a freak storm came through Los Angeles. A storm

that has been crouching and pissing all over us for three days straight. The disappointment on Hazel's face when she woke up this morning gutted me. I launched into action mode, made calls to bowling alleys and the local indoor mini golf courses, and came up completely empty. Seems it's the one day of the year that they're at capacity. I checked with our condo complex about reserving their activity center, but it's also booked. I even offered a Disneyland day in a fit of desperation, but Hazel's face crumpled.

"*Too many lines on a Saturday, Dad,*" she'd signed. "*And you hate Disneyland.*"

"*I don't hate it. And today's your day, Hazel,*" I signed back with as much forced levity as I could.

"*I just wanted to swim and go on the waterslides with my friends. We've been talking about it all week.*"

"*Don't worry, birthday girl. We're going to have the best day. Let's go get your friends.*"

INSTEAD OF GIVING HER THE best day, I am sinking in something that feels eerily similar to stage fright. I cannot think of what to do.

I'd called Lance, the owner of the comedy club that I first started gigging at—where my pre-writing comedy career was born—and asked if we could come here. I've got a pizza order and cupcakes on the way, but it's not like I can play music and give them a dance party.

"Lance. I am panicking here," I plead.

Lance looks taken aback. "Meyer, all I know is comedy, music, and drinks. Why don't you give them a little stand-up show or something?"

"With what material, man?" Everything I've written since Hazel was born has been for TV shows and scripts. My old material from my stand-up days is not appropriate, nor is it the stuff that a seven-year-old would consider the pinnacle of humor, anyway. Not to mention, any material I do have would have to be combed through and tweaked so that I could make it less "Hearing Funny" and more "Deaf Funny."

So much of stand-up is in the delivery and inflection, even when it's subtle. The dips and tones added to voices are what make a C-level joke funnier. Take that away, and the jokes had better be *sharp* if they're going to be funny in ASL. Plus, the girls definitely wouldn't get (or care about) my nuanced take on the adult single world, which is what my writing and collaborations have been focused on lately.

I turn on the stool when I feel a tap on my shoulder.

"Can we open our favor bags and have the snacks now, Dad? Or do we have to wait until after pizza?" Hazel asks.

"Go ahead, sweetheart. Pizza will be here soon."

She smiles and nods, a good sport as always, but I don't miss the hint of sadness in her expression.

"Fuck," I hiss, before I remember myself, and Olive whips her head my way. Shit. "Sorry, Olive."

"Don't worry. I won't tell my mom," she says out loud.

THE DOOR TO THE CLUB flies open. Bright gray light streams in and silhouettes a figure in the doorway, the sound of the pouring rain hitting the room in a rush.

"Dammit, I thought I locked that." Lance growls. "Jones! The answer, for the millionth time, is NO!"

The figure—Jones, presumably—lets the door slam closed behind her before she straightens and stomps over to us.

"Lance. You old fuckwad! Give me my job back or at *least* let me do my set tonight!"

"*Hey.* I have kids here," I say to the girl—woman—on instinct. Her hair is flattened to her head, dripping water everywhere, like she's just stood in the rain and let it wash over her for hours.

"You have kids at a bar in the middle of the day?" she says to me, scrunching up her nose. "Sounds like a well-placed f-bomb is likely to be the least of their troubles." She whips back over to Lance. "Lance, I apologized. But customers were leaving because everyone else that night tanked. You should be *pleased.* Tickled, even! I made this place good money that night."

"You abandoned the bar to do a set, Farley."

"One: Because you kept denying me my spot or scheduling me on open mic night instead of letting me have it off like I continually asked for. And two: Everyone else was dying up there. When I got up, the laughs were so loud that people started piling in from the streets. It was standing room only in this place! Even without the booze people were laughing, Lance. Give me my spot tonight." She throws me a look that clearly states *the hell you looking at?* before she turns back to Lance. Then, with a blink, she jerks her head back to me, some of her sopping wet hair splattering across her chin with the movement.

"Oh, shit. I know you."

"You do?"

"You're Meyer Harrigan." Amber eyes grow bigger, and her dark brows shoot up.

"How do you know me?" I shake my head, confused. She's too young to recognize me, surely.

"I saw you. A couple of times! Okay, *fine,* not really. But, I have watched every stand-up set you've done that's available on YouTube probably a thousand times."

I grunt an acknowledgment, unsure how else to reply.

"Help me convince him I deserve my spot tonight," she demands, leaning in eagerly.

"Uh, no?" It's like there's a hummingbird in my face, wings beating so rapidly the movement is a blur, its beak needle-like and jabbing at me. The urge to figuratively swat it away is strong.

She looks me up and down, studying my face for something before she glances over my shoulder.

"You don't seem like a drunk or a deadbeat," she says.

"That's nice. You very much *do* seem like you might be on . . . *something.*"

She shakes that off with an eye roll. "If you're not a drunk or a deadbeat, why do you have these kids at a bar for a birthday party?" The party hats I picked up on the way must've clued her in.

"It's a comedy club, not a bar."

She smiles wickedly. "Funny, you'd think it was just a bar with the shit this guy keeps giving me over closing it down for a few minutes to focus on the whole comedy thing." She stabs a thumb toward Lance.

I look over at him and snort. Fell into that one.

Lance reddens but appears resigned as he mutters to his inventory clipboard. I catch movement in my peripheral and spin to see the girl approaching Hazel's table.

"You guys could at least put some music on for them or something."

"Hey. No—" *Shit, what was her name?* "Jones. Stop."

Her steps stutter a bit when she gets over there, pausing as she looks at the side of Daisy's head, noticing her cochlear.

"How you girls doing today?" Jones asks then, as well as

signs, and I suck in a gasp. Each girl sits up in her seat, instantly a little brighter. None respond.

"Whose birthday is it here?" she asks, and signs perfectly again.

Hazel raises her hand. "And how old are you today?" she signs as she speaks.

"*Seven*," Hazel replies.

"Seven?! What the hell are you guys doing sitting in here instead of out celebrating being seven?! Seven puddle jumps, now!"

They're all smiling at her, looking a little awestruck. *"My dad won't like me jumping in puddles,"* Hazel says with a laugh.

Jones glances around, not overselling it, but making it appear like she's searching. She lifts her hands with a smile and signs, *"I don't hear him complaining, do you?"* and all four of them burst out in laughs.

Good God. The woman hit them with a *hearing* joke, within a minute of meeting them, completely unafraid.

Needless to say, we all head to the alley out back and jump in gigantic puddles while the rain pours down, until we are soaked to the bone.

When we head inside for hot pizza, Hazel says, *"I guess I still got to splash around with my friends today after all."* She beams up at me.

Hazel had her first cold when she was just a few weeks old. Suffice it to say she was *pissed* about it. She'd screamed and cried endlessly—great big tears that only led to her being stuffier. I was terrified, alone, and utterly clueless. So, like any standard twenty-six-year-old man, I called my mom. "Mom, I don't know if I can do this."

"You can, Meyer. Keep her elevated. Let her drink as much

as she wants, whenever she wants . . . and have you tried a bath? If the rest of the cord has fallen off all the way, you can try a bath."

I checked her belly, peeling her off of me just enough to see. I couldn't set her down long enough to dress her without her screaming, since my clumsy, shaking hands made the process last way too long. Even diaper changes required bracing.

I drove out and bought her a baby bath as she screamed the entire way to, in, and from the store. The moment I set her in the little tub, against the little bouncy chair, her eyes went wide, and her lips pursed. She hiccupped and kicked her legs, splashing, finally happy.

She's always been a water baby.

"DID I HEAR LANCE CALL you Farley earlier?" I say to Jones when Hazel goes back to the table with her friends.

"You did. It's my name."

"Your name is Farley? You some scion of a comedy dynasty or something?"

She laughs bitterly. "Nope. Just a family name. The only family I have left hates this," she says, gesturing to the club, her finger whipping around in a circle.

She pivots on a heel and goes back to the girls, naturally taking them through what feels like a set designed for them, without the unnecessary theatrics behind it. She doesn't stand up, doesn't use a mic (which is good since it would be pointless in ASL); she just makes it feel like conversation over pizza, but has them all giggling and snorting uncontrollably. She pokes plenty of fun at me, at Lance. She jumps up and leaves for a second before running back in and presenting something to

Hazel. As she takes it in her palms, Farley signs, *"It's a tattoo. Now you can say you got a tattoo for your birthday."*

I feel my eyebrows pinch together. "No tattoos!" I call. Farley ignores me, and since Hazel isn't facing me, she's not privy to my objections. Farley looks at me and grins, eyes twinkling even from a distance.

As her hair dries, I notice that it's got quite a bit of red in it.

She brings Hazel to the sink at the bar and applies the temporary tattoo on the back of her hand while I look on, trying to settle the strange feelings muddling in my chest.

It's a colorful umbrella with flowers raining from the canopy.

Hazel runs over to show the other girls, the tattoo making her smile and flourish her hands as she signs. The manner that she holds her hands and twirls them makes something heavy catch in my throat. She clearly feels proud, and pretty . . . even more special for the way that she communicates in this moment. I'm actually jealous that I didn't think to do it first.

Farley finds a bowl of cherries behind the bar and starts eating them one by one.

"I think this party is a hit after all," she says.

"Thank you." I clear my throat. "You saved it. I'll, um—I'll make sure Lance gives you your mic time tonight."

She frowns and sets down the bowl of cherries. "I didn't do any of this just to make you do that."

"I know. But now I'm genuinely curious. I'll come back and watch your set later."

She eyes me suspiciously, chewing, before her face breaks into a huge smile.

She extends a hand for me to shake. "I've got a funny feeling this is the start of something great."

THREE

NOW

All my life I've wanted to *be* somebody, but I see
now I should have been more specific.

—LILY TOMLIN

FARLEY

"A beer," I announce in a panic to the waiter.

"A *beer*, Jones? You've never ordered a beer in your life,"
Meyer says, exasperated.

I'm so worked up that I can't seem to think of any other
drink in existence, though.

"Miss, what *kind* of beer?" the waiter asks patiently.

"Oh. Alcoholic, please."

"*Jesus*, please excuse her. She'll take whatever sugary lemon
drop thing you serve," Meyer says. The waiter nods and scurries
away. I grimace when Meyer squints at me.

"You mind telling me what's got you so spooked? I'll remind
you that the last time you drank some of my beer you said it

tasted like something that was fermented inside of a belly button," he says with thinly veiled worry.

"Alright." I sigh. "I guess it's only fair to prepare you before Kara and Clay get here." I take a few breaths and spot our waiter returning with our drinks. "Oh, good. One sec."

Mine hits the table, and I promptly toss it back.

When I reach for Meyer's beer next, he lays his palm over mine, gently flattening it to the table to stop me.

"Jones, whatever it is, it's okay. If they're offering you something that requires you leaving . . . me . . . or whatever, and you want to take it . . . Don't feel bad about it. Whatever it is, I promise you, I'll support it."

He doesn't meet my eyes, though. Just keeps his gaze fixed on our hands.

"They want us to date," I blurt, and now his eyes snap up to mine. The band that keeps his expression tightly wound appears to have snapped, his eyes wide and searching.

"For PR. Kara wants me to go on tour and open for her and Shauna Cooper, but they want us to beef up some publicity beforehand. Kara has *SNL*, and Shauna is dating the sportsball guy."

"The three-time Super Bowl champion, Fee."

"Yep, that one."

My breathing becomes audible, and Meyer seems to suddenly realize that his hand still lies over mine a moment before he snaps it back.

"Why would they think that anyone would be interested in us? We're already together all the time," he says.

"Well, I gather that it's *you* who's the real allure. Just like when we got all those comments on Instagram from people assuming you were writing my jokes," I say, and his face pinches, remembering. "Before I took the one picture of the two of us down, of course. And I imagine that curiosity will grow when they announce the tour and their opener. Your name attached to mine . . . publicly . . . will be good, and I guess they want to play off that. I—I don't really know how it will all play out, Meyer, honestly. Kara barely told me the idea before she asked us to meet here."

"She doesn't think I'm too old for you?" he sneers, his lip curling. It's a gut-punch.

"Ten years is hardly scandalous, Meyer." Maybe he thinks I *act* too young for him.

His only response is a snort. His expression grows furious.

"You don't have to do this," I whisper.

His frown deepens in intensity. "Neither do you, Fee."

I want to curl in on myself, noting the apparent disgust on his face. He is *disgusted* that I would ask him to do this with me.

"Fee. You don't have to do this because your talent speaks for itself. It should be enough. I'm fucking pissed that anyone would insinuate otherwise."

Oh.

Kara and Clay arrive then, sliding into the booth with the smooth confidence that comes with knowing you're expected, knowing you're important. The waiter immediately pops over and takes their drink order. *He sure is quick and attentive,* I observe. And then, over his shoulder, I notice two other waiters hovering by the bar, one of them raising his phone to snap a picture of us.

"So, did Farley give you a rundown on what I presented her with?" Kara asks Meyer, before she takes off her bright red frames and begins cleaning them on her Biggie Smalls T-shirt.

"She did," he says, jaw rolling.

"And?" she asks.

"And I think it sounds like pandering bullshit. We both know she is good and that you want her. She doesn't need to do this. And frankly, I think it's beneath you to even ask her to."

I jerk back at the deadly tone he's taken. While I can appreciate the protectiveness and the strong moral stance he's taking, I reject the judgment implied. If it helps us achieve the hype we undoubtedly deserve, then who is he to judge us?

I have my reasons for my initial hesitation, but half the battle in this field is getting your name out there, gaining a following. And unfortunately, women still have extra hills to climb when it comes to stand-up. *He's* a man. How dare he hold me to some arbitrary code when he's got no clue?

Publicity stunts, as a rule, aren't limited to women, either. I may not have been privy to the fact that these stunts might include pairing up for show, but I do know *that,* at least. Plenty of men do it without catching an ounce of flack for it. It's business.

"Who are the other options you're considering for me?" I ask, before Kara can respond, or leave.

She turns her glare away from Meyer at the same time I feel his turn on me. "There are plenty. In fact, there are three I confirmed on the way here that would be up for it, so I'm willing to leave that up to you. There are two of Tyson's teammates who could use a bit of PR to help secure some brand deals and such. The comedian angle is enticing, though, and I happen to know that Declan Crowe is looking for some positive attention."

Meyer shakes his head. "You mean folks don't respond *positively* to heroin and slapping around your girlfriend?" he seethes.

"Allegedly," Clay corrects.

"I'll do it. One of the sportsball guys, though," I say before Meyer can explode.

"Perfect. We'll get plenty of public appearances in that way through football season before the tour starts in spring. Some group photos could be cute and cozy, too," Kara declares with a smile.

"Just *hold on* one fucking second here. I want to understand what the thinking behind suggesting me was in the first place," Meyer chimes in.

"Clay?" Kara prompts.

Clay nods, prepared. "Well, to be honest, you're a bit of an enigma. You disappeared right as you peaked. People in the business know you're still actively writing and managing Farley now, but there's a general curiosity around you when it comes to the public. Once we announce that she's going on tour with us, and start testing out material at smaller venues, she's going to be in the limelight anyway. It would stir up that curiosity more to have you publicly acknowledged by her side. Especially when people connect some of the material," Clay declares.

"If we agree, I'd want outlined specific events and to know when we're going to be photographed. No one just randomly following us around. I have a daughter," Meyer says, pointing a finger on the table with finality.

Guilt rushes through me, hot and sour, at the mention of Hazel. "Meyer, I'll just date a footballer. Really, it's fine."

He only glares at me harder. "Is that what you want?" His nostrils flare out and his eyes dart between mine.

"Well, no, obviously I think it would be easier for you, and I just . . . you know, based on semantics alone, but . . ."

"I'll do it," he says, more to Kara than to me.

"Clay and I can work with Shauna and her manager to get together a schedule and a list," Kara replies, after a cursory glance my way.

Meyer nods, and we all shake hands when we emerge from the booth.

In true comic form, since we are unable to handle things with seriousness for any stretch of time, Kara breaks up the silence with a joke.

"Honestly, *I* tell jokes about my son's baby boners and licking my husband's asshole. So, I exploit the hell out of them. Don't feel bad about putting on a little show. We're going to have the best fucking time, I promise."

I BEAT MEYER TO HIS car so that I can avoid him opening my door for me, but, with my typical subtle grace, I fling the door too hard and myself along with it. He steadies me from behind with his palms on my arms, his breath puffing out against my hair before he lets me go and stomps around to the driver's side.

It's after 10 P.M., but it's a Saturday night and the L.A. traffic behaves accordingly. We sit in bated silence, crawling along the freeway for twenty minutes—and probably just as many yards—before I cave.

"Meyer, I'm sorry. But listen, you really don't need to do this if you don't want to. I don't want to burden you with me any more than I already do."

He responds with a scoff.

"What?! I'm telling you that you're off the hook!" I say.

"I'm not playing into your bullshit, Fee. You're not a burden and you damn well know it. I agreed to do this, so I am doing it. Your success is my success, too, and I want you to have this."

"Then why are you so angry about it? I'm wondering if I should start to get offended."

"Well, wouldn't that be something? I can't even imagine it. *You*, offended?"

"*Meyer*."

"Jones."

"Just tell me what's going through your head. *Please*."

He sighs and hazards a glance my way. "What if you meet someone? I worry that you already spend all your time with Hazel and me as it is. You're young, beautiful, and clearly have a bright future ahead of you."

My brain does me a solid and decides not to process him calling me beautiful, for now. Traditionally, sweet compliments outside of my work make me want to break out in hives. "I am on the verge of officially making it, Meyer. Of positioning myself to do whatever I want in this business. It would be the wrong time for me to meet someone, anyway. Not to mention, I love spending my time with you guys, and you damn well know *that*." *I also just love you, but you don't need to know that. Ever.* "Also, can you stop acting like you're ancient, grandpa? For fuck's sake, Meyer. You're a catch, too, and I don't see you doing anything about it."

"Why would I when I have a hot twentysomething clinging to my side all the time?"

I scoff, repeatedly, lamely, scrounging to respond.

"Jesus, Jones. Listen to yourself. You can't even handle when I *pretend* flirt with you. How are we supposed to date? You don't think they're going to expect us to be flirtatious, at least? Affectionate, even?"

Oh, God.

"I didn't know you were testing me!"

"Well, if we're doing this, you're going to have to commit to the bit here, Jonesy. It's already October, so my guess is that they'll expect this little dog and pony show to begin as early as November if the tour is going to start in March."

"Oh, I'll commit to the bit so hard, don't you fucking worry." I feel my anger growing now, even though I can't pinpoint why. I've conquered too much to get to this point, mastered too much doubt to make it here. Only a little left to go. The least I can do is pretend to date the man I'm probably in love with but keep at arm's length because of the combination of my emotional stuntedness and my respect for our friendship.

"Good, you better, because so am I."

"So hard," I confirm.

"Oh, you don't even *know* how hard, Jones," he says deeply, slowly, deliciously.

My mouth falls open as heat floods my face, and I turn to him. I can just make out his satisfied smile in the darkened car, the lights from the surrounding traffic and the city reflecting and throwing their colors onto his face.

He catches my expression and starts to laugh. Actual rumbling, continuous laughter.

I'm momentarily suspended between shock and indignation before his laugh catches on and I start up, too.

When it dies down, he reaches across the console and grabs my hand. "We're going to be fine, Fee. You deserve to be on that tour and for it to be big. We'll be fine. Let's just . . . be careful around Hazel, though. I don't—I don't want to get her hopes up or confuse her."

The warmth from his hand travels up my arm, through my chest and the rest of me. This makes four times in one night now. And how pathetic is it that I am counting? That my heart feels like it's one of those speed bags being rapidly pummeled just by glimpsing this flirty side.

There's been a *maybe,* before. A few nights here and there where his guard was down and friendly remarks felt heated. One particular drunken night in Vegas that still makes its rounds in my dreams. I can't—don't—trust that it wasn't just me reading into things, though. That it wasn't just emotions amplified by drinks and a clumsy tumble that pressed us close. . . . He'd been such a wreck that night. I shift mental gears away from the memories.

"I'd never, ever do anything to even risk hurting her in any way, Meyer. I promise. And if this gets to be . . . too much . . . we'll stop it. Without question. Deal?"

"Deal."

He takes his hand back, and it requires every ounce of self-preservation in my soul not to grab it and remind him how committed I am to this bit.

HE WAKES ME UP WHEN we pull into the garage at his house. "Jones. We're home."

"Hmm? G'Alright. Thnsfertheride," I slur through a yawn.

"Guest bedroom is set. Marissa got you the bath stuff you like," he grumbles.

"Nah, I'm fine. I'll get home and out of your hair," I reply, forcing the words out clearly and stretching my eyelids open.

"Don't be weird about it, Fee."

"Yeah, okay," I concede.

We head in, as quietly as we can since Marissa, Meyer's all-encompassing, worth-every-penny help, is asleep in her designated room over in the same wing as Hazel. I head to the hallway on the opposite side of the house where the master and guest suite are found.

I'm hyperaware of our steps being in time with each other, of the heat coming off his body as we walk side by side, until we approach the split and need to part ways.

"Night, My."

"Good night, Fee."

FOUR

38 MONTHS AGO

My focus is to forget the pain, mock the
pain, reduce it.

—JIM CARREY

MEYER

"You sure you're up for a late night?" I ask a freshly dried and
changed Hazel. She keeps staring at her hand, so I have to get
her attention and ask a second time.

*"And you're sure you don't mind going to this on your birth-
day?"*

"Dad, stop asking. This will be fun."

WE GET BACK TO THE club and I order Haze a Shirley Temple before we snag a table. As soon as we sit, Farley appears from the
ether, visibly percolating with excitement.

"You weren't full of shit!" she says (and signs), and I sigh
tiredly as Hazel snickers.

"Not full of shit, no. *Please,* though, something tells me to ask you not to sign during your set?"

"No worries, not in my plan tonight. I do hope she'll still have fun, though?" she asks, nodding down to Hazel.

"She's great. She'll be locked into a game on my phone in no time, I'm sure."

"Okay, then." She laughs. The auburn in her long hair brings out the similar color in her eyes. She's changed and dried as well, now wearing a maroon sweater that clings to small curves.

Nope. Absolutely not, you lecher. You are here in a professional capacity only.

She sprints over behind the bar and comes back with a bowl of cherries that she plops down in front of Hazel before flitting back to the stage.

When she approaches the mic, she greets it like a friend, an illuminated smile already in place. . . .

"Good evening, friends. Happy to see you all. . . ."

Her timing is natural. She lets everyone's attention gravitate to her.

"Thanks for spending your Saturday night out here with me. Personally, I find myself trying to avoid going out on Saturdays lately, because I've recently started attending church on Sunday mornings." She pauses, and I gather that there are a few returners, because they let out some laughs and a few *Yeah, right*s.

"No, really! Listen up. This is a hot tip that I'm sharing with you all. . . ." She glances around, gathering some light tension. "If you haven't been, let me clue you in: Modern church is literally—and I mean *every* syllable of this—literally like going to an Ed Sheeran concert, but *for free,* you guys. Listen to 'Castle on the Hill' and tell me that's not the same fucking song they play at any suburban middle-class church every Sunday!"

The laughs immediately start rumbling, whether knowing that this rings true from experience, or just finding her take funny—either way, it resonates.

". . . and, exactly like an Ed Sheeran concert, at church, there's also a bunch of white ladies with their hands in the air. White men with their hands in their pockets, shifting their weight from foot to foot . . . occasionally clapping along." The room erupts at her spot-on impression. I look over and see Hazel laughing brightly.

"The snacks and drinks are oddly small, but even those are free!"

SHE'S A NATURAL.

The way Farley continuously moves her face and body without reservation commands my full attention, as punch lines are exclaimed with a perfectly timed hip pop, or a pose. She hops and hunches and is the closest thing I've witnessed to a human version of Kermit the Frog running around, completely untethered and shameless. The jokes all generally relate back to things that equal the simplest joys in life. . . . Kids and their ability to cut you at the knees with the smallest, most brutally honest assessments. How, with every aging year, food becomes more and more of an all-consuming experience that borders sexual gratification.

The bit that is, without question, the least intellectual, and yet elicits the most tears of laughter and keening wails between bouts, is her impression of a goddamn *bumblebee*.

She starts the bit talking about boredom being a necessary evil, and how it can make you turn your thoughts inside out. She tells everyone about losing her phone for an afternoon and everything she discovered about herself during that introspective time.

"... I realized that I always thought that the buzzing sound came from the bee's mouth, not from its wings. Do you guys realize how *stupid* that is? That I thought that bees were just flying around, sputtering on, yelling '*I'm a beeeeeeee!!!! Lookatme!!! I'm flyyyyyinnnnngggggggg!!!!*'" She roars it so ferociously and animatedly, sprinting back and forth across the stage, that I have to swipe a palm over my face to stifle the stupid grin that wants to surface. When she stops, she polishes off the impression by doing a terrifying squat-and-thrust dance, the most possessed version of a twerk I've ever seen, like a bee pollinating.

Hazel hasn't asked for my phone once, just continues to laugh and beam on.

For being raunchy at times, and flat-out silly in others, Farley's set has the room grinning in ... a strangely *wholesome* way? I gather that it's because of how she manages to tie most of these things into a life philosophy or positive observation.

The transitions between jokes are clunky, and they jump around a bit abruptly, but it's because she is attempting to be a freight train—charging on through the set and leaving it all out on the table for her allotted minutes.

The potential is a palpable thing, but I can't help but think about how exhausting it must be to live in that brain.

Comedians tend to be some of life's most ardent observers. Often, it's born on a personal level. Find a way to laugh at your family's (or your own) dysfunction, and you've somehow found a manageable way of enjoying it, instead of letting it drag you down.

Self-deprecation is also the best way to keep from feeling laughed *at,* after all. Intercept the joke and make it yours first, and it can't hurt you, right? Learn to diminish the pain by reducing it to a laugh.

I admire that reducing, simplifying ability. I *miss* that ability. Though, I have to admit that I don't know if I ever truly had it to begin with. I can write jokes from a more detached, abstract angle now. I can't do it from my soul the way this woman so clearly does.

Constantly searching for that angle can eventually take you out of yourself, though. Out of actually experiencing your life, since you become too preoccupied with observing it and writing it down to make a bit from it.

She heads over to our table when she's done, after raucous applause. The smile on her face broadcasts itself from across the room. I motion for Hazel to get ready to leave as Farley waves her goodbyes and follows us out.

"You guys don't want to stay for the rest?" she asks when we hit the cool night air. If I didn't know the signs and the feelings myself, I'd probably miss the way the corners of her smile and the muscles of her cheeks tremble with the force of keeping up right now.

"Nope, just came to see you. We're heading next door for ice cream." I hand her a water bottle, knowing she needs it. "Let's eat and uh . . . let you settle first and then we can talk about it a bit if you want?" I don't know why I am so possessed with offering this girl advice when she hasn't solicited it. I feel a compulsion to share, though, to make sure she knows that I think she's great, but that I also saw her earlier today . . . as she breathed life into some kids' day.

I want to know why she knows ASL. What her eventual hopes are for her career. If she takes care of herself . . .

Fuck. Calm down.

She tosses back a few gulps and sighs, letting the smile relax even as she eyes me suspiciously.

When everyone is settled into our booth, eating leisurely, I say, "I always found that I needed something else to do with my mouth after a set."

She quirks an eyebrow at me with her spoon paused midair. "Was that a line?"

I cough on my ice cream, choking. "What? No! Oh, fuck. No, no. I swear." I hold up my fingers in a "Scout's Honor" salute. "I meant that I remember how my face would hurt and the only thing that would help it relax would be eating and drinking something."

"Relax," she laughs, "I was fucking with you."

Ah. I scoop up another bite to cover up a smile. Little shit.

"So, constructive criticism first is my speed. Would you mind?" she asks.

"First, you're a liar. No comic wants anything less than resounding accolades," I respond.

"Not me, Meyer Harrigan. I want the criticism first so that I can actually *believe* you when you shower me with the accolades after." She smiles, her chin tilting between us.

I nod, but before I can start, she points to herself with the spoon. "Overly critical father. Can't accept love without a catch."

I sigh at the familiar song and dance. "Listen. You don't have to do that here. You don't owe anyone the quid pro quo on your trauma, or your background. I know it's the standard with comedians—especially with each other because we tend to take those digs when we see them, but I won't do it to you if you don't to me."

She sits back against the booth and cocks her head at me with a pout. "You're surprisingly grumpy in real life."

"Sorry to disappoint."

"I didn't say you disappoint me," she says with enough force to make me pause a beat.

"Alright." I set aside my empty cup as Hazel leans against me, growing visibly tired. "My only suggestion would be to have smoother transitions in a short set like that. You're cramming a lot into a small time window, so you don't have the luxury of pausing and letting the laughs die out from one joke to another. You have to find a way to connect them."

She nods, then smiles sweetly at Hazel before she signs, *"Are you tired? I have more room on my side if you want to come over here and lie down?"* Hazel looks to me for approval before she moves over there and settles.

"I have a hard time coming up with some of the connections because that's just not how my brain works. Each bit comes to me when it happens, I write it down, and I work it into a set. The connecting piece is just . . . me."

"Well, that's where you gotta tweak the truth. Come up with something or use someone else arbitrarily. Like, I don't know . . ." I search my brain for an example. "One time I used my mom. I talked about how she and I were in a fight because of something I'd used in my set. And then I went on to tell them about how she proceeded to say extraordinarily weird shit during that visit, things that I couldn't *not* share with them. Then, when it was time to transition to something else that was a little disjointed, I made up some more dialogue with my mom and used that to connect it."

"I remember that," she says, eyes rounding. And I'm immediately disturbed by how proud I feel to have something to offer. She looks up at the ceiling in contemplation. "God, why didn't I think of that? I could've started by saying my dad dragged me to church, which is true. And then talked about him being worried about my love life. . . . Then I could have even tied it back to him somehow with me not having my phone."

"Yeah. Keep it simple, though," I reply. "Say he didn't have a charger or say it broke on Christmas Day or something. I also thought about how you could say you were at a family event and you could pick out a specific kid that was at this made-up event to talk about those bits where the kids trolled you."

"Mm-hm. Yeah, I don't have any siblings or anything, though. So, no nephews or nieces to speak of. I try to avoid *completely* fabricating things, you know?"

"Totally agree. There has to be some kernel of truth or at least something that *could* be true."

She nods and grabs a napkin and a pen to scribble triumphantly. I can just make out the top of Hazel's side as she breathes steadily, fast asleep.

"How are you so good with kids if you're not around them much?" I ask, curiosity getting the best of me.

"I'm a tutor and an aide at Brooks Elementary for ASL students there. It's only a few days a week, which is why I was bartending at the club until fuck-pig Lance canned me."

"Fuck-pig?" I wince.

She finishes whatever she's writing and grins at it, biting the tip of her thumb with a quiet laugh, too distracted to answer me.

"If you want, I'll see if I can put a good word in with Lance. Get you your job back." Even as I say it, I feel my lips turn down.

"Why do you look like you're holding in a fart?"

"Because I don't know why I just keep offering shit."

"Well, you won't hear me try to turn you down. I am a twenty-three-year-old woman sleeping on a bunk bed so that

I can afford a shared room in L.A. Last night, my bunkmate-slash-roommate, Marissa, woke me up to ask me to move to the top bunk so that she and her boyfriend could have sex in the bottom one."

I grimace. "That lacks ingenuity. I'm sure there's a perfectly good floor there they could've used."

"The floor's the only thing left in that place that *hasn't* been tarnished by their sexcapades. They already broke the toilet seat off the hinges, stained the suede couch, and got the cops called on them the last time they did it in the backyard. . . . Besides, Marissa shares her weird sex stories with me, for material, in exchange."

I laugh through my nose. "Not out there collecting your own weird sex stories, huh?"

"No. You offering to mentor me through some of that, too?" She wags her brows until I rear back, horrified at myself for letting this conversation get away from me, my daughter sleeping next to her lap. Her expression falls.

"You're just . . . don't get me wrong, Jones. You're fine. There's nothing wrong with you, or anything." *Good God, man.*

"Relax, grandpa. I was kidding." *Oh, thank God.* My ego doesn't have legs to stand on for it to be offended by the grandpa remark. She's attractive and bright, but outside of my role as a father, I've been living in a consistent fog. Without knowing how to—or having any desire to—put it into words to this person I just met, I know, undoubtedly, that my fog would only dull her shine.

"I *am* interested in you in a professional capacity, though, Farley. Not that my word is gold or anything, but I at least think you're good enough to make it."

FIVE

NOW

> Life is a tragedy when seen in close-up, but a comedy in long-shot.
>
> —CHARLIE CHAPLIN

FARLEY

I manage to avoid Meyer for five days.

The way I snuck out of his house the morning after deciding our scheme may as well have been the walk of shame, rather than the neurotic panic-run-after-we-touched-four-times that it was.

He avoids me just as much for the first two days before he breaks radio silence with texts that seem innocuous, which I still manage to apply a deeply weird vibe to.

3 Days A.D. (After Decision)

Meyer: Jones, we need to talk.

About what, I wonder? My own stream of consciousness sounds obtuse even to myself.

Is he going to want to *practice?* Jesus, the idea of that makes my cheeks and chest go hot. . . . I'd certainly thought of suggesting it myself, but . . . well, I couldn't claim that my intentions would be entirely innocent. I know myself better than that.

And, no . . . Meyer never fails to remind me that I am "too young."

My mind trips on memories of those few occasions over the years, though. The ones where glances lingered and actions were spurred on by some external force or event; a small collection of maybe-almosts. But outside of those, he's always responded to my sarcastic flirting with abject horror. I've managed to keep the flirting to a minimum since we added the professional element to our relationship. Even when I've slipped he's been tolerant at best. Allowing myself to consider him sharing my attraction would be like pulling on new skin. Like stretching freshly healed chapped lips. Too easy to crack and bleed. Must smother some more instead.

Still. That night feels like a turning point. A decision was made, and there's not going to be some *Sliding Doors* type scenario available to me, for me to see how it will play out, and choose another direction should it all go wrong. If I go through this Decision door, that's that.

3 Days A.D.
4 Missed Calls from Meyer

Meyer: We should probably establish some rules and guidelines, Fee. And I need to talk to you anyway. About after the tour. So, call or text me back, please.

Marissa: Why does Meyer keep asking me if I've talked to you? He seems even more agitated than normal.

4 Days A.D.

Meyer: For real, Jones. Clay just called me, and they want to set up a meeting date. You agreed to this.

Marissa: I have tutoring with Hazel again tonight. What's the update on the weirdness with you and Meyer? I'd like the heads up if I'm stepping into anything between my boss and my closest friend. . . .

5 Days A.D.

Meyer: Dammit, Fee. Are we in sixth grade? We establish being boyfriend and girlfriend and now we don't talk? CALL ME BACK.

I screenshot that latest text because that would make a good bit someday—someday when I can look back and laugh at all of this. In fact, I specifically remember my sixth-grade boyfriend Nick Farnum, and how we entered our deep relationship via origami folded notes passed between friends. And then we never spoke or made eye contact again.

Oh my god, maybe Nick Farnum is out there in the world wondering if we are still together? The stupid thought makes me laugh out loud for the first time in nearly a week. I wonder if Meyer knew it would. If he realized that laughter is always the safest channel for me to communicate freely through. . . .

Day six is a typical Los Angeles October day. Unseasonably

warm; pool weather. I bought Meyer and Hazel's former condo for a screaming deal when he bought their new house, the pool being one of the major selling points. The average age in the complex is, at minimum, 75, so the pool feels like my own private one more days than not.

I do my laps, mentally charting how I need to call Meyer and apologize for acting like this. It's *for* me that he even agreed. It's for a major tour. One that will be filmed, that might even end up on its own special. Plus, he already made it clear that we will have a whole outline, a clear and effective approach. I know that Meyer is too good, too balanced, and too intelligent to do anything that would put either of our careers at risk. The only base we need to cover is our friendship, and me hiding out for days certainly isn't doing that any favors.

I break the surface on a gasp and haul myself out of the water, anxious to get to my phone and rectify the situation. I hit call and start biting my nails, feeling inexplicably on the verge of tears. It starts ringing, and there's an echo—or rather, I hear a secondary ringing. When I turn toward it, I spot Meyer, hanging on the outside of the pool gate with his phone dangling casually from his hand.

"I was just calling to apologize!" I yell out.

He crosses his arms. Waits.

"I'm sorry!" I call, still hovering on the other side of the pool.

His arms remain folded. The only indication that he's heard me is that his chin dips to his neck and pauses before he looks back up in my direction.

I begin my plank walk over his way, continuing down my verbal spiral.

"I just got a little freaked out. I know this is big. And I feel bad that you're even doing this for me when you've already done so much . . .

". . . I also worry about Hazel. But I know that it's not even really my place to worry about her. I know you've got her covered, of course you do. . . ."

I reach the gate and hazard meeting his gaze, only to find a stricken and horrified look.

"What?!" I yelp.

"What in the—your swimsuit . . . ?"

"Oh!" I look down at the one piece with the hairy nipples and beer belly printed on it. "I got this because I kept catching Arthur in 14D staring at me while I swim." I smile, proud of my ingenuity. "No feet for free and all that."

He shakes his head with a sigh. "If anything, you now owe Arthur and me, Farley."

I pull up my palm and pretend to write on it. "Duly noted. Must show boobs in bikini for the period of three months as compensation for damages to spank-banks incurred."

"Always with the last joke." One side of his mouth turns up. "You letting me in or what?"

"Oops. Duh."

As soon as I let him in, he shoves his hands into the pockets of his shorts.

"And Farley, I'll forgive you just about anything if you *talk* to me about it. Just don't disappear on me."

"I know. It was stupid of me. I'm sorry."

"You're forgiven."

I turn and lead him over to my lounge chair.

"Christ. The thing has back hair and an ass crack, Jones!"

I laugh and do a little wiggle.

WE LOUNGE IN THE SUN quietly for a bit, and I revel in the peace. Meyer's the only person I've ever been able to maintain this comfortable silence with. With everyone else it always feels . . . expectant. Which might just be my own projections, but nevertheless, I always feel like I need to do or say something for a laugh with everyone else. I always feel *on*.

"You ready for tomorrow night?" he asks.

"Yep. Sold out again like last week?"

"Yep. Clay and Kara want to meet on Sunday to go over your contract. Obviously our little arrangement is more of an informal understanding, but Clay called to tell me that there will be some separate paperwork for that, too."

"What's it going to say? 'At minimum, we expect to get these photos of you guys grab-assin' on these such occasions'?" I laugh.

"If that's the case, we'll need to negotiate pay or make sure it's you that's required to do the actual grabbing. I'm scarred and traumatized by this thing." He gestures down the length of my swimsuit. "It really doesn't help that it's exactly your flesh tone."

I laugh at his annoyed pout. "So. We've covered the main work points. You mentioned something about guidelines?"

"I did. I think it goes without saying that while we're doing this publicly, we, uhhh, shouldn't be dating other people."

"Aw. I'll break the news to my harem." I smirk when he turns his stern gaze on me. "Obviously I'm kidding. That's easy enough. For me, I mean. I have shockingly few prospects for a woman who openly tells a sexy tale about the time I puked in my purse and carried it around all night." I sigh mournfully.

"Yeah, who's not into that," he deadpans.

"Right? What about you?" I ask, keeping my eyes closed and facing the sun instead of making eye contact.

"What about me?"

"I mean, are you going to be okay keeping yourself off the meat market for the time being?"

"I'll be just fine, Jones. The other rule I think we need to stick to is avoiding the internet drivel. Do what you gotta do in terms of promo stuff, but don't read the articles that will inevitably have shit wrong, don't look at the pictures floating around. We'll do the . . . *things,* but let's avoid that side of it all, please." He looks down at his hands and tugs at a piece of a blister there. "If you cave and do, just . . . don't tell me. I don't want to acknowledge that part if that's okay?"

"Of course, Meyer," I say quietly. He nods in thanks.

"What else did you want to talk to me about? About after the tour?" I ask.

"Oh. No. Nothing. That was just me trying to get you to call me back." He shrugs, oddly—a quick yank of his shoulders. I mimic the gesture, not buying it.

"Oh. Okay?"

"Anyway, I have another thought. And I'm going to need you to put on your grown-up hat for this one," he says.

"But that hat clashes with this swimsuit." I pout.

"*Jones,*" he warns.

"Got it." I mime placing a hat on my head. And then I cut him off before he can speak. "Oh my god. Are you going to ask me to practice?"

"Uhhh. . . ." He blinks slowly and flicks his sunglasses back on.

I blink slowly back and do the same.

He clears his throat. "I don't think I was going to refer to it as *practice,* per se. I just would like to know what you're comfortable with. I want to know where the lines are drawn here. I'm not okay with putting you in any kind of position where you're even slightly less than comfortable."

I swallow. "That's very . . . considerate of you." Thank God we are both wearing sunglasses now. Otherwise I'm certain he could see the back of my skull through my eyes because my brain has vacated the premises.

"This conversation is not exactly cozy for me either, Fee, but let's get it done. Even if it's pretend, I need to know it's consensual," he sighs.

"Jesus. Please don't say *consensual* again."

He slaps his palms on his thighs and gets up to leave.

"I'm sorry!"

"Stop apologizing. Just call me when you're ready to talk."

I scramble up to go after him, the slap-slap of my flip-flops matching the pounding of my heart.

"Wait. I'm ready now. Let's talk now." I grab his upper arms to stall him.

He turns, and my hands fall to my sides.

He shoves his hands into his pockets firmly again. "It's very obvious that you're uncomfortable touching me, and I'm not stating this observation to you to make you feel like you need to correct me. I understand why that is. We have a friendship, plus a working relationship, and I've always respected our collective boundaries so that we don't muddy those lines too much. You've always been . . . openly affectionate, with other people, though, so I just want to make sure I don't make you uncomfortable, okay? That's all I'm saying."

"Okay," is all I can come up with. But then he turns to leave, and I grapple for more time. "Are you hungry?" I ask.

He turns to me. "Very."

AFTER A TERRIBLY SILENT AND awkward car ride, we settle down at a table outside at our favorite sushi restaurant. Meyer's developed the habit of just picking where we go without asking, and I love him more for it. He somehow manages to know what

I want without me having to think and lead and pick all the time. It's a superpower that I pretend is solely used on me. The gesture motivates me to concede some vulnerability.

"Meyer, it's not that I'm uncomfortable touching you. It's that I appreciate you too much to chance making *you* uncomfortable. You . . . you've made your fair share of remarks about my age and all that, and I just have tried to be diligent about not crossing that line with you, in an attempt to be . . . fuck, I don't know—mature?" I pull a mock barfing face.

"Fee, you've called me *grandpa* at least a thousand times."

"I know. But . . . I promise. I won't have a mental breakdown over this if you won't." Might when it's done, but if I think on that too long I'll back out entirely.

"I won't. But this is why I think it'd be good to . . . practice, I guess, so you're not jumping anytime my hands come in contact with you." His big shoulders inch toward his ears, tense.

"I agree."

"Yeah?" The tension wavers a bit.

"Yes. But I don't want to have to specifically define it. Let's not make it too exact here."

"We'll just take it as we go?"

"Exactly."

Our waiter comes then and puts the bowl of spicy edamame on the table. We place our orders, and I dive into the beans when I notice his hand . . .

He's laid out one forearm on the table, palm just slightly turned up. It might be an invitation, but it's not so blatant that it might *not* be, either . . .

I decide to experiment and lay my own forearm down so my hand sits just on the inside of his. We're both still wearing our sunglasses so I can't see his eyes to determine whether he's noticed.

When he doesn't move again, I hold my breath and graze my fingertips along his palm, which he unfurls instantly. I peek at him through my lenses, at his throat bobbing on a swallow and his nostrils slightly twitching. His fingertips rise up just so, smoothing along the underside of my wrist.

I physically *feel* myself wanting to ruin this moment with a dumb remark or—God forbid—a sound effect. Rather than chance it, I shovel back some edamame with my free hand, silently begging for him to be the one to speak first.

"So . . . anything new you plan to add in tomorrow's set?" he asks.

When I lick the spicy garlicky remnants from a finger, his thumb wraps around to push my palm into his. A million synapses begin to buzz, and I will that hand not to sweat.

I search my brain, thoughts ping-ponging around in my head. "Um . . . nothing profound. But I did decide to start trying natural deodorant this week. You know, because the regular stuff just has all kinds of chemicals and is actually pretty toxic. And then it didn't take long for me to decide that I'd just rather die a little bit sooner with some of that crap in my system than gain a few extra years having to *smell* that toxic."

"Always love a good public service announcement."

"Except my sex toy one, of course."

He laughs through his nose as his thumb continues its circles across the top of my hand.

Sushi arrives, and it's not until halfway through the meal that I notice him using his fork to eat instead of the chopsticks. It's also when I notice that he uses that fork with his opposite hand, so he can keep hold of mine with the other.

It's the best lunch of my life.

SIX

34 MONTHS AGO

I used to think the worst thing in life was to end up all alone. It's not. The worst thing in life is ending up with people who make you feel all alone.

—BOBCAT GOLDTHWAIT

MEYER

You wouldn't think that many people would spend Christmas Eve out at a comedy club, but you'd be wrong.

It's packed, overheated, and overflowing with the drunk and jolly. Hazel and I agreed to spend this Christmas Eve with Farley, who has ferreted her way into our lives and asserted herself as a regular fixture.

I don't know how to define our relationship. Friends? I give her occasional advice on her stand-up, but I wouldn't go so far as to say that I'm mentoring her. Friends is accurate, I suppose. The amount of space she takes up in my brain certainly feels friendly.

She and Hazel have a unique bond, and in spite of Farley constantly making jokes about how she should not be allowed to be an influence, I do think she's good for Hazel. She makes her laugh, at least. And, more than that, she helps handle some of the stuff that I muck up—like issues with friend groups, a boy that shoved her down in some game called wallball—and she handles it with *productive* advice. I, on the other hand, was ready to yank her out of school entirely and find a private tutor and not let her out of the house ever again.

Instead, per Fee's instruction, we all met at a park three nights a week and practiced until Hazel kicked the kid's ass handily in wallball. He completely avoids her now.

She helps Hazel with her dance routines—which, I might add, is a highly specialized skill. Not being able to hear a rhythm requires a different kind of memorization and feel. I'd been extremely wary—angry, even—when Farley pushed me to let her join. But the brat has proven me wrong again.

"Just because she can't hear the music doesn't mean she can't feel it, Meyer. She likes to move, and is begging to do this. It's good for her. Let her try," Farley had said.

I'd felt powerless and immediately tired by the mere idea of arguing about it, so I did let her try.

Watching her learn a dance . . . *God,* it makes me sick with pride. Fee makes Hazel want to be brave, and then she follows that up with helping her apply it. They memorize a succession of gestures to indicate the start of a song and then Hazel takes it from there. It's not lost on me that Farley ends up having to memorize the dances herself in order to help Hazel in certain sticky spots.

So, when my parents told me they were headed to Hawaii for Christmas, Hazel asked if we could go to Lance's club and see Farley's last show of the year, and I agreed. Although, as I watch what appears to be a group of frat guys in from out of town, greeting each other with varying degrees of chest bumps and yelling about "Shots!", I wince and wonder if we should have just met up with her afterward.

Farley gets up to do her set and the part of my brain that I usually donkey-kick into submission rears up and catches me off guard when she sidles out under the lights.

She's . . . she's beautiful.

It's not as if I haven't noticed that she's attractive all this time, but there's some force that opens my eyes fully in this moment. Maybe it's the sum of Hazel's recital yesterday, ice skating the day before, and that whole Christmas spirit thing. Whatever it is, I take her in and feel like she's in focus. Like one of those pictures that starts out looking like a multitude of different tiny photos but turns into a portrait when you back away from it.

She's up there, with her little red boots, some band T-shirt I don't recognize, and a skirt that showcases creamy ivory legs. The shadows from the spotlight and the green and red Christmas lights play on the hollows beneath her cheeks, making the lines of her jaw stand out.

I realize that I know the shape of that jaw and how her cheeks pull up when she grins. How she smiles at Hazel and signs—not speaking for my benefit and *only* signing so that I know when it's just between them. How she bites the tip of her thumb when she's excited about something. I know how the corners of her lips try to pull down when she frowns—like the time I firmly declined when she hinted at setting me up with a friend of hers. How the apples of her cheeks make her eyes nearly disappear when she laughs full-out.

Fuck.

I have to tell her. As emotionally suppressed as I am, I know that I have to tell her that I'm developing feelings for her . . . I need to give her a chance to separate herself a bit while not cutting her out of Hazel's life completely. I'll have to find a non-lecherous way to tell her that it would be more appropriate for her to maintain some space, to somehow define the boundaries of this relationship. All of the late-night texts come back to me, and I feel a rush of embarrassment. Embarrassed to be pining after this young woman when she's been nothing but a friend to us. She might jokingly flirt, but that's just her. She *jokes*.

Dammit, Meyer. You can write a script full of comedic foreshadowing, and yet you still didn't see this shit coming?!

And then the other, much tinier voice in my brain has the balls to chime in.

What if she's feeling the same way? What if this is more than friendship, or work, or whatever, to her, too?

I haven't dared to let myself think this way in so long. . . .

BEFORE I KNOW IT THE applause is crackling and I've stared, stupefied, for the entirety of her set. My mouth goes dry as she walks toward us, as she looks . . . *different*, somehow. Almost shy.

"Can we talk later?" I hear my own voice ask.

"Yes." She smiles. Just, yes. No questions or hesitations or worried eyes. Just yes.

I feel myself smile back; a quick, small laugh barks out of me. She smiles bigger but looks down, again being demure. Though that's impossible, because this is the same woman who once told me (in these mere months that I've known her) that she likes to make lists in the Notes app on her phone while she masturbates, in an effort to try and "train her brain to be more *into* organization and structure." She wants organizing to make her excited and is attempting to Pavlov's-dog herself into it. *Shy,* she is not. I clamp my lips down to stifle another laugh at the memory of it.

We start making our way to the exit after I grab Farley's jacket from the spot behind the bar where she keeps it. We say our quick goodbyes to Marissa—tonight's bartender and Fee's friend since elementary, her bunkmate-slash-roommate. Marissa also fluently speaks ASL, and Farley's been trying to get me to hire her for tutoring, which I plan to take her up on soon.

As I help Fee into her coat, that hopeful, optimistic feeling continues to rise. That feeling starts firing off sparklers when she holds my hand on her shoulder and looks up to smile at me briefly.

Thwap.

A towel slaps the back of my head. When I whip around and find Marissa at the end of the bar, she yells over the noise, "Mistletoe!" and points to a spot above us.

Fee's expression pales and she says, "Marissa, stop it!" before she bolts out the door, holding Hazel's hand.

I turn an annoyed glare back at Marissa, but she's already been called over to the frat guys again.

"Jones—" I start, trying to catch up to her.

"Dad?!" she says as I get through the door. I frown as I follow her line of sight and see a man, with her same-colored hair, scowling down at her.

"Dad, what are you doing here?" she asks, her entire demeanor shrinking in on itself.

"I thought I would come convince you to join us for Christmas. When you weren't at your place, I figured I might find you here." He shakes his head, his lip curling in disappointment. "I wonder if you can imagine how proud I am? How *proud* it makes me to see you putting that 720 verbal score to such spectacular use, up there telling stories about shitting yourself and giving blow jobs," he spits.

"Dad, stop," she whispers, voice catching on the words.

"Farley, when are you going to learn that this is not a serious career? Don't you want to contribute something to society? Actually, to hell with society. Don't you want a steady income for yourself? Medical insurance?"

"Dad—I'm . . . I'm actually starting to do pretty well for myself. I've been asked to do shows at quite a few different places around town, and I do—I do work hard." Her voice is a hollow shell of itself. Unrecognizable compared to the sweet, booming cadence of her normal tone.

"You're taking nothing seriously. *Nothing.* I know you're hanging on to some misguided vendetta against me, but I only want what's best for you. This—there's no stability. You're treating your life like a pinball machine. And you're the ball! And who's this?! Some guy you're sleeping with?" He points a finger at me as I tuck Hazel more firmly into my side. "You look like you might have your shit together. Maybe you can talk some sense into her."

"I'm her manager, actually," I say. "Your daughter here is extremely bright and extremely talented. I've been trying to get her on as a client for quite some time. She's going to do big things."

I catch Farley's tear-filled eyes, and the gratitude behind them solidifies it. Fuck it, I'll be a manager. I'll call in every single one of my favors around here and get her name out there, if only to prove this motherfucker wrong. The rising shock and rage on his face is already worth it.

But that also solidifies another thing. I won't—*can't*—abuse that position by getting romantically involved. If I manage her *and* date her, no one will take us seriously when I promote her.

Just like that, the hopeful feeling dies.

A different kind of determination takes its place.

Fee turns toward the car before saying over her shoulder, "Bye, Dad. Merry Christmas."

LATER, BACK AT THE CONDO, she pours herself another glass of wine as she stuffs candy into Hazel's stocking.

"Meyer. I've never . . ." She blows out a breath. "Thank you, for what you did back there for me."

"You're welcome, Jones."

"What did you . . . what did you want to talk to me about?" Her knee bounces anxiously.

"Oh . . . uh—just that. I was going to ask you if you'd want me to manage you."

"You were?"

I shrug. "Yeah."

"Thank you. I can't believe it. But thank you."

Determined to undo whatever damage was done earlier, I tell her, "We'll work out the details later, but I mean it when I tell you that you can make it, Jones. You do this shit for the right reasons. I can tell."

"What are the right reasons?"

"Making people forget that they're sad. Bringing people together by making them laugh. It's actually fucking beautiful, what you do. What the best comedians do, really . . .

"Some people make jokes, and, even when it's about political stuff, since it's in the form of a joke, people actually listen to it.

Even if they don't typically want to hear another side, when it's disguised as a joke, it clicks in your brain even if you don't want it to. You make people see that other angle in *life*. In uncomfortable situations, you make them want to look for something funny about it. You sneak it in on them in your way."

She starts to cry, so I apply that logic and jokingly slide her wineglass away from her.

It works, and she laughs. "Stop," she whispers, swiping at a tear and lightly punching my shoulder. And the whiplash I gave myself earlier in realizing my feelings—and then promptly tucking them away—makes it too hard to hug her right now, so I just rub circles on her back.

"I've never really told you . . . why I stopped. Why I stopped stand-up for a long time . . . ," I say.

She looks up at me, her eyes now a fiery gold from the tears.

"Hazel's mom and I . . . we weren't . . . we weren't together or anything, which was fine with both parties. It had been a one-night stand. But she was a little bit older, so when she found out she was pregnant, I guess she debated even telling me at first, worried I'd have wanted her to have an abortion. I was twenty-five and peaking in stand-up at the time, and if I'm being honest with you, Jones, I probably would have. I would have respected whatever her decision was, of course, but I think if she'd come to me right away, I'd have said something extremely fucking stupid, so I'm really glad she didn't.

"As it was, by the time she told me, it was too late. Also, by that time, I'd already known people in this industry who'd OD'd or developed some kind of addiction. If you don't stay grounded, you get so addicted to that adrenaline—to having that feeling that you get up there—that a lot of us chase it when we're not. So, when I found out about Hazel, I knew it was my sign to stay tethered . . . that I had some real shit to live for off stage, too.

"But then . . . It was a freak thing. After Hazel was born, her mom, Hallie, had what's called an amniotic fluid embolism. It's extremely rare, but within twenty-four hours she was gone." I rush through the rest before I can second-guess myself.

"I felt like—like I couldn't find a single fucking bright spot in that situation, obviously. That this person, who wanted *nothing* from me, but was so excited to be a mom . . . she brought this perfect, beautiful thing into the world, and she didn't even get to enjoy her. Doing it killed her. And I—I know it's not logical, Fee, but I felt like I killed her." I swallow.

"Meyer—"

"No, let me finish, please. Because you need to know why what you do matters. Because it really does." I pause, collecting myself. "I swear, I thought I would never laugh again after that. I thought I didn't deserve to. And I was drowning, clueless when it came to a baby. My mom came out from Ohio and helped me when she could, but the thoughts that I had, Fee . . . God." I feel like I could choke on the shame now, thinking back on it.

"It had been a rough night—day, I don't know. At the time, they were all blurring together. But then I turned on some stand-up. And I laughed. And obviously, now I know she couldn't hear me, but my laughing face made her smile for the first time.

"So, I started writing stuff down that would happen. Stuff that honestly fucking sucked, but that I thought I could find funny if it was happening to someone else. Finding baby shit under my nails, tearing a ligament in my ankle tripping on a play mat. I wrote it down, and eventually was able to turn that into a pilot that I sold.

"So, comedy may have taken me out of my feelings at times, but it helped me make them manageable, too. I made sure whatever I put in front of my face was funny, so I had no other option but to try and laugh. And even when I couldn't laugh, making my pain into something that someone else could laugh at somehow made me feel less lonely."

She looks at me and I look away, having spilled my guts as much as I'm willing to at the moment.

"My mom died," she says. "When I was sixteen. A heart attack. At way too young of an age. And my dad . . . he didn't have any kind of custody agreement or anything. I saw him some years and others I didn't. My mom didn't even use his child support payments. She put every penny from him into an account for me. The woman struggled to put food on the table, and yet still did *everything* for me. She never failed to make my life feel like magic." She smiles as a tear glides down her cheek.

"I'm sure it will come as no surprise that I was a very rambunctious kid. Teachers *hated* me. I just had a really hard time sitting still, was highly emotional. So, my mom had the idea to put me in ASL lessons. She figured if I had to occupy my hands and pay attention, it was the one thing that would help me focus. She was wrong, by the way, but still . . .

"Anyway. I wish you guys could have met her. I wish she could have met Hazel. My mom was just . . . fearless. Bright. Silly. She played with me as a kid and wept with me as a hormonal teen. I know they say you can't be friends with your kids, but she proved that wrong because I would have done anything to make that woman proud of me . . .

"I took every penny that she'd put into that account and gave her an epic service. Bought her the most beautiful casket.

And when they were lowering her into the ground and my world was crumbling before me, a bird crapped on it."

"What?" I ask, trying not to snort at that abrupt turn.

"A goddamn bird crapped on my mother's casket. And I laughed. The worst moment of my life was made just a little less worse by a splatter of shit." She starts laughing maniacally and wiping away tears. "The priest didn't know what to do. He tried to wipe it off with his sleeve and kept apologizing, but I was near pissing myself with laughter because I knew she would have loved it.

"And you know what, Meyer? I've been living my life that way ever since. Looking for the laugh."

SEVEN

NOW

*If you're creating anything at all, it's really danger-
ous to care about what people think.*

—KRISTEN WIIG

FARLEY

"Is it going to get you into trouble if I tell the story about the
PTA ladies?" I ask Meyer from behind my goblin mask. Hazel
decided at the last minute this year that she wants to dress
up and give trick-or-treating a go, and this Halloween store is
down to slim pickings.

He frowns as he places a sad puppy mask on his own face.
"That depends. Which story?"

"*The* story, Meyer. When they invited me to their night
out?"

He grunts. "I don't remember."

"Yes you do. It was like *Girls Gone Wild* meets *The Purge*.
One woman squirted her breast milk at a bouncer, one ended

up with stitches, and that one who always harps on the school lunches ate an impressive thirty-seven dollars' worth of Taco Bell at the end of the night."

"Oh, *that* one."

Hazel comes over then, sporting a white wig and Coke-bottle spectacles.

"Can I be an old woman for Halloween? That way, if anyone yells at me and I don't respond, they'll just think I'm being 'method'?" she signs. This girl's brain never misses.

I look at Meyer, who's slid the sad puppy mask off and is smiling that megawatt smile I rarely get to see. *"Absolutely."*

When she scampers off, I realize I forgot what I was asking. . . .

"Regarding the PTA mom thing," Meyer says (*Oh, that's right*), "do you plan to paint them in an unflattering light?"

"Not on purpose or anything. I mean, I *do* think it speaks to the unrelenting pressure that moms are under for them to cut loose *that* violently, but I personally loved every second of it. I will say, though, that it was made very clear that they only invited me around to try and get the scoop on *you*."

"What do you mean?" he asks as he puts the puppy mask back on the shelf.

I make a "psshhh" sound, and he stops and looks my way.

"No, really? What scoop?"

"You've *got* to know that they all think you're the hot, broody, single dad, Meyer. One of them asked me if you, Marissa, and I were a throuple."

"You're lying."

"I'm not. And once they found out that we're friends, they each pulled up a list that they'd compiled of people to potentially fix you up with."

"*No.*"

"Don't worry. I covered for you. I backpedaled and told them all that I'm secretly in unrequited, passionate, bittersweet love with you and they shut up real quick." *God, Fee, what in good fuck possessed you to say that?!!!* I laugh awkwardly behind the goblin face. I hate it here.

"Ummm. Alright. Well—thank you?" he says, clearing his throat. "Back to your question, though. You won't get me in trouble. Just round the joke out with that part about the unrelenting pressure put on moms."

"Can do."

"Why do you seem more neurotic than normal about offending anyone in your set?" he asks, cocking his head. "You already know that you have to dive in, and you know there's always going to be someone who misunderstands, or someone who *does* understand and just doesn't like it. Since when are you so concerned?"

"I don't know. I guess maybe since Kara is a mom, too, as far as that particular bit goes. And since I want to come up with a lot of fresh material. I kind of feel like I'm . . ." I take a deep breath, reluctant to put a voice to the worry. ". . . blocked, or something. I'm having a hard time coming up with new stuff."

"Well, what are you doing to *get* new stuff?"

"I mean, nothing specific yet. It's only been two weeks since we did all the paperwork, but . . . alright, well." I make an unflattering sound in the back of my throat. "Why do you always have to approach shit with logic, Meyer?"

He laughs. That deep rumbling, tumbling of gravel being poured. "Sorry. But I do have a logic-based solution we could try?"

"Yeah?"

"Yeah. You up for killing two birds with one stone?" He

picks up and sets down things continuously along the shelves. "When we do our practice dating, let's make actual plans and go do things out of the ordinary together. Some level of ridiculousness is bound to take place."

"You mean outside of the staged stuff?"

"Yeah, in addition to the staged stuff, instead of just practicing, let's actually go out together and be a little more intentional about it. No Hazel, no activities centered around work or Hazel, and no hanging around at either of our houses. Let's force ourselves out of the box a bit. Maybe being distracted will make the practicing come easier, too."

"Sure," I say breathily. *Marry me, while you're at it. Let me bake something for you. Give me a pet name and let me massage your palms when you're tense.*

He laughs again. "Having this entire conversation with you in a goblin mask was surprisingly productive."

"Well, I guess that's good, because the damn thing is caught in my hair somehow and I can't get it off," I say as it hangs from the tangled mass in my hair somewhere off to the side.

"Here. Need me to help?"

"Please?"

I turn and take a step backward toward him, until I feel the warmth of him on the backs of my shoulders.

"Your hair worked itself into the knot back here."

I hold my breath as he runs his fingers under pieces of my hair and parts them to the side. He grazes a spot on my neck and the spot feels instantly colder, like I need his hand to return to it immediately.

"Hang on . . . I'm just going to have to tear it," he says as he moves to my front.

His beard scrapes against my ear as I feel him tear the string with his teeth.

"There . . . you're free," he says softly, his voice only inches from my ear.

I could just turn my face and kiss along the column of his neck like this. I could run my tongue up the length of it. I could slip my arm around his middle and slide my hand down slowly, pressing, gliding to the back pocket of his jeans where I could lightly squeeze an ass that rivals America's. . . .

His chest collides with my shoulder on an inhale, and I peek up at him to see that he's staring that same angle down back at me. My eyes leave his furrowed brow and dart to his mouth. To that mouth that's almost too pretty to belong to a man.

"My—" I croak.

He blinks, his thigh bumping into mine as Hazel darts into, then around him before he steps away.

"Let's go!" she signs emphatically. *"I need to find a cardigan and some beige tights, now!"*

He turns back to me, but before he can say anything, I look down at my watch (that I don't actually have on), then I say and sign, *"I'm actually running late to meet Marissa. I'll see you guys tomorrow for trick-or-treating, though."*

"See you! You better dress up!" Hazel replies.

I dart out without chancing another look at Meyer, certain that I'm about to burst into flames.

I'M PULLING INTO THE GROCERY store parking lot when his text comes through.

> **Meyer:** Hazel's headed to her aunt's for a sleepover to-
> night. Want to go to the outdoor movie? Or do you actually
> have plans with Marissa?

I pout a little at being called out, until I remember that we share a Google calendar and I'm anal about adding everything to it, since my brain cannot be trusted to memorize or track plans on its own.

I dial Marissa as I'm walking through the doors to the store. "Hey-o!"

"Meyer asked me on one of his proposed practice dates, and we had a moment earlier, and even though we already talked about this dating thing in vague terms, now he's putting a plan to it and I *know* I'm going to screw everything up and explode and jump on him."

"Hold on. You're going to need to break it down for me a bit here."

I tell her about our lunch. About the touches. About how tightly wound I've become and how I don't see a way to navigate through this without things getting carried away.

"Okay. Don't take this as me being dismissive, but, when's the last time you got some?"

"Myself and I had a beautiful time together just this morning, thank you." An elderly man frowns at me in the produce aisle before I turn away.

"Even though it's often more productive, that's still not the same, friend. It's not the same as the weight of a man or his attention. That push and pull in tension. It's not the same as the heated glances and sweet compliments, the small gestures of affection and long kisses."

I look down at the Brawny man on the paper towels in my hand and sigh mournfully. "Yeah . . ." I place Brawny in the kid's seat facing me. "Jesus, Miss, I'm lusting after cartoon men. I'm a wreck." Also, it's not just lust that I feel for Meyer. It's so much more overwhelming than that.

Unfazed, she asks, "What's the worst that could happen, Fee?"

"I tell him that I love him more than a friend, that he's everything to me, I make him wildly uncomfortable, and it ruins our friendship as well as our working relationship. I lose him and Hazel."

"Damn. Okay. Well, honey, I don't think that will happen. Meyer's hard to read, so I can't say that I think he feels the same way with any kind of confidence, and I'm not some fake friend who would say that to you without knowing. But, there's a chance that that's the case, babe. You just have to decide what you can handle. I also think if he doesn't feel the same, that yes, it might change *your* relationship, but he'd never cut you out of Hazel's life."

"So, go to the movie?"

"Sure. Go to the movie. Make him fall in love with you while you're at it."

"No pressure, huh?"

MEYER'S NEVER BEEN ONE TO compliment my appearance, aside from the odd detached remark here and there. The one thing he has acknowledged before, with a gruff compliment that seemed to surprise even him at the time, are my little red boots.

So, I wear them. More of a red-brown, they're these little patent heels with a squared off toe and a crocodile pattern. They were the first frivolous thing I ever bought for myself when I booked a show that sold actual tickets.

I put on a dress and a leather jacket, and I do everything else in my routine as if it were a normal date. I remove every hair from my body below the neck, slather myself in a variety of creams until I could be used to refract light, and take care with my makeup. And, just like a date with any other man, I act certifiable from the moment Meyer shows up on my doorstep.

"Hello, sir," I say when I open the door. I polish off the weird greeting with a little half butler bow.

"Uh—hey? You having that mental breakdown you promised me you wouldn't have?"

He's in his normal attire. A gray henley and dark jeans, with some brown variation of sneakers. I'm suddenly overcome with the realization that I don't know what his feet look like. What if he has hairy hobbit feet? Or even a millimeter-too-long toenail? I know he's been barefoot around me before because we've all been to the beach and swimming plenty of times. Maybe that's a good sign that there's nothing overly strange about them since I can't bring them to mind? But I've never seen the man wear a flip-flop. Is Meyer a flip-flop man? Why does that idea kind of gross me out? Am I discovering a shallow prejudice of mine? An anti-foot fetish, if you will?

"Jones. Blink, please. You have crazy eyes."

"Sorry!" I look up to find him suppressing a smile.

"You about done?"

"With what?"

"Your one allowed freak-out for the night," he says, shaking his head at me.

I sigh. This is Meyer. At the end of the day, I love him. And I'm a self-indulgent woman that wants to let myself enjoy this, consequences be damned.

I am also the type of woman who buys bags of Mini Cadbury Eggs at Easter time and tells myself I'll ration them throughout the year, though, so perhaps I *should* be a bit more wary of the consequences of my indulgence.

Nah, fuck it.

"You look nice," I say, and the smile that touches my lips is genuine. The returning curve in his soothes my frazzled nerves.

"You look beautiful. I've always liked those boots."

"Thank you," I reply before I turn around and lock up. "I— um, I knew that you did."

His jaw rolls once before he nods over his shoulder to the car. "You ready?"

"Yep."

I SMILE STUPIDLY WHEN HE slides into the car after me, as I inhale his familiar scent. It's pleasant and comforting, clean and seductive. It's petrichor and his fancy sandalwood soap that I know he loves, because he has the same one in a hand soap version in all of the bathrooms at his house. It's him.

When we pull away from the curb we fall into our typical easy small talk. Everything continues along merrily, with him making me laugh and me making him smirk and shake his head, until we get to the amphitheater.

The great sloped lawn is littered with chairs and blankets, all the way down to a massive screen at the front. The perimeter is packed with a variety of food trucks, lines of people snaking their way through the crowd.

"If this were a real date, would you let me pick which food truck to order from?" I ask when we arrive. I'm already cycling through analysis-paralysis on what to order.

He sighs a little and looks over at me. "Humor me, Jones, and try not to start every sentence with some variation of 'if this were real.' Because, fake girlfriend or not, I know you want something from each of them, and I'm all for sampling anything that sounds good right alongside you tonight."

"Oh—okay." I don't know what to make of him this way. So relaxed and . . . almost wistful. But it's that wistfulness that compels me to grab his hand, to want to be reassuring. Of what, I don't know, but that little eclipse of sadness I'm seeing makes me want to squeeze it away. He wraps his big palm around mine and then slides it to link our fingers.

We get up to the window too soon, but when he has to let go of my hand he nudges me in front of him and wraps his arm around my chest, across my collarbone. "This okay?" he asks the top of my head. I nod, my chin bumping into his forearm. We get truffle fries and chocolate sesame shakes to dip them in. Then, when we turn to head over to the next truck, his arm slides to rest over my shoulder as we walk.

"You're surprisingly smooth with this," I say, pointing at the hand.

"It feels surprisingly good."

I realize that I keep expecting sarcasm or a joke, but he's disarming me with his simple and honest replies.

"Have I said thank you yet?" I ask.

"For?"

God, so much. The thought makes me choke up. *For helping me achieve my dreams, for believing in me, for having the coolest kid on the planet. For grounding me, for being a friend.* "For agreeing to this."

"It's not like it's some hardship, Fee." He smiles a crooked smile down at me and lifts a brow. "I will say that I'm going to be more comfortable if you keep making the first move as far as this goes," he adds, nodding to his hand on my shoulder.

I wince when he looks away at the chalkboard menu. Me being in the driver's seat means being the one who might take it too far. . . .

Stop it, Farley. He's an adult. You're also an adult, contrary to popular belief. You're both a part of this agreement. Have faith that the man will let you know if you're making him uncomfortable. He's already had this conversation with you.

My inner voice sounds an awful lot like my therapist when she's rationalizing with me.

We each order a couple of tacos and all the offered sides, pickled red onions, and a green spicy slaw. I decide that there's something deeply sexy about a man that can manipulate his hands in order to carry five cardboard food containers along with a shake. I still end up carrying two, then stand guard over our smorgasbord when we find a spot while Meyer goes to retrieve our chairs.

I see a few people point and talk to him at a distance, obviously recognizing him. He smiles politely but continues walking on. While it's normal for him to be recognized, it's not so much that it's bothersome, and anyone who seems to know him is a fan, so they're always respectful.

When he comes back he gets us set up on a blanket, but I quickly realize that this short dress won't allow me to settle in the low beach chair without some part of my ass being exposed. Meyer picks up on it right away and takes off his henley, revealing a simple white tee.

"Aren't you going to be cold?"

"This is L.A., Jones. I won't be cold until December."

"True," I laugh, and drape the thing across my lap, immediately digging in.

A preview comes on advertising the next season of my favorite show, *Dollar Mountain,* and I clap gleefully. "Oooohhh God, I can't wait," I declare.

Meyer scoffs and shakes his head ruefully. "It's surprising to me that *that's* what you're into."

"What do you mean?"

"I mean I've heard you and Marissa drooling over the men in that show and they all look like they require subtitles to understand despite speaking English."

I bark out a laugh. "Have you even seen it? They don't have accents at all. It's set in Idaho."

"I don't need to see it to know that when those guys say 'boy' it sounds like it ends in an extra syllable."

"What the hell are you talking about, Meyer?"

"BOWAH!" he bellows out the side of his mouth with a deep twang, and I toss my head back and dissolve into a fit of laughter. That sight and sound will live in my head for ages. I wish I could set it for his ringtone, as my alarm for every morning. The first feeling, first laugh of every day could belong to him.

"You're watching it with me soon," I tell him.

He chuckles back. "Fine."

He seems to be watching the previews a little more intensely than normal, staring up at the screen in between impressively large bites.

I'm stealing another glance at him dipping three fries into his shake when I recognize my own voice, in an impression that closely resembles the lead singer of Korn, scream-yelling, *"YOU THINK THAT'S SEXY, BIG MAN?! I'LL SHOW YOU SEXY!!"*

I drop a fry of my own when I turn back to the screen and see myself, blown up to ungodly proportions, crouched and giving aggressive chimpanzee energy. The video quickly pans to Shauna doing a bit, then Kara with her sound bite, with a voice-over giving ticket sales information, dates, and then a shot with a list of locations.

I turn to find Meyer glancing at me expectantly, clearly suppressing a laugh.

"You knew about this?!"

He nods, smiles. I start laughing uncontrollably and move the detritus of my food aside so I can stand and hop up and down. He stands with me.

"Hey! That was you, wasn't it?" a woman behind us calls, pointing up to me. I nod through a smile, my eyes watering. It's such a quick sequence of moments. A matter of seconds, really . . . but it confirms that these years of late nights, the neuroses, the doubt, the emotional rollercoaster of both pride and shame . . . that it's all going to be worth it.

Meyer grabs me and wraps me in a hug, pushing my face into his hard chest. I squeeze him harder back, wanting to crush this moment into my soul, to press my gratitude for him into his very bones.

A few people around us snap some photos occasionally, but we end up getting to watch the movie uninterrupted overall.

It's a little over halfway through *Grease,* after I cackle at Danny's dramatic "Oh Sandy, *Sandy!*" when I notice the goosebumps on Meyer's arms. The sheer giddiness from earlier ignites some weightless bravery in me, so when I give him his henley back, I scoot over to him and sit on his lap, peeling up the corner of the quilt to cover us.

"This okay?" I ask over my shoulder.

"Yes. Yeah." He laughs through his nose. "You're surprisingly smooth with this," he says, repeating my line from earlier, his voice tickling my ear.

"It feels surprisingly good."

EIGHT

NOW

The reason I talk to myself is that I'm the only one whose answers I accept.

—GEORGE CARLIN

MEYER

"You need some friends your own age. Or therapy," Lance says tiredly as he massages his temples behind the bar.

"I've seen a therapist biweekly for eight years, Lance, and I have friends."

"Then why aren't you going to *them* with this Gossip Girl shit? I'm tired, Meyer. I'm sixty-three. I can't pretend to give a shit," he groans.

"I thought you being older and wiser might offer some insight here." Also, I don't know that I can admit this entire thing to my therapist yet. Dr. Dale would have a field day.

"I've been married to the same woman for forty years. And when *I* liked her, *I* asked her out. I kissed her on our first date and I snuck a base on each date after. I didn't keep that shit a secret for years."

I think back to almost a week ago now, to mine and Fee's first date. Letting myself fall into the comfortable touches was one thing. A form of torture, to be sure, but a good one, nonetheless. Like a deep tissue massage from a man built like the Terminator. But the moment the ad came on and I saw her face light up, my heart stuttered to a stop, then shot right back off like a rocket. I had to crush her to me to keep her from seeing the emotion on my face. I know we both felt the weight of that moment for her.

Then there was the lap sitting. I tucked her back against my chest while I worried I'd crush the arm of the chair that I gripped with my free hand, willing myself not to slide it along one of her thighs. I wouldn't trust myself not to slide the pads of my fingers up and down her soft skin, to skate them in circles up to tease the hem of her dress. The comfort and sheer fucking *goodness* of having her there only intensified my physical reaction.

I walked her to her door that night, but before she could ask or even *hint* at asking about kissing, I kissed her goddamn hand like some stuffy Victorian psycho, before promptly turning on my heel and practically speed-walking to my car.

Thank fucking God Hazel ended up wanting to trick-or-treat with friends the following night and saved me from having to see Fee too soon after that.

I groan, letting the embarrassment wash over me again. "God, you're right. I need to back out of this. I can't fucking do it." My face falls to my palms before I take a drink and grimace. "Jesus, man, what is that?"

"Red Apple Pucker. Straight."

"I figured you'd pour me a whiskey or a scotch like literally any other bartender on the planet would."

"A sweet and sour drink for a sweet and sour man," he says with a dead-eyed expression.

"Lance, we're supposed to meet in an hour to go over the pre-tour schedule. I need to figure my shit out."

Lance sighs, the sound coming out heavy and rattled. "I don't know, Meyer. You know I love Fee, but I'm not certain it's good for you to put yourself through this. I get that it's good for her and the tour, and Lord knows the kid has fought for this. But as much as I want it to be great for her, too, there's gotta be an end date, or some kind of limit on the threshold of pain that you can take."

I nod and accidentally take another swig of the drink. "*Shit.* You're right."

I put my heart on the back burner and got through it once before . . . at least, I got myself to a place where it was more important to prioritize our working relationship and not risk anything further. It's obvious that this forced proximity thing is going to flambé all that for me, but I think I could find a way to get through it again when this is done. I'll *have* to find a way to get through it again. "I can't take her away from Hazel, though. I won't do that . . . but I think—I think I can do this if I know there's an end date. If I know I won't be her manager anymore after this, I think I can pull it off." Like running a marathon. One mile at a time. If you know the finish line is there, you take it in bites, reminding yourself that relief is coming.

Relief that, poetically in this little symbolic scenario of mine, will also accompany a great deal of pain.

"Once again, Meyer, I've been with the same woman for forty years and I'm fairly certain that she has slowly incapacitated me to the point that I am completely dependent on her for all of my thoughts and opinions. Therefore, I can only tell you that I guess it's better to be a man with a plan than one without."

"Thanks, Lance."

EVERYONE IS ALREADY SEATED AT a table when I get to the restaurant, a fact that throws me off-kilter a bit since I'm twenty minutes early. Kara, Clay, Shauna, and Fee all laugh heartily at something and that sense of resolve settles in me.

Farley won't need me after this. And I know I'll need to have some modicum of distance, friends or not. The one element of our relationship that can be cut is work. She was already good enough without me, but now she'll have made a name for herself, big enough to leave no room for doubt.

"Hey!" she calls brightly when she sees me, and hops up to give me a quick hug. When she pulls away she doesn't meet my eyes, and I wonder if she's shocked herself with how easily she jumped to do that.

"Hey, everyone." I shake hands and go through the standard greetings around the table.

After the waiter comes over and takes drink orders, Clay wastes no time getting into it.

"So, first things first. I have the NDAs for everyone to sign, along with additional ones for the two of you." He nods to Fee and me. "Take them to your lawyers and send them back at your leisure."

I give it a once-over and don't see anything unexpected, so I nod and set it back in the folder before I slide it off to the side.

"How's the new material coming along?" Shauna asks as she sips on a drink, raising her brows at Fee.

"Good. Pretty good, at least. When do you want me to have some stuff ready to test out by?"

"That's what we wanted to meet about. I split my time between here and the Bay Area, and there are some great smaller clubs up there, too. I thought it would be a fun kind of bonding thing if we planned it all out and took the tour bus together? We could leave from here and head up north, pop into the Valley, the Bay, then head back down the coast until we get back here. Would you be up for that?" Kara asks.

"Wait—how long would we be on this? I don't know that I can be away from home for too much consecutive time," I say before I can think twice about it.

"Well, we'd do it just like a regular tour. You can fly home when you need to and meet up with us when you're available and all that. We just figured it would be fun. If we can, we'll time the Bay Area stuff so we can all go to one of Tyson's games together. Kara and I talked about a series of shows spanning three weeks after the holidays," Shauna adds.

"Yeah, and I'll definitely have to be home during plenty of that, too. I've got three kids, and no nanny. Just my mom—who will probably murder my husband if I don't show up to intervene regularly. She's a fan of periodically boycotting English when he irritates her, and things get tense, to say the least. So you won't be the only one leaving here and there," Kara says.

"That sounds reasonable and fun. I'm in. Do you think you can swing it, My?" Farley asks.

Not just comedy clubs, but brainstorming and hanging with other comedians, constantly laughing and being challenged, shenanigans highly likely. Things I haven't immersed myself in since before Hazel was born.

A tour bus. Sharing a tiny space together on wheels between hotel rooms. No breaks to escape and collect myself. Consistently being expected to be affectionate, and in all likelihood, share a room. And when we come home, I know she'll want to see Hazel almost as much as I will, so we'll have to transition right back into not being affectionate. Which will only get more difficult, seeing as I'm already dying to grab her hand right now.

"Of course."

NINE

NOW

It's a helluva start, being able to recognize what makes you happy.

—LUCILLE BALL

FARLEY

"Okay. Where did Clay say they'd be again?"

"Somewhere outside," Meyer replies with a beleaguered sigh.

"Uh, it's an outdoor mall. So . . . ?" I start scanning the perimeter, looking for the photographers Clay said would be around.

"He didn't exactly draw me a map, Jones." Meyer shakes his head before muttering, *"Shockingly."*

I roll my lips and nod, confirming that the last of Meyer's patience is already slipping with this charade. And we're only three days in.

A day after finalizing paperwork with Clay and "the team,"

we met with him again for a social media consult. To summarize how that meeting went: He spent half of the time telling Meyer and me what to do, how to act, and what to post, and the other half of the time convincing us that just by injecting and circulating photos—so, just flashing our faces—people would be convinced to care.

"So essentially, you persuade people to take an interest in us—in Fee's work—by circulating uninteresting pictures of us doing innocuous things, but then you want us to fire up this interest with more carefully curated photos that require maximum effort in order to look, in fact, effortless. Got it. Makes sense," Meyer had spat.

I decide to try and push onward, and aim for a carefree tone. "Well, My, we're here. And I'm so—"

"Don't apologize. I'm sorry I'm being a dick." He scrubs a palm down his jaw and the sound of it makes my own skin feel like it's being scratched in the process, tingling. "I just . . . don't like knowing I'm being watched, is all."

"I know. I'm—" He glares at me and I hold up my palms in surrender, stopping myself from apologizing. I gesture to the arm attached to the hand shoved in his pocket. "May I?" He nods in response, and I loop my arm through his.

"You have anything you need to shop for? May as well knock out some to-do's if we can?" I ask cheerfully. "Low on your supply of Aspercreme or war memorabilia?"

"War memorabilia?"

"I dunno. Old-guy things? I know I'm reaching here."

But the comedy gods are smiling on me today, despite my sad joke, and with perfect timing, we pass a store for orthotics. I make to drag him in before he hip checks me.

"Need to get a shingles shot?" I try next.

"Ha," he says, but his smile twitches up. "No, but speaking

of that, I got another calendar alert for your birth control shot appointment tomorrow. If you could please put those on your personal calendar that would be ideal. Explaining to Hazel what a series of knife, eggplant, and babyface emojis meant together was not a conversation I was totally prepared for yet."

I wince. "Sorry. I swear I thought I did this time." His reply is a rueful smirk.

"Does my hair look stupid, by the way?" I ask, eager to keep him distracted.

He scrunches his nose with a shrug as he looks over my braids. "Why would it look stupid?"

"I don't know. Kara looked cute with hers. Edgy, even. But I think with *this* face and this long hair that I might just be toeing the sister-wife line." This makes him laugh immediately, a full, rich sound that makes me want to dig in more. "Or at least makes me look like I have two first names, for sure." I grin, and he reaches across his chest to tug on a braid.

"I think you're one of my top three wives, at least," he teases.

I'm near giddy that he's playing along. "Oh, come on, now. I put out the most. I'm your favorite."

"But you also stir up the most trouble."

"I do," I lament. "I do stir up the most trouble."

"We should get you an umbrella while we're here," he pivots, and my face falls into a frown. "What? You're always saying you need to get one whenever you borrow mine."

He sees something in my expression and cocks his head suspiciously. "Why are you weirdly evasive about an umbrella?"

I sigh. "It's dumb."

"You're many things, Jones. Dumb isn't one of them."

We keep walking at a leisurely pace. The day is gray and cool. The kind where you know the sun is just behind the clouds, even if it never peeks through, shadows shifting and moving on the ground continuously.

"My mom always liked to remind me of this story of when I was an early teen, and going through a terrible phase. I was awful to her, Meyer, and she was amazing at handling that kind of thing. She never punished me for my outbursts or emotions even though she probably would've been justified in it. . . .

"Apparently it'd been a special week of me slamming doors, crying, screeching at the drop of a hat." I blow out a sigh. "My dad was getting remarried at the time, and even though we weren't close, I'm sure that was manifesting in negative ways, and yes, I'm sure hormones were involved as well.

"Anyway, I guess on this certain morning I was shrieking from the moment I opened my eyes. And I do remember bits of this. I remember feeling like there was a monster living under my skin, like I was going to rip at the seams, you know? And she just kept acting like everything was fine and normal, calm in the wake of my storm, and it kept making me angrier and angrier at her. At the world, at everything, I guess.

"I should add, we were living in Seattle at the time, and in Seattle it's really only tourists who use umbrellas. It's just, like, a thing. But I always wanted to stand out—I know, crazy, right? So, of course, I always used an umbrella. My mom had given me one for my birthday a few weeks prior to all this, with all these flowers on the underside and tassels. It was bright and moody and I just thought it was the most beautiful thing I owned. But then, on this particular morning, when my mom wouldn't buy into my wretchedness, I looked outside and saw that it was raining. And it was the excuse I needed to just have an absolute fucking meltdown.

"I remember looking over at my mom and noticing how

tired she was, but she just shook her head and quietly chuckled at me, told me I was going to miss my bus."

I think of her face, now, and the tears instantly spill over. How she struggled not to laugh at me, how I made her flinch, shoulders jumping, when I continued my screeching.

Meyer replaces the hand in his pocket with mine—to keep me secured or contained, I suppose—and wipes my face with his sleeve. When he's satisfied, he pulls my hand back out, laces our fingers together, and patiently waits for me to continue.

"I, um . . . I went to leave, and I was so angry I wanted to break something. I remember thinking that. But I didn't actually intend to do it, you know?

"But, I grabbed my umbrella, and in my tantrum I shoved it open so hard that it went completely inside out. All the spindles on one side poked through, and I tried to right it but . . . it was already torn. I burst into tears and my mom was *still* gentle with me. Gentle, but firm. She calmly walked up to me, turned it the correct way, handed it back to me and said, 'Serves you right for getting mad at the rain, Farley.'" I exhale a shaky breath. "When I got home that night I cried some more, and apologized. She told me she forgave me, told me that it was okay, to forgive myself. She said that it was going to be one of our favorite stories one day because that was *me*. I was always going to have big feelings, and it was going to be up to me to make sure they were worth it. She told me I was going to have to learn to wear those feelings proudly, without doing damage to the things or people I love, that I'd only hurt myself in the process if I did." I look back up at Meyer and let my eyes slip along my favorite corners of his face. The ripples of his forehead, the jut of his jaw.

"What happened to the umbrella?" he asks.

"I used it for years, actually. Up until it basically disintegrated outside of Lance's—on the day I met you." I laugh, remembering. "Because of my many shoddy patch-up jobs over the years, it had become a little sloped in one section and would *collect* rain. So when it fully broke, it dumped more water on me than if I'd have not used it in the first place." I smile as another tear falls. "So, yeah. I guess I've always had a thing for umbrellas."

His mouth lifts into a sad smile. "But you don't want a new one?"

I shrug. It doesn't make sense to me either. "I'll just keep borrowing yours, if that's alright."

He nods.

"She sounds like she was pretty great, Fee," he says, swiping his thumb over the back of my hand.

"She was."

He reaches between us with his free hand, stalling midway before he tucks a stray lock of hair behind my ear.

"You know," I start, letting it barrel out of me in a moment of bravery, "she and I watched a few of your sets together. Not in person since I was too young, obviously. But she loved your stuff. She used to call it 'caustic.'"

His eyes widen and his face falls. He visibly struggles with a reply before he comes up with, "That makes me really happy, Fee. Thank you for telling me."

Click.

I blink, then look to my right and see a man with a camera.

So, I smile and wave.

TEN

32 MONTHS AGO

My doctor said, "You're crazy." I said, "I want a second opinion." He said, "You're ugly, too."

—RODNEY DANGERFIELD

FARLEY

My footsteps hit the ground hard enough to reverberate up my shins as I get to the parking lot. I swipe angrily at my phone, which naturally results in it not registering anything, until I slide into my car and slam the door. After a soothing breath, I manage to scroll to Meyer's name and hit call.

"Hey."

"She doesn't fucking like me, Meyer."

"Today was therapy?"

"*See!!!* You know what I'm talking about before I even have to explain!!!"

"I know because it's on the calendar and because I know *you*," he replies, offensively calm.

"And you know how inherently unlikable I am? Respectfully, Meyer, what the fuck?"

He sighs wearily and says something to someone away from the phone.

"Oh, I—I didn't know you were busy. Why would you answer if you're busy with someone?"

"What makes you think she doesn't like you, Jones?" he breezes past my question.

"She didn't laugh or even smile at any of my charming quips. Not one, Meyer."

"Farley. She is your *therapist.* You are not there to entertain her."

"Oh, bullshit. Why would anyone be a therapist if they didn't want to be entertained by other people's issues?"

"Also, this just confirms why therapy is important for you. For me. For all of us, but especially people in this field. Your likability is not directly correlated to how much you make someone laugh."

"First of all, how dare you. Second of all, she wouldn't even meet me halfway, Meyer. She straight up ignored my self-deprecating comments. I even told her that story about how you made fun of my run, and how I didn't think I actually cared, but then I had that dream—"

"Fucking hell, Jones, you performed a bit for her?!"

"I didn't *perform* it. I asked her to translate the Freudian meaning behind the dream. I told her how I was being chased by killers and how they stopped and started laughing at my run. So, I asked, does this just mean that I need to take running lessons, or does it mean that I am so deeply self-conscious that I worry that even a killer would find me lacking-slash-unworthy?"

"Meet me for lunch somewhere. I need to see your face to gauge how serious you are with this shit."

"*Fine!*"

"The kebab place down the street from Lance's in thirty?"

"Fine."

MY STEPS STUTTER AS I take in Meyer at a table on the patio. He's already got an empty platter of hummus in front of him, with my favorite marinated chicken pita half-eaten on another.

"What the hell? You ordered without me?"

He slides his palms down his parted, jean-clad thighs, and something hitches in my lower gut. It's a constant with him lately, yet I'm caught off guard every time. I wish I could at least predict which things would make my stomach dip so I'd know what to avoid. But it's always some tiny mannerism, some passing comment, or even some sound.

Last week, he pumped my gas for me and wiped off my windshield, his shirt riding up to expose a strip of toned torso, a dusting of hair trailing down from his belly button . . . I broke out in a cold sweat.

"I did. I didn't know if this was a professional lunch or not, after all."

"What does that mean?"

"It means that I don't know if I'm still going to be your manager."

"Meyer—" I whine.

"Jones. Listen to me. Therapy is a condition of me working with you. I've got no interest in working with you closely and watching you fade. And you fucking will if you don't learn how to balance your shit out. You can still use your humor, wield that like a whip, but keep your mental health a priority. Which means learning tools from an expert. Like healthy coping mechanisms, how to check in with yourself mentally and emotionally . . . I feel secure in saying this to you, and not at all lame, and I'm not even tempted to make a self-deprecating joke about it *because*—you guessed it—I go to therapy." He folds his arms onto the table and cocks his head, looking me directly in the eyes.

"Well, you're kind of unfunny for a comedian," I retort primly.

His palms go to his heart in mock horror. "Just wait until I tell you about your meeting with a financial advisor and how I plan to make you set up a 401k."

"Lovely. Do you jerk off to Dave Ramsey, too?"

"No, but I did find a podcast of women who talk about NFTs and sometimes I'll have a go at myself to that."

I know he's kidding (I mean, he has to be, right?) but the mental image of Meyer gripping himself in the shower sweeps over me and pulls me under. I can't swallow air back fast enough, my stomach left somewhere above my skull in the atmosphere. *Nononono.* . . .

"Jones? Come on. Jesus, I was kidding. You can't dish it and expect me to not *ever* give it back."

I grab his beer and take a gulp. "Ughh." I shudder. "Fine. But can I please have a different therapist? I felt stupid today."

"Nope. She came highly recommended by mine."

I do an undignified stomp, letting my head fall back on a groan.

"Fine," I say, and I take the rest of his pita.

* * *

I CALL OUT TO MARISSA as soon as I get into the house.

She levers up from her horizontal position on the couch and I squeak. "*Jesus*, I didn't see you there."

"What's up?"

"We have a problem, Miss."

"Oooh. Go on," she says, grabbing the bag of Doritos from the floor by her side.

"No, for real. This isn't a Doritos thing."

"Day wine?"

"Yes, day wine."

Moments later, day wine in hand, we sit side by side on the couch staring at the blank TV.

"I officially have a crush on Meyer," I admit.

"Like, a harmless, 'ha-ha' silly little flirtatious crush, like you've always had?"

I turn to her. "Like a heated, vividly-pictured-him-naked, sharp-longing-from-my-vaginal-soul crush. Throat-thickening desire and pining. Distracting, life-altering. I've kept it under control, but then he sends me to one therapy session and I'm suddenly a little *too* in touch with my feelings if you know what I mean."

She crunches a stack of Doritos while she searches my eyes.

"Okay. . . ." She swallows. "Well . . . I want you to know that this isn't coming from a selfish place—though obviously, it *would* probably be uncomfortable and shitty for me if you started banging the man who is about to be my boss, who is giving me my dream job. . . . But, I also genuinely think that this is not a good idea for *you*."

"Marissa, I know this."

"Well, I just mean that working with Meyer is a great opportunity for your career. If you guys start hooking up, unfortunately, it could lead to you not being taken as seriously.

Then there's Hazel and how any potential fallout would affect her—"

"Miss, I *know*. And Meyer is good for me. He's a good friend and I already know he'll be a good manager. I don't want to ruin that. I just need to figure out how to handle it."

She reaches a finger into her mouth to pick the Dorito gunk from her teeth as she considers.

"Wanna go out?"

I sigh. "I think it's the only thing we can do."

A COUPLE FRIDAYS A MONTH, Lance's club has a DJ instead of any comedians or open mic nights. It's still rarely crowded, and it certainly doesn't turn into a young, hip dance club of any sorts, but that's precisely why we love it.

The crowd is a blend of all ages, and the music is the same. DJ Jerald takes any and all requests, treating us all to a journey through time and sound every night that he works.

We strut through the doors to "Don't Stop Believing" and shimmy directly over to the bar. I've proudly managed to wrap myself in a shirt that looked like a scarf when I began the application process, and I start perusing for a man that looks both worthy and capable of taking it off later. Prospects appear to be low so far, but it's early yet.

Marissa presses a tequila drink into my hand because she knows what tonight is about, and because she is a good and supportive wingwoman.

She is a wingwoman who is being diverted over to a man at the end of the bar smiling her way.

She is a wingwoman who appears to be ditching me. . . .

Marissa is a shit wingwoman, apparently.

I fold myself onto the stool and blow out a breath, wondering if I should just say fuck it already and unbutton these jeans. They look damn good but are the kind that require a process of jumping and using gravity and momentum to get them up in the first place, and then lying down and attempting to flatten myself to Gumby proportions in order to get them buttoned.

Lance ambles over as I slurp the last drop of my drink audibly. "Tequila soda?" he asks.

"Sure? I think so?"

DJ Jerald starts playing "Lover" and I make a cynical noise from the depths of my sinuses as Lance slides me my second drink.

"Yikes. Not a Swiftie, I take it?"

I turn to my left just as the observer sits, and I can't help the smile that bends my lips. He's got the kind of cute, guileless look that I always go for. Warm brown eyes and fluffy blond hair with a slight curl to it. A Labradoodle in human form.

"Of course I am. There's a Swiftie song for everyone."

"Oh, so it's just *this* song, then." He grins, dipping his head conspiratorially. "Care to let me take a crack at what yours is?"

I shrug. This isn't the worst way I've been hit on before. I'm intrigued.

"It's gotta be 'Me!,' no?" he asks. He's wearing one of those shirts that's like six inches longer than a normal one—a style, apparently—one that I know Meyer hates. He's also wearing a chain necklace. Another prejudice of My's. And goddamn it, I'm thinking about Meyer while this objectively attractive man is flirting with me.

"You nailed it," I lie. He doesn't need to know that I coincidentally do have a Swift-specific song of the moment, nor does he need to know what it actually is. The only reason one even surfaces in my mind is because I heard it play the other day at the beach, watching Meyer fly a kite with Hazel for the first time. It's encapsulated into my memory now, imbibed into my core. Just a sweet melody made sweeter by the people and moments it played to. "Run," I think it's called.

This guy's smile grows. Does he smile a lot, or am I just stuck on someone else's frown?

"I'm Joe," he says.

"Farley," and I reach out my hand and smile back.

ELEVEN

NOW

My favorite kind of humor is basically, if it was happening to you, it wouldn't be funny, but to observe it, it's hilarious.

—BILL BURR

FARLEY

"Whatever happened to that Joe guy you dated for a while?" is the way Meyer greets me when I open my door.

"Meyer, it's our third date and you want to talk about exes?" I try for light and teasing, but it comes out annoyed and huffy, like this is really our third date and I am actually miffed that he's putting a damper on it.

"I just saw a lady pushing some sort of poodle in a stroller and it reminded me of him, is all," he snorts.

The truth is, Joe was a one-night stand that just kind of . . . stuck. His expectations were low; he was easy, affable, and accepting. He gave great oral but didn't let his ego get in the way of breaking out a vibrator. We'd go days without talking without either of us getting upset about it . . . at first, at least. It was light, fun, and nice.

He was the perfect brain break when things started picking up with my career. Once Meyer and I worked out a contract (alongside a benefits program, excellent medical insurance, and even a retirement plan), Meyer's name made a huge difference in scoring me great gigs and better, consistent pay. I did a few short openers for bigger names, built a solid reputation quickly, and the gigs snowballed from there. Within four months I quit my other jobs altogether. After a total of three paying gigs in the span of two years prior to that, I was booking that many a week, consistently.

The travel was a bit rough. Cheap flights, even up to San Francisco or Sacramento, were still full-day affairs—with multiple plane changes and stops to keep them under budget. But the trajectory of my entire career was skyrocketing.

Joe fit into that.

Until he didn't. . . .

"Hey. Why don't you want to tell me?" Meyer says, pulling me out of my wandering thoughts. He leans on the car door in front of me, legs crossed at the ankles, all casual ease. Today's henley is a rusty brown, which makes the brunette parts of his hair and beard seem to stand out and nullify the gray. "You don't have to tell me if you don't want to. I just realized I didn't know."

"I knew you didn't like him. I didn't think you'd want to know either way at the time." A half-truth.

"He was a doofus. It's not that he was unlikable, I guess. He just wasn't likable, either."

"You were a dick to him and you know it."

"I was the same to him as I am to every little *boy* you've had hanging on your coattails that is undeserving, Fee," he spits.

"He was the same age as me, Meyer."

"You were dating down, Jones. He was small-minded compared to you. That's all that I meant by that."

I adjust my purse on my shoulder, wondering how to put this to him honestly while saving face.

In the end, I'd read Joe wrong. I thought he was as invested as I was, which, if I was to quantify it, would probably have been about 50 percent. We wouldn't talk every day, but we weren't sleeping with other people or anything, either. We certainly weren't making declarations of love, but I did see him at least once a week for about five months.

But then there was his birthday. I'd felt terrible that I didn't realize it sooner, but Meyer and I had a seven-day trip scheduled up in San Francisco to do a series of shows. It was to start in S.F., immediately followed by Oakland and San Jose. And we'd planned it out for Marissa (who was working out amazingly as his new tutor and quasi-nanny) to fly up with Hazel halfway through so that we could go to Alcatraz, as well as a play for her early birthday gift. *Harry Potter and the Cursed Child* was playing, and the translators were *incredible* . . . I'd scoped it out myself to make sure.

I could tell that Joe was already a little perturbed to come second so easily, but he didn't make a fuss over it, so I just figured it wasn't worth hashing out . . .

Until Hazel got a nasty flu two days into us being away. Meyer flew back immediately, and I came as soon as my last show was done two days after.

I walked through the front door of the condo he'd been packing up to sell to the faint smell of bleach and sickness. He and Hazel were convalescing in separate rooms, but Haze was already through the worst of it. She was tired and living on whatever Marissa would drop off on the doorstep (sporting no less than a hazmat suit), but she had her TV and Netflix with subtitles in her room.

Meyer, on the other hand, was *ill*.

I am all for poking fun at the man flu, but this man was truly sick: a 103-degree fever that I could only get to break by alternating Motrin and Tylenol, and even then would only get down to 100, for over three days straight. He could hardly keep down water, to the point that I had one foot out the door ready to drag his ass to the emergency room before he finally turned the corner.

He'd only ever had a goatee or nothing before then, but the days of barely coming to life, only to move from the bed to the bathroom, had given him enough stubble to pass for a beard.

I propped him up in bed, a freshly cleaned sheet tucked around his bare, clammy shoulders, and started spoon-feeding him broth.

"I'm surprised you're not complaining about this," I said to him with a frown. He just looked at me with sad, bloodshot eyes.

"You've already heard the sound that comes out of me when I vomit. I can give you this," he'd croaked, his deep voice made even deeper by hoarseness.

And that was Meyer at his most vulnerable, I realized.

He'd made himself into a man that really *didn't* use humor or sarcasm to shield himself anymore, unless it was for my benefit. He'd worked tirelessly to be a better version of himself for his daughter, to constantly take care of everyone who mattered to him. But he'd slipped just a little in that moment with me.

It made me realize what a gift I'd been given in him allowing me—in all my sarcastic, bawdy glory—into the steel bubble that he'd built around himself and Hazel.

For some inexplicable reason, he'd let *me* knock on the secret door and waltz right in from the moment he met me. Now this was a small moment, when he was feeling incredibly weak and probably deeply embarrassed, where I could see him figuratively trying to tidy up, trying to keep me at the threshold.

I chose to shove past it. I put my palm to his cheek and ran my thumb against the new stubble there. "I like you with the beard."

Once he'd kept the broth and some crackers down for over six hours, I decided to head home, indescribably worn out from days of worry and little sleep. When I showed up to the rental, Joe was there, sitting on my front step.

"Joe . . . hey."

"Don't worry. I won't take up any of your time."

"What? What do you—"

"I was at Lance's last night, with my buddies, for my birthday." He looked at me and let that realization set in.

Fuck. I hadn't even texted him.

"He told me you've been home for four days, Farley. I thought you were still in San Francisco this entire time, and you couldn't even give me the heads-up that you were coming home."

"Joe. Shit, I'm—I'm sorry." *I'm also just so very tired and would like to get past you and get into my bed,* I'd thought.

"It's . . . well, I'd love to say it's alright, but you know what? It's not. I've tried to be whatever it is that works for you. I've tried to just fit, in whatever capacity you'll have me. I've been extremely respectful of the fact that you are passionate about your career, and have supported you putting it first. But, Farley, I think it's to the point that you'd put your career—that version of you that lives on stage—above every other part of *yourself*. It's like it's this whole separate you, and you're willing to actually set aside your own happiness, and every other part of your life, in order for that one part of you to thrive. You can't make it through a meal without having to write some bit down. You can't go to a restaurant without having to watch other couples and what they're doing so you can invent some joke about it. You couldn't even fucking *call* me on my birthday," he sighed, and I was overcome with the realization that Joe was actually *not* unaffected, and that everything he was saying was true.

Except, it wasn't true when I was with Meyer, or with Hazel. Sometimes not even Marissa.

But especially, above all else, never with Meyer.

Sometimes when I was with him, I would get annoyed that I'd even *have* to write something down, because I was too busy enjoying myself. I'd do it anyway, of course, because I knew I'd forget later. But the material that would come to me when I was with Meyer was organic and easy. Bits inspired by our conversations, or whatever innocuous things we'd do together. I didn't have to entirely fabricate anything with him, ever.

Joe left without saying more, and I let him.

He's only ever late-night texted me once, and he followed it up with an apology text the very next morning.

I never cried over it. At least, not until I realized that I didn't even feel his absence from my life, which prompted me to truly open up to my therapist, Dr. Deb, for the first time. It was the first time I was sincerely worried about who I was becoming as a person. About my detachment.

I realized that I had been using one human being to meet a need, all while having my heart occupied by another.

"Fee. Did he—he didn't do something, did he?" Meyer asks, pulling me back to the present, his voice dipping to a deadly tone as he stands up from the car. I shake my head to clear it.

"No. He didn't. Do anything, I mean. We just grew apart. We broke up over two years ago, Meyer."

"I knew you broke up. I just . . . had never asked."

I shrug. "It wasn't worth mentioning."

He nods, accepting the answer despite eyeing me strangely. "Alright, then. You ready for this?"

"For apple picking? Of course. It's every girl's wet dream to go apple picking in fall. The question is, are *you* ready?" I laugh.

"What could go wrong?" he asks, and I can't help the thought that emerges in response: *Famous last words.*

TWELVE

NOW

Sometimes the road less traveled is less traveled for a reason.

—JERRY SEINFELD

MEYER

"Closed?!" I blurt, and it's the closest I've ever sounded to an appalled teenager who's just been told that there's no Wi-Fi. "How can you be closed? It's the height of fall!"

"Which is exactly why we are closed in the middle of the week on a Wednesday and not on a Saturday, sir. We're closed for a private party," the teen manning the gate says with a bored look.

"Meyer, it's fine. Let's just go," Fee says to me soothingly.

I give the kid another frustrated glare-and-sigh before I turn and take Fee's hand. We held hands for most of the two-hour drive here, her sweeping her thumb across my skin occasionally, and while I wouldn't say it felt natural, it sure as hell felt nice. To me, at least.

She's silent as we get into the car, though, and as we pull out of the parking lot. I know she's not disappointed in the loss of apple picking, exactly, but I also feel the weird, strained energy blanketing us.

When we're together with Hazel, like we were multiple times this week while they practiced for her upcoming recital, things are smooth and easy and normal. Conversation is still fairly easy and normal even when we're alone, but the air feels heavier, my pulse feels thicker in my veins. I feel like I'm holding my breath too much. I'll start to catch myself filtering what comes out of my mouth or questioning it more because I want her to *like* me more. The admiration that I've always carried has heated to something that I can't just veer away from now. It's making me feel flustered and awkward. Like I'm made of teen angst and gurgling hormones. It's not exactly unwelcome, I guess. It's just . . . precarious. Unsteady.

In essence, this is already starting to feel like it was a bad idea.

Before I let those thoughts take over (and because I'm worried that something similar is rolling through her head too) I peel off the side of the road and onto a dirt path.

"Meyer, what are you doing?" she asks.

"We're picking some fucking apples, Jones."

The dust cloud settles around the car, and I turn to Fee's bewildered face.

I can't even define why I need this to work so badly, but I need this date to fucking happen. It's like I can feel the sand sifting through the hourglass on this arrangement, and I want every grain to go unwasted.

A few too many moments hover in my mind, reminding me of times when something could've happened and didn't.

"It's just that . . . we drove all this way and we can just walk into the orchard right here and go, right? Let's make the best of it?" I offer.

The look on her face melts from bewildered into amused. "Sure. Screw it."

I grab her hand when we meet in front of the car and we start walking.

"JESUS, MEYER," SHE PANTS, "IT'S too big."

"You can take it, Fee. Just one more."

"I have nothing left. My legs are going to give out," she keens with a whining sigh.

I halt and blink when the playback hits me. Fee stops short and stands up straight, still panting, and starts to laugh.

"I just heard it too," I snort, wiping my forehead with the back of my hand.

I turn to the hill, one of countless that we've trudged up so far, and wince. My long-sleeve shirt is tied around my waist and I'm sweating a bit, too, but Fee is more vocal about her discomfort.

"I didn't dress for hiking, Meyer. I dressed for apple picking. We have yet to pick an apple." She catches up to my side and bends over, bracing her hands on her knees as she catches her breath.

I'm aware of how she's dressed. I had to stride faster just to get past her in that cute denim getup. It's a one-piece outfit thing with buttons all down the front, and it hugs her entire body like it's been painted on. My eyes kept veering to her pert, heart-shaped ass when she was in front of me, until I muscled my way around her, stomping the ground in frustrated strides as the years of comments I've heard and read about that ass replayed through my mind. . . .

I take in the forest of trees surrounding us. I just wanted to get to the top of the hill to check out what I assumed would be a nice view and capture our "required" pictures—another fun little assignment for the publicity stunt—but each hill we've scaled has just led us farther into a labyrinth of trees. It's a clustered cloud of varied fall shades, and in spite of the sweaty sheen and irritated look she's sporting, it happens to be a backdrop that looks *made* for Farley. Browns, russets, yellows, and reds.

I resent the heat that lingers despite it being November. She belongs in some Lifetime channel small town with three months of pure fall; all her colors. In crisp, cool air, even under the sun.

"L.A. in fall is bullshit," is all I manage to say.

"Honestly, Meyer, *actual* apple picking isn't really what this was all supposed to be about, anyway."

"No?"

"No. I wanted some kind of apple-flavored drink, to feel some leaves crunch underfoot, and to eat some goddamn pie. I also thought I could get you to pose like a stuffed pig with an apple in your mouth. Maybe make a candle. Churn some butter. Buy a wind chime from a man that whittles wood in his mountain cabin and only comes down to sell his wares at the local craft fair. He's a loner with a chip on his shoulder, but has a soft spot for his one-eyed dog and for the woman who runs the bakery. . . ."

"Hang on," I say, her monologue lost on me. The woman could write a biography for a stranger in her mind if you gave her sixty seconds. I spot something in the distance and decide to cling onto this plan a bit longer. "I'll be right back."

"Meyer!" she whines.

I jog back, new treasures in hand, feeling hopeful. But when my gaze meets her mildly disgusted one, I frown. "What?" I ask as she looks around me, searching. I start to deflate. "It's an apple picking tool, Farley. With a . . . basket thing." I urge them both toward her, stupidly. "Now we can actually *collect* some apples." She steps to the side and looks harder, so I turn. "What the hell are you looking for?"

"The time machine or portal you just stepped through to retrieve that."

I roll my eyes and drop them both.

"Meyer," she laughs. "Come on. *Look* at that creepy thing. You walked over here looking like that old painting of the angry farmer. I had to."

I do look, and she has a point. It's a petrified wooden pole sporting what looks like Freddy Krueger's curled, rusted hand at the end. But, as Fee herself would put it, I'm *just over it* now, so I start to make my way back in the direction of the car.

At least, I think I am? Shit, this place is a maze.

"Wait. Are you actually mad?" she calls.

"No, Fee. I'm not mad," I say, sounding exactly that.

"Annoyed, then?" I level her with a look as she skips to my side. "Good, because so am I. I'm sure I have blisters on my pinky toes, and sweat stains under my ass cheeks. Definitely working on a Gold Bond–required–type chafing situation. If this were a real date you would *so* not be getting to first base."

"I guess it's good that this is all just fake, then, isn't it?" I spit, before I can hold it back. I know she was just trying to get a reaction out of me, and I know I played right into it. "You know what . . ." I sigh, frustrated and defeated. "This wasn't supposed to go like this. I'm sorry. I'm just trying to make the best of it, and I'm clearly failing. Maybe you *should* go with one of the football players."

When I meet her eyes, they're nervously assessing, even as I'm thinking of a way to backpedal out of that last statement. "We should just kiss," is the last thing I expect her to say, and yet I'm almost certain it's what she's just said.

"I'm sorry?" I shake my head, trying to clear it.

"No, really. Nothing particularly funny is happening, so this isn't exactly helping me with my material. So don't you think we should just work on the second part of the assignment? It's just that, if I need to pose for pictures and practice PDA with some stranger it's going to mess with my head and be an even bigger distraction, right? That's, like, one of the biggest hurdles, at least *I* think, don't you? I mean, *obviously* I don't want to coerce you into feeling like you *need* to kiss me or anything. But I also refuse to jump on you in public and make you feel manipulated or forced *then*, either. And we can't do anything in front of Hazel. Not to mention, we have that football game coming up that they want to photograph us at, plus they want the social media manager to start working on my accounts, which means more pictures and PDA. But, of course, if you don't want to do this with me anymore that's fine, *obviously*, totally, but if you are still open to it then maybe we should just kiss and—"

"Do you *want* to kiss me?" I ask, even though I hate cutting her off and usually find her word vomit endearing. This thing is urgent, though, and I need to know. My voice comes out rough, strained, and I hope she doesn't pick up on the desperation.

"Yes," and then she blinks. "For the reasons stated previously."

What are those again? I can't recall. . . . My mind goes blind in some sort of white flash. Like staring into the sun too directly and then trying to blink it away, starbursts of light behind eyelids, I'm still attempting to clear my head when she asks, "Do you want to kiss *me*?"

"Yes," leaves my mouth. "I mean, I think it's a good idea. For the reasons previously mentioned."

She takes a step and so do I. I'm mentally mining for the justification in this, but coming up empty. Do I care? She seems to think she needs this. I *do* like to think I'm a helpful guy.

"Fee," I say, reaching for her hand. "Are you sure?"

She answers me by pushing up onto her toes in slow motion and sliding her palm from mine, up my arm, fingertips grazing beneath the edge of my shirt there. I see the damp hair stuck to the corners of her forehead, the little smudge of makeup under one of her eyes. She seems possessed, compelled by something, the edges of her gaze uncertain. But she's so soft in this moment that something in my chest squeezes. I feel greedy for this side of her, for all of her quiet moments. Never for her uncertainty, though. *God,* I want to kiss that uncertainty away.

I lay my hand against the slope of her neck, stroking the thrumming skin at the base of her throat with my thumb, floating it up along her rosy bottom lip before I lean to take it between my own.

She meets me, gently, at first. The kiss somehow feels like her in the most Fee-like way; like how she came into my life, how she conducts every show, and every conversation. It's a firm press, followed by a softer one, a little more open. Something tart—some fruity-mint gum she must've been chewing at some point. A surprising, almost-too-hard nibble here, a wet, sweet glide there. And when her tongue meets mine, my fingers curl in her hair, just as my back hits something. A tree? I don't know, but she's backed us against whatever it is and molds her body to mine as my palm presses into her lower back. I break away and a noise slips out of her—a short, huffed whine that shoots up my legs to my groin, effectively crushing the last vestige of restraint I have. *"Fuck,"* rasps out of me, unrecognizable, before I turn us, gently place her back to the tree, and slide a thigh between her legs, my hand clutching at her hip.

"HEY! WHAT THE HELL ARE YOU DOING OVER THERE?!"

THIRTEEN

NOW

The love that comes from friendship is the underlying facet of a happy life.

—CHELSEA HANDLER

FARLEY

Meyer tenses above me, eyes wide on my face. They flicker to my mouth quickly before he turns, shielding me from sight.

"Sorry about that!" he yells out toward the stranger.

I peek around his broad frame to see a small older man in overalls marching toward us. Meyer steps away and grabs the haunted farm tools, thrusting them out to the man. "I, uh, think these are yours?"

The guy gazes down at the tools, his frown cinching before he looks back up at Meyer and puts his hands to his hips. "Just how old do I look, then? Those there are from the 1800s, son."

I snort-laugh and pop all the way into view. "Hi, sir. We're sorry if we wandered into the wrong area here." I jut my hand out to shake the man's and his frown melts away. He's shorter than me, with unkempt pure-white hair and black caterpillar eyebrows, brown eyes, and rosy, plump cheeks. He's grinning openly at me now, and I can't help but return it. He's a garden gnome come alive.

"It's not that it bothers me, miss, it's just that you two are lost," he chuckles.

"We'll get out of here. We apologize again," Meyer says before turning and crowding me protectively, positioning himself between me and this ostensibly harmless old man. *Ridiculous.*

"And just where do you think your car is?" the stranger asks.

"We'll find it," Meyer retorts.

"If you keep heading in that direction, you're going to go over a damn cliff. This part of the orchard is notorious for getting folks mixed up. Especially if you're . . . *distracted.*"

I poke my head around again and he winks at me.

Meyer turns back with a grimace and sizes up the guy. "Would you mind pointing us toward the main road, then?"

"I wouldn't, but I'd rather you come up to the house and get a ride down, instead, so I don't worry about finding your bodies somewhere later." He lifts a single eyebrow so high it disappears under his downy hair, and reaches out with a gnarled hand. "I'm Abel Larsen. Owner of the farm."

"Meyer Harrigan." Meyer takes his hand and starts a little, apparently surprised at Abel's grip.

"And you, Red?" Abel twinkles at me.

"Farley Jones."

"Lovely to meet you. Hasn't anyone ever warned a beauty like you not to wander around with city boys who'll get you lost? Or were you *enjoying* getting this guy all mixed up?" He maintains his grip on Meyer as he addresses me.

I laugh, charmed, if not a little chagrined. "No comment," is the only acceptable response that comes to mind.

"Alright, then. You two follow me."

"CRAP. I'M DRUNK," MY REFLECTION says to me in the bathroom mirror before letting out an award-winning belch.

It's the first time I've seen a mirror since this morning—a mistake in more ways than one. Not only has my makeup been smeared, courtesy of sweat and laughter, but I'm only just now seeing the little red, irritated skin on my chin, my lips that still appear nettle-stung. Meyer's kiss comes bursting to the forefront of my mind, and I reach up to touch the mild beard burn with my fingertips. It doesn't hurt at all—just feels exposed, hypersensitized.

It was born from an intrusive thought that popped into my mind, really. One that had whispered on a loop, from that part of my brain that I typically reserve for comedy: a deep-seated instinct that always tells me, *Just say it, what's the worst that could happen?* One that eventually won out again, giving me the gall to straight up *suggest* kissing when I noted how defeated he looked after I needled him about the shortcomings of the date.

Sometimes I really think my mouth is an entirely separate being from my brain, or that it's running at a different speed. Maybe in a completely different race.

The fact that he jumped to do it, though. . . .

Was it to shut me up or calm me down? I did start verbally spiraling, but he's never really been fazed by that. It's typically me who sends a self-conscious text about it later or makes a joke.

He'd stepped up to me after agreeing so simply. The swallow

that bobbed his throat and the determination in his eyes had heat pooling in my core. A heartbeat tugging behind my belly button, through my chest, at the base of my throat.

And *God,* his hand at my pulse—at the juncture where my neck meets my collarbone . . . the way he ran the tip of his thumb along my skin was so redolent of *longing* that the moment his lips touched mine, something broke loose inside me. He tasted so new and exciting, and yet like I somehow always knew he would. And the way he kissed me . . . it was as if it was just the first bite in a seven-course meal. Like he was savoring it and letting the flavors coat his tongue. Like he planned to take his fucking *time* with it.

I was utterly lost, ready to climb him and let him take me beneath a tree, out of my mind . . . *clearly.*

Whatever it was that broke loose in me is still in there rattling around, despite my attempts at drowning it with various apple-flavored libations. There was no way I didn't expose myself a bit with that kiss, whether by my prompting it, or by the way I lost control. It was blatantly clear that there was nothing *practiced* about it.

And then Abel marched us over one more hill, to a huge clearing covered in long wooden picnic tables and about sixty confused faces.

As it turns out, it's Abel and his wife Betty's fiftieth anniversary. Betty's family descends from another neighboring farm—the Starfelds—who were once the Larsens' sworn enemies. A real Capulet and Montague situation by the sound of it.

But Abel and Betty's relationship led to the eventual union of their families, along with the other local farms, all of whom have supplied this party with a mishmash of goods.

I indulged in the hospitality after Abel introduced us as "a couple of wandering orchard neckers"—a title that was greeted with acceptance, like it's a regular occurrence or something. I was offered apple beer, and, not one to be rude, I accepted.

I suspect it's just apple cider mixed with beer, but it's apparently my new favorite thing. I was also given an apple rum cocktail (or two), with a cute cinnamon stick and a caramel, sugared rim. I'm a sucker for a cute themed beverage.

A knock on the door startles me, and I cringe, wondering how long I've been in here and how much time I lost track of. "Just a sec!" I call.

"Farley, it's me," Meyer says through the door.

Blood skyrockets in my veins, and I look around for an escape. I've avoided making too much direct eye contact with him this whole time, engaging in the history of the farm, being rapt in our tour of the giant farmhouse and everyone's goods.

I've felt his eyes following me, though, felt everywhere they touch me and press. I feel stupidly shy, embarrassed at the strength of my reaction to this new side of him. The rate at which I've been consuming drinks and conversation with anyone *but* him is likely evident of that.

"Talk to me through the door?" he says. I sigh. *Bless this man.*

"Okay."

"Are you feeling alright? I, uh, got you some food."

"*Shit.* Meyer, what time is it? We have to get Hazel, don't we?!" I just realized.

"No, I already called Marissa. She's got her. And I'm not drinking so I'll be fine to drive . . . whenever. We're free to stay and hang out."

"Oh, okay. Um. Okay, great." *Jesus*, it's like I don't speak in front of people for a living.

"Jones. I'm sorry, okay? I'm sorry I was so bent on making

the date happen, making you hike and then making you feel like you had to kiss me since nothing else was going according to plan. Let's just—take a mulligan on this one?"

I peel my forehead off the door with a groan. "Meyer, no. Stop." I open the door too abruptly and he steps forward to catch himself, apparently having been leaning on it also. My face bumps into his chest in the movement. "Ouch."

"Sorry. Again," he says, taking a step back, plate of food held up like an offering.

"*I'm* sorry. I shouldn't have implied that things weren't going well so you should just kiss me, I shouldn't have manipulated you like that, and then I shouldn't have . . . um." *My god, I am blushing, I can feel it. I have simulated doggy-style on a stage in front of a crowd and this goddamn conversation about a kiss is making me blush.* "Well, it was a good kiss," I say with a shrug, the words coming out too quickly and too close together. I can't apologize for it in earnest because it *was* good and I'm not ignorant. He was enjoying himself just fine.

His expression cracks, the laugh lighting up everything about his face and pulling my eyes to his. I automatically start to laugh back. "It was a fucking *great* kiss, Fee," he replies, his eyes landing on my mouth and heating.

Not willing to risk the buzz making me misread the moment, I take the plate of food and thank him shakily. We head back out to the party, the smells of barbecue and pies perfuming the air.

Meyer was recognized by a few of the guests earlier, and I now catch one of the grandsons taking a picture with his phone in my peripheral.

"Meyer—just a heads-up, that kid over there has snapped a few pictures of you."

"Fee, it's you too, not just me." He smiles down at me as we find our spots at the end of a picnic table.

"No chance."

"Absolutely a chance. I overheard him talking about it." His eyebrows pinch even though he smiles, like he can't understand how I don't realize this.

I don't manage a reply, not sure how I feel. I focus instead on getting food in my system to counteract some of my reckless decisions.

Glasses clink around us, then, a tinkling sound that gathers and grows. Abel walks over, ruddy faced from indulging himself, and raises his glass at Meyer. "Tell us the story of how you met."

Meyer's eyes skitter across the crowd as cheers and encouragements go up in the air. "No, no. I couldn't. This is your celebration, Abel," he says.

"Nonsense. We already know our own story. We want to know yours," Abel replies.

I work to swallow my bite quickly and put my palm on Meyer's arm. "I always tell the story better, My, why don't I?" He lets out a breath through his nose and nods in thanks, his eyes speaking volumes.

"Well alright then, stand up so we can all hear you," Abel booms. Meyer slides off the bench and holds out his palm to me, jaw working. I stand up alongside him.

He looks down at me, his eyes never leaving mine, and all I can manage is to tell the truth. I can't come up with much else under the weight of his gaze and the feeling of his palm at my hip, tucked into his side this way. I embellish some parts, saying things that apply to our friendship but read like they apply to love in this case. Things like, "and that's when I knew I'd charmed him and he'd never be rid of me." Or, "he was pretty standoffish at first, but he kept coming around."

The glasses start clinking again, spoons tap-dancing against them when I'm finished. So, I look to his fierce frown, reach up on my toes, and peck his lips. They soften *just* so to mine, just enough to give the people what they want.

"Thank you," he huffs against my ear.

"I've got you. Always."

"You do. I've got you, too."

FOURTEEN

Just because nobody complains doesn't mean all parachutes are perfect.

—BENNY HILL

FARLEY

The energy in the club is frenetic. There are pub tables littered throughout the dingy room, but not a seat to be found. Shoulders are rubbing like flint and steel, tempers rising. The air is stale, smelling like cigarettes in spite of the fact that it hasn't been legal to smoke inside here for decades. Someone is shoved and it dominoes through the crowd; the sound of a bottle breaking crashes. Variations of *"Where the fuck is this guy?"* and *"We want our money back!"* are slung out.

"Meyer. Should I just go out there? This place is about to blow."

"No, Tweed is supposed to go out first and warm up the crowd. You shouldn't have to. It's not your set." No shit. But

Tweed is thirty minutes behind schedule and nowhere to be found. This is a paid gig, in Vegas, of all places—my first out-of-state event. These people paid for a *group* of comedians tonight, not just for me.

Just then, the MC of the night comes barreling around the corner backstage, his face pinching when he finds us. "We've got a slight problem, guys," he says.

"No shit, Ralph, where is this kid?" Meyer barks. I struggle not to roll my eyes at him calling the guy a kid, even though Tweed's a couple years older than I am. He's good, too. Always dresses like a hipster Sherlock Holmes, covered from the neck down in tattoos. His material is mainly just making a parody of himself and the questions and comments he gets over his look, but it's the perfect opening act. Attention-grabbing and easy.

"He's not going to make it. He's nervous," Ralph replies, and I flinch because I just know that My's about to shred him.

"He's *nervous?*"

"Yes, nervous."

"Did you just say . . . he's fucking *nervous?*"

"Meyer, yes, I know, okay? He's been great before, though. Totally calm on the surface. The stuff I sent to you was him at smaller venues, I guess, but he seemed ready."

"He can't get *through* the nerves?"

"No, when he got here there was vomit on his sweater already."

"Ooh, I know this one!" I chime in gleefully. *"Mom's spaghetti?!"*

Meyer closes his eyes next to me and breathes out through his nose; a three-count that he follows with an inhale of the same. "My, maybe *you* could go out first?" I say, and his eyes blast open and laser down at me.

I've honestly always thought that making out with super tall men is annoying. I can't seem to get out of my head enough to *not* be hyperaware of how uncomfortable the sensation is on both of our necks the whole time, and find myself rushing to get to the next step. But when Meyer's imposing six-foot-two frame withers before my eyes, I'm tempted to reach up and kiss his chin, bolster him back up. His belligerent frown tilts at the edges, looking more afraid than angry.

"Or not. I'm sorry. Just let me go out there. It'll be fine," I say.

"What, are you *nervous* or something?" Ralph asks him slimily.

Another tussle breaks out by the bar, but is just as quickly squashed.

I don't see it when he makes the decision or when his expression changes, but Meyer glares at Ralph, then at me before he shoulders past us without uttering another word.

The moment he steps under the spotlights, the comments begin to trickle through the crowd.

"Is that—?"

"Wait, I know him."

"Wasn't he on that improv show?"

"Isn't he on that Netflix special?"

"Yeah, I think he actually writes for that show now—the one about the dads that gigolo, I think . . ."

"Oh my god, someone get this on video!!!"

The hush sweeps over like a wave, followed by ear-splitting cheers and applause.

And Meyer looks like he wants to drop dead.

The color drains from his lips even as he smiles out at the crowd over the mic.

"H-hey, how you all doing tonight?" he greets them, but it judders out of him, slurred, trembling.

Holy. Shit.

He has stage fright.

He shoves his hands into his back pockets to hide their shaking, looks down at the microphone, and swallows, not just audibly—amplified.

What have I done? I need to go to him and get him out of there.

Am I the only one who sees this? My heart gives a sick, hiccupping thud in my chest.

"There's been a little mix-up tonight, so the guys back there asked if I might come and hang out with you for a few before the next act, but I gotta be real, I haven't done this shit in years."

Okay, he's sounding more like himself again at least. Though he's still just looking down.

"It's weird when your life fundamentally changes, isn't it? I used to come up on these stages and *your* laughter and *your* reactions are what made me, *me*. They were everything. All I had. Then I had a kid and it was just her and I . . . and I only had myself and whatever was in me to wake up with every day.

"Any parent can tell you that your kids sure as hell won't give you any kind of validation. They constantly humble you. You have these brief, fleeting moments of feeling like you've figured something out only to realize how fucking clueless you are shortly after." He's met with some nervous laughter. . . .

"Now, instead of coming up here and making fun of my friends or myself or the futility of life, I get to go to therapy." *Oh thank God,* they all smile and let out small trills of laughter.

"No, really." He looks up, a little more confident. "I think that we all need to go to, and talk about therapy more. Going to therapy should be like getting coffee. It makes us feel good even though it also makes you feel a little jittery and bad, it helps you get your shit out, and it makes us better to people around us." Warm, easy laughter reverberates through the room.

He blows out a breath into the mic. "With that being said, I'd like you to give a warm welcome to *your* therapist for this particular evening, Farley Jones."

He turns and claps, smiling stiffly at me as I make my way on stage. He flees as soon as I'm within range.

I EXIT THE STAGE AND let my smile slingshot off of my face, even as the applause continues. Ralph notices it. "What? That was great! You did great!" he says.

"Where's Meyer?" I demand.

"Uh, I think he left?"

Shit. I start marching toward the exit as I pick up my phone, ignoring the remarks and congratulations trailing me.

He picks up right away. "Hey. I'm—I'm headed back. I'm sorry I left."

"*No,*" I say. "No, don't come back. I'm headed to you. Are you back at the hotel?"

"Yeah," he sighs, sounding relieved.

"Meyer, I'm sorry."

"Jones. Don't," he groans. His voice still sounds shaken, and my stomach manages to sink further. I'm disgusted with myself, a relatively foreign feeling that I can usually suffocate, but fail to in this moment.

"Meet me at the hotel bar?" I ask.

"Yeah, sure. I'll head down."

* * *

HE'S ALREADY STANDING AT THE bar when I get there, tapping the side of a fist rhythmically against the counter, next to an empty glass.

He doesn't look up until I'm in front of him, his eyes the only things that move my way. Bloodshot, with dark circles underneath.

"Meyer. I am—I am *so* sorry I threw you into that. I should never have put that on you." My big mouth and rashness have gotten me into trouble before, but never with a friend, not with Meyer.

He sighs and reaches around me to pull out my stool. When I sit, he follows.

"Jones, I should be the one apologizing. I'm sure I brought down the entire vibe of the room and made it harder for you to bring everyone back up. I should've been able to at least pull off a few minutes, and I couldn't even do that. *God,* I told the equivalent of a dad joke and then bailed," he groans. The bartender slides another drink in front of him and he takes a sip before nodding my way. "Ralph texted, though. Said you did great. You want one of those lemon drink things you always get?" He blinks lazily, his eyelids slightly out of sync with each other—he must be buzzed.

I look over the cocktail list and choose one at random, waiting until the bartender walks away again to ask, "Do you want to talk about—what happened? When did that all start?"

His sigh is deep as he wraps both big hands around his already half-empty glass. He never drinks like this. He's always controlled, always steady.

"I don't know, exactly. But, I guess it's some form of PTSD. Dr. Dale and I have surmised that it has to do with the couple years of isolation I had when Hazel was born." He rubs a palm along his stubble and finishes his drink. "It wasn't like it was anything that could be helped, though. I was unprepared, completely, to be a dad. I thought I'd . . . *fuck,* it sounds so lame saying this . . . but I thought I'd have her for only short, small periods of time. I didn't know I'd . . . and then, I felt like I was doing everything wrong, when she wasn't always meeting the milestones that they say they should meet at those certain points. But she was so brilliant and beautiful and I loved her. I just—I guess I insulated us? Especially when we learned that she was Deaf, and no one had caught it prior to that. I had to teach myself a new language, along with teaching her. I didn't realize just how much I was isolating myself since I was working, still. Writing, at least. But I didn't need to be anywhere in person and going out was such a hassle. I didn't trust anyone to watch her back then."

"Meyer. That's all *completely* understandable. No one could have prepared you for all of that at once. You didn't do anything wrong."

"Well, I know that *now,* Jones. But back then it also felt like I was giving up on myself. None of my stand-up material was super sharp or high-caliber, since everything else had turned into these stories that had to have more meaning, more depth. They worked for shows but not so much as jokes. I had to be able to show the whole picture, you know? Still, I was determined to get up there and do it because it was what I'd always done.

"And then I couldn't. I didn't just fall apart, Fee. I evaporated. I didn't even *like* it—at all—anymore. I hated all the faces and all the noise and there was no part of me that wanted that attention anymore.

"I still love laughter. I still love comedy, but I didn't want to get up there and tell jokes about being a dad and how shitty it can be when I couldn't go on to elaborate about how goddamn Earth-shattering it is when she smiles or learns something new, too. And it's not like I had any dating stories, certainly not anything sexy to talk about." He chuckles darkly, tossing back the ice and chewing on it. "So now, I write. And I'm okay with it. Sometimes I miss that adrenaline, but it's very, very rare, Fee. Doesn't change the fact that it's fucking embarrassing, nor do I totally understand why that changed so much for me. And I really don't love not understanding myself. I used to feel like the smartest fucker in the room. Hell, that was why I loved it, why I did it. Now, I know better."

A tear slides down my cheek and I restrain myself from reaching out to him. "The mind is a fickle bitch. I don't know how I get places 99 percent of the time when I'm driving. My brain just manages to take over even when I'm consciously in a completely different scenario. I constantly wonder 'how the hell did I get here?' I'm sure it's the same, in a way."

His eyes close in agony and he sighs through his nose. "God, please don't bring up your driving right now. It might be the one thing that terrifies me just as much." He finishes the drink as he shakes his head.

"I'm sorry again, My. I hope you'll forgive me."

"Stop," he says, holding up a palm. "It's already done." He tries to smile.

It doesn't sit quietly in me, though, my insides still twisting in guilt. "Doesn't this make you miserable? Taking me to do all this all the time?"

If I couldn't perform anymore . . . So much of my self-esteem is wrapped up in it now that I can't quite imagine the feeling.

He turns my way again, a drop of whiskey or melted ice

glistening on his lower lip. "Surprisingly, not at all." He doesn't elaborate further. And I decide I don't want to push him any further.

"You wanna get drunk?" is what I offer instead.

He shrugs, his shoulders giving a weary little jump. "Fuck it."

FIFTEEN

NOW

If love is the treasure, laughter is the key.

—YAKOV SMIRNOFF

MEYER

I remember my mom complaining every year without fail about the speed at which the holiday season flies by. Something about the short days being shorter than normal, the early dark, and the cold. I suppose the cold was more of a factor back in Ohio versus here in California, but the sentiment still tracks.

The two weeks after the apple picking date go by in a flash, mostly spent in more paperwork and scheduling arrangements. We've worked out the pre-tour tour schedule, and I've worked out a vacation back to Ohio for Hazel to spend with my parents, sister, and nephews.

My parents, especially, are both thrilled and shocked. My mom started crying on the FaceTime call and I realized that perhaps I have been too stingy with my trust. They both learned fluent ASL, after all, and have asked to spend more time with her over the years, repeatedly.

I had a perfectly good upbringing, milquetoast by definition, but always felt loved and cared for. And they still loved and supported me even when they didn't quite understand my desire to pursue stand-up. My sister and I were never particularly close until I had Haze. Now we are as close as siblings who live states apart can be, I suppose.

Nevertheless, I'm realizing that I've been pretty immovable when it's come to letting Hazel stay away for too long, even under their care. So I'm sure that this is going to be good for all of us.

We've also got the NFL game and seats all arranged for some photo ops, but, without planning it, have already earned some extra credit as far as all that goes. There are officially photos and articles circulating online, thanks to Apple-ocalypse (Fee's term, can't take credit for it), and even a few from our mall stroll. I've done an excellent job of not looking at the pictures or any captions, though—as has Fee . . . at least I assume, since she hasn't brought anything up.

She enters my mind and the barbell flies up, suddenly light even after numerous sets. I rack the thing and get up, sliding my headphones out and cutting the workout short.

I hit dial on FaceTime before I can calculate what I want to say or talk myself out of it, and it's ringing as I walk into the locker room.

Fee's face pops onto the screen, brightly smiling until she sees me and it twitches a little. "Oh, hey, Meyer—I was expecting Hazel."

"You always expect Hazel when I call?"

"When it's on FaceTime, yes." Oh, *duh*. I guess that makes sense.

"Ugh *oh my*—Meyer!! ACK! Where the hell are you?! God, *my eyes!!*" she wails, and I turn to see what looks like a frog in a human suit, standing on its hind legs. A naked old man with an indent where his ass should be—*fuck*—yep, my eyes sadly went there. The man turns and Fee's screams echo through the room.

"MEYER WHY!!!!"

"Shit, I'm sorry, sir," I say to the man before I scoop my belongings out of the locker and bolt, he and his naked-old-man-clan shouting expletives behind me.

"Why did you apologize to *him?!* Jesus Christ, apologize to *me!*"

I slide into my car and shut the door before I completely lose it. I don't know how long I laugh but by the end of it I'm clutching my ribs. "I'm sorry, Fee. I didn't even think." I finally look down at her as I swipe a tear away.

She's smiling her biggest smile, chin cupped in her hands, clearly enjoying herself. "It's alright. You have a great laugh, you know that?"

"So I've been told." Only by her. "Hey, I wanted to ask you, do you want to get dinner with Hazel and me before the recital tonight?"

"Of course. I came up with some stuff I wanna show you, too." She inhales excitedly, her shoulders lifting. An excited Fee is an adorable Fee.

"Sounds good. Can't wait. How about we pick you up around four thirty? Haze wants pizza." Surprise, surprise.

"Sounds good. Can't wait," she replies, and why does that make me grin like an idiot? Why am I loving this little streak we've got of repeating things back and forth? This little game of tit for tat.

Oh shit, I'm still just smiling at the screen. I wipe the grin from my face. "'Kay, then. See you later."

"Bye." She waves.

I put my phone away and catch my reflection in the rearview mirror. "You need to get it together, old man. You are not sixteen. Be cool."

But the dumb grin keeps trying to pull on my lips, and I laugh to myself countless times on the short drive home.

I look back at the mirror after I pull into the garage, and sigh. "You're so fucked."

"DAD, NO ONE CARES WHAT you wear to my recital. No one will be looking at you," Hazel signs as we walk up to Fee's door. She's in her full leotard getup, but not entirely ready. And I can't even respond because my arms are full as I trail behind her with various hair gels, sprays, and glitters. I'd just asked her if my tie was okay—apparently a moronic thing to even wonder, if her facial expressions indicate anything.

We already got into an argument before heading over because I do a *fine* job with her hair and the dance makeup stuff, but she was adamant that Farley would do it better.

So, we're here, imposing on her an hour earlier than I planned.

Tonight is about Hazel, though, and I hate that the lines continue to blur in my head. That even though it should be separate, should be just like any of the other recitals we've dressed up for and attended together, that tonight already feels charged.

It boggles my mind that you can know someone—every angle and curve of their face and figure, every quirk and dislike—and in an instant that comfortable familiarity can change to this adrenaline-infused, nervous excitement. That especially because I know her, and now know the taste of her mouth and the cadence of that sound she made, that I only want to know more. To see what other sides and sounds and discoveries I can uncover, even more than I may have wanted to in the past.

I register an erratic motion in my peripheral and my vision refocuses on Hazel, waving irritably. *"Dad. Let's go."*

Fee opens the door, then, smiling radiantly. I trip a little, my toe catching on a crack in the concrete, if I had to guess.

Definitely not just because of how fucking beautiful she looks.

Because this is like every other recital, like the other five or ten or whatever number of times she's joined me, been the great fucking friend that she is to me and to my daughter, who loves her.

Tonight is about Hazel, but I'd truly be as moronic as Haze thinks I am if I didn't admit to myself that it weighs more. That time is once again making me zero in on this moment, realizing how thankful I am to fate or God or the Universe or Walt-fucking-Disney—whoever's up there pulling the strings— that Fee stomped into my life, as inconvenient and powerful as the storm that same day.

FARLEY

Hazel's slap on my thigh stings and I catch her eyes in the mirror as she laugh-apologizes. *"That was harder than I meant to! You and Dad both have the same brain bug tonight!"*

"What do you mean?" I sign, dropping the mass of her stiffly sprayed curls.

"He was doing the same thing. Spacing out. And had the same dumb look on his face." She tilts her head and stares off to the side, an open-mouthed, lopsided smile, miming exaggeratedly.

I tap her shoulder with the back of my hand, admonishing her with a laugh. She tilts her face up to me and grins. She's got the same colored eyes as Meyer, that clear blue that's so crystalline it can be hard to look at. Like a block of ice, just as difficult to hold for long. Just as sharp. I set the brush down again.

"I have a lot going on with work. And your dad is helping me, like always. I'm sorry if he's acting . . ." I struggle for the right way to say it in ASL. *"Tired because of it."*

"I know he's not tired. He's bouncy."

"I thought you just said he looks like this." I mimic her impression and she laughs.

"He's either bouncy or he stares like that. And you guys are weird with each other."

"What on Earth are you talking about?" I pick up the brush to occupy my hands and limit myself from saying anything further.

"I'm Deaf. Not blind," she manages to deadpan in ASL and I clamp my lips together, refusing to laugh, trying to look stern even as a snort escapes.

"That joke is inappropriate, Hazel."

"You can't be funny if you don't take risks. It would have been bad if you said it. It's okay if I do."

"I'LL GO CHECK HER IN if you want to grab us seats," I tell Meyer as we walk up to the auditorium.

"Alright," he replies, smiling at me. I idly wonder if his smiles are getting tired from how much more frequently they flicker lately.

"Go kick ass, and be proud of the work. The reward is in the work. I'm proud of you. I love you," he signs to Haze. The same

dad speech he gives before every recital. The first time he said it Hazel and I frowned at each other, then at him, until he explained that it was what came to mind since it was what his dad always said to him before his football and baseball games. "I thought it still applied." He'd shrugged.

She laughs as usual. *"I'll kick ass, Dad. I love you, too."*

I get Hazel backstage and get her settled with her teacher before we do *our* affirmations.

"What I don't hear, I feel. What they lack in knowing, I make up for in showing," we sign together. The rhyme itself is not translatable by rhythm or phonological sound, but its meaning is the same. We've said it since she first began doing this, back when she was worried she couldn't do it well enough because of her frame of understanding. I told her how every artist feels that way. How we all wonder if what we feel is making it to the stage, microphone, page, or canvas well enough. That we can't ever know what they understand; all we can do is use our tools and what we feel, put our hearts into it, while keeping it good for *ourselves,* first and foremost. I don't actually know if Meyer himself has heard this, but I suspect that it's just for her and me.

We salute each other before I turn to head out, my smile stuck on my face, not able to loosen quite yet, when I hear an overloud chuckle and a *"Hey!"* off to my right. I turn to a man I vaguely recognize.

"Oh, hey," I offer back, still walking.

"It always surprises me when I see you at these things," the man says. "I'm Pete, by the way. Riley's dad."

I continue to smile politely, but crane my neck to look for Meyer.

"Yeah. It's like I can't reconcile it, you know?" he adds. And I do suspect that I know, actually, because I've caught this guy's eye before at these things. Have felt his judgmental stares. And yet, I ask.

"What do you mean, Pete?"

"Seeing you here, at these kids' events all the time. I see you with your little girl, all cute and heartwarming, but all I can hear is you talking about wanting men to up their dirty talk game, and that bit about being Dora the Expl-whore-ah in college with a backpack full of condoms and dreams. That shit is funny as hell, by the way."

"It's called a joke, Pete," I say with force. *Not here, just not here, please.* It touches some raw and tender spot in me, a hot iron to broken flesh.

He seems like he means no harm, and I'm sure he only meant to be relatable, but the last thing I want is to wonder if everyone here is judging me, thinking I'm not fit to be in Hazel's life.

"Hey, angel, you doing okay here?" Meyer's voice finds me as his hand presses into my back, and I turn to see him glaring daggers at Pete. "Pete. Riley's about to head onstage. You're going to miss it."

Our dear Pete remains completely unaware. Clueless as to the emotional grenade he's just pulled the pin from. "Ah. Okay. See you guys," he says with a pointedly dumb smile and wave. *Hope your pillow is always hot, Pete.*

Meyer's eyes lower to mine, then. "What the fuck did he say to you?" He seethes.

"Nothing that I didn't already think myself, My. It's okay. He's stupid, but meant no harm."

"Meant or not, if there's harm we're going to address it."

"Oh, are we now?" I raise a brow. He raises one back. "No harm here," I say, blinking lazily, wishing my mind was like one of those View-Master toys I had as a kid. I'd simply click away from that last picture, focus on the next one. The one that's right before me and the one that's coming up on that stage soon. I smile.

"You know you have the best smile? It's really hard not to automatically smile back, even when it's one of your sadder ones," Meyer says.

It's almost an audible thing, really, the way my heart punches against the bones in my chest. It's like the drum solo in that fucking Phil Collins song, it becomes so all-consuming. "Maybe you shouldn't fight it so hard, then." He just nods in response, his head swiveling down as he steps even closer. "I—I didn't think about people being here and asking you about . . . about us. Or trying to take more pictures or anything," I say.

His frown snaps up to my face. "Don't worry about that, Fee. It's in the contract for the school and for their dance program. Too many other famous people's kids go here for them to be lax on those things. It won't be an issue."

"Oh. Okay. Okay good." I suppose that posturing must've been just to put Pete in his place, then. . . .

"You ready to head in?"

"Yep."

He lays out an arm and holds open the door with the other for me. As I pass him and step into the darkened room, his free hand slips up to the back of my neck and lightly presses as we walk. He keeps me close to his side this way, I feebly try to tell myself. It's just to guide us to our seats. It's not a possessive hold. It's a practical one.

It's for show. It's in case anyone's watching.

But it's difficult to see anything outside of the illuminated stage in this room.

No one would be able to see the way his thumb lightly traces the knobs of my spine there.

No one would be able to see the way his arm dangles over his armrest and onto my seat, either. The way his knuckles trace the skin of my thigh every so often throughout the show. The way I lean to the side to get closer, until the outside of my breast touches the side of his bicep.

Even if they were all looking this way, they'd surely miss how he looks down at me and smiles, mouths "Thank you" silently after Hazel's contemporary solo moves me to tears.

They wouldn't see the way he leans down to kiss my cheek, or the way I shamelessly turn into it at the last second so that it lands on the corner of my mouth. How, in the dim lighting, I see one of my tears glisten on his bottom lip, and the tip of his tongue as it darts out across it.

No, no one else could see that but us.

SIXTEEN

NOW

> When humor works, it works because it's clarify-
> ing what people already feel. It has to come from
> someplace real.
>
> —TINA FEY

FARLEY

I'm a woman distracted.

A woman on the brink of my truest vision of success, and yet one who can't seem to think up a joke to save my life.

Anytime I attempt it, my mind wanders to Meyer. To the way he looked when Marissa and I joined him and Hazel on Thanksgiving. The house was warm, with music on full blast as we walked in. We'd knocked, but weren't heard over the volume. He never has music going on continually in the house, let alone blaring like that. I've always assumed this was just a by-product of having his only other cohabitant unable to hear, of course. Still, it caught Marissa and me both off guard when we let ourselves in, only to find them dancing in the kitchen. What caught us more off guard was how, when he saw us standing there, wearing dumbfounded expressions, he wasn't at all deterred.

He'd been wearing a simple black T-shirt, a dish towel slung over his shoulder and a toothpick in his teeth, and kept right on singing into a turkey baster microphone.

I'll start toiling away at a vaguely food-related bit and my mind will veer off to the way the tendons and muscles in his forearms worked as he chopped the celery, onions, and apples for stuffing that day. Or to the way he'd roll the toothpick to the other side of his mouth with his tongue occasionally as he spoke. To the way he stood behind me at the sink as I struggled to peel a potato, wrapped his palms around mine to demonstrate, *"It's just a matter of applying the right pressure, and then it slides easily, see?"*

I'll be attempting to write a joke on how men are babies, but then Meyer's concerned face will project itself in my brain. The way he'd jumped up when I clumsily grazed my wrist against the hot burner on the stove. I can still feel the way he blew on the burn, the way he applied a Band-Aid with a featherlight touch.

Then there are some things I find I can work with, but in their inception, they're a tiny grain of truth that I'm forced to embellish based on my observations of other people's relationships and conversations. Like how I start an entire piece on being suspicious of your significant other's happiness—all based on how even Marissa is picking up on the changes in Meyer's demeanor, and how she goes on high alert because of it. Some hug, or a few extra grins slide out of him, and I'll catch her squinted, smug gaze as she mouths *what the fuck* at me from behind his back. Granted, her suspicions lean toward him wanting more from our arrangement than him hiding something bad, but still.

It makes me think about normal, real relationships, and people wondering if their partners have some other motivation when they seem extra attentive. Perhaps they're amping up to ask about butt stuff, or planning a trip with their parents? Maybe they took out a credit card and racked up some debt they neglected to share?

It's the hardest I've ever had to work to *try* to be funny, and ironically, it's the depth of that endeavor that has me questioning if it's even any good or not. Like if I dig too far, or just a foot off of where I need to, I'll find shit instead of treasure.

This is just the beginning of where I start to unravel.

IT'S OFFICIALLY THE DAY OF the football game, the first scheduled "event" where all three of us—Kara, Shauna, and I—will be together prior to the pre-tour tour. I'd flown in last night, fully prepared for a night on the town, three funny females taking San Francisco by storm . . . and ended up in the hotel alone and asleep before 7 P.M. Shauna was with Tyson, and Kara was at home. Meyer flew in this morning, not wanting to be gone from Hazel any more than necessary before the extended trip.

When he emerges from his Uber at the curb, his breath curls in the chilly air, stern face held tight. An angry dragon forced from his lair.

"Was your driver rude or something?" I call out, and the change in his expression when he finds me has my ears pulling back, has me swallowing a stupid chuckle.

In just a few of his long strides he's there, less than a foot from me. "It was the opposite, actually," he says. "She talked the *entire* time. We took a selfie for her niece, Willow, who's an undergrad at Cal Berkeley, with a roommate named Kale. She told me she asked Kale if he liked spinach and I had to pretend to laugh at that, Fee." His chin dips meaningfully and I snort. "She kept trying to maintain eye contact through the mirror while she spoke instead of focusing on the road. Her brother, Raul—Willow's dad, in case you were wondering—is getting married for the fourth time next summer and Marcia, my driver, has a *lot* of feelings about it."

I snort again. "Oh my god. It was your actual nightmare." I smile so hard my vision is obscured.

"Nightmare." He smiles back, searching my eyes. "Riveting stuff, really. I felt like I was being poisoned. The only thing that could have made it worse would've been talking about the weather." The grin grows.

"God, you're such an asshole." I give a little punch to his chest. "But I know you were polite still."

"Of course. Took a lot out of me, though. I'm weak and famished." He grabs my wrist and plants a chaste kiss on my knuckles before scooping me into his side.

We eat outside, the steam from our drinks and breath mingling in the December air. I'm grateful for the sun warming my face and giving me an excuse to wear sunglasses again, so I can surreptitiously steal glances at him. The chill paints his cheeks with a rosy bloom above his beard, legs akimbo with one palm braced on a sturdy thigh. His own sunglasses fog occasionally when he brings his drink to his lips. This whole image is explicit, somehow. *Feels* even more so when he snatches the leg of my chair suddenly and pulls it—including me—over to him, to his side of the little bistro table. I drape an arm around his middle, palm falling to his chest in the abrupt movement—to catch myself, of course, not to feel the mound of a hard pec beneath my palm. He wraps his arm around my shoulders and kisses my temple before dipping down to my ear. "Photographers. Eleven o'clock." I let my eyes dart that direction, where I spot two leaning over a car.

We sit this way for a while, eyes closed to the sun and limbs draped over one another like vines.

It isn't until later that I realize just how comfortable this has started to become—the touching. There's still a jolt to my system, but it's one I relax into now. Like slipping into warm water after being submerged in cold, or vice versa. Just feels like a refreshing surge each time.

AT THE GAME, SHAUNA SITS to my right and Meyer to my left, with Kara on the other side of him. He's brought me a spare jersey he had, a 49ers one I'm informed. The whole thing is surprisingly fun, easy to follow, easy to get into quickly. Before I know it I am screaming alongside everyone else. I find a few key phrases that seem to apply for multiple scenarios. *"Come on!"* being the most universal.

I'd felt that standard feeling at first—that "on" feeling with Kara and Shauna. I'd be lying if I said I don't feel the need to impress them, even if I do already have the gig.

It's actually pretty common to meet comedians and find that they're not all that funny in mundane life. It's like they hoard up that energy, any quips or banter to use onstage. Plenty of them are still masters at their craft, though, so I try not to pass judgment when I come across these individuals. After all, you wouldn't judge an author based on their text messages or

Instagram posts, or expect an actor to slip into a new identity without a camera or an audience.

But Kara and Shauna are naturally hilarious, easy to get along with, and irreverent. What many would consider over-sharing is what disarms me with them the most.

Shauna tells us about hooking up with Tyson on their first date, while Kara jokes about thinking she was headed for a life of leisure with her husband—a graduate of MIT—but instead *she's* managed to become the primary breadwinner by talking about bodily fluids ad nauseam. It's obvious that they're both deeply in love, though—at least to me—based on the number of jokes they make at their own expense alone.

When they pick up on Meyer's blushing at certain comments, they dig in ruthlessly. It's a bit that they fall into, but they stick to it flawlessly when they see it working on him.

"I honestly thought I'd miss getting to be a ho. But then Tyson had to go and give me multiple that first time we hooked up, and now my standards are awfully skewed. I'm not willing to play the market after that, you know?" Shauna says.

"Praise be. My only complaint is that now that I make all the money, I don't think he spanks me as hard as he used to, and he doesn't want to try anything with any kind of risk factor," Kara replies with a mournful sigh, and Meyer chokes on a pretzel as I start howling. I smack his back as his eyes water and he continues to cough violently. "He definitely won't even *attempt* to choke me," she pouts.

The public affection is easy in this setting, surprisingly. There's no stream of self-conscious babble in my mind anytime my hands land on him.

I think it's because expectations aren't overly high. Even if I was trying, it's not like I'd be able to differentiate who might be taking pictures of us versus the game, since so many cameras and phones hover in every direction. I find myself easily patting a muscular thigh, leaning into a hard shoulder as I close my eyes in a laugh. We stand up to cheer for a touchdown and my hip bumps into the front of his after I jump up and down. He's continually placing easy kisses to my hairline, or wrapping me against his front with his forearm across my collarbone—just like that first date by the food truck. My palms hold it there every time. Sometimes his chin rests on top of my head and I imagine I'm buoyant, that I'd float away without the weight of him securing me.

But then it's over, and I couldn't tell you what team won because all I know is that despite feeling like I'm on the verge of disaster in my work life, I feel like the most victorious woman alive.

I let myself hook a finger through Meyer's belt loop on our way out, and wrap my other hand around his arm as we walk.

Shauna, Kara, and I make plans to meet up and go out that night, before they go their separate ways. When they're gone, Meyer frowns down at me and asks, "Are you sure you don't want me to stay? Marissa is there anyway tonight, and Haze will be asleep by the time I get home . . . and I could still be there in the morning." He looks unsure even as he says it, but my mind swan dives into the gutter at the question, nonetheless. I'm thinking he means *stay,* stay. Like, with me. For the night. "Uh . . . ," I stammer.

"I mean to help, like, socially," he clarifies, clearing his throat and folding his arms across his chest. "Go over the parts in your set you're trying to work out and stuff, too, maybe."

"Oh! Okay. Well, no, that's okay. No social lubricant required here." *God, poor choice of words, Fee. Thank God you stopped before*

you said you were wet and ready or something equally terrifying.
"I'll be totally fine. And we've got time to work on the material.
It'll be good for me to do a girls' night." I shrug. Marissa and
Meyer might be my only close friends, but I already feel a kin-
ship with Kara and Shauna, so I don't feel anxious about that,
exactly.

He smiles lopsidedly and nods before he looks down at his
phone. "Alright. Uber's two minutes away."

"Oh okay—you don't have to go get your bag from the concierge?"

"I do, but I just added a stop. I, uh, figured we'd just share it
back to your hotel and then I'll take off from there."

I already regret not taking him up on staying, but don't see
a smooth way to rewind. "Oh! Okay, well . . . do you have time
to get some food before you gotta hit the airport? I actually
kind of do think that maybe we should start going over some
material." That was lame.

But he looks down at his phone and winces apologetically,
so I speak again before he can. "No, no, never mind. Of course.
Honestly, I'm so full of nachos at this point anyway, my reflux
is going to be a bitch later."

The car pulls up, and we ride back to the hotel in that weird,
strained, smothering silence that we've managed to avoid lately.

We get back too soon, and before I know it I'm looking up at
him on the sidewalk in front of the hotel. At the muscles in his
jaw as they work, flaring out. His hands slide into his pockets.

"You're sure you don't want me to stay even for a bit? I
could just catch the later flight. There's one more first thing in
the morning."

Years of manners have me speaking on auto reply. "No,
really. I don't want to keep you from Hazel any more than I

already am. It's all good." There was my chance, and I blew it. Again.

He nods, then turns around and walks through the revolving doors, but stops short when we step into the lobby. I run into him with a little *oof,* ass to abdomen, before he turns back to me.

"Should we have a . . . a check-in conversation? On this?" He gestures back and forth between us. "I'm not—" His sigh is so frustrated it blows a lock of hair off my face. "—I'm not over-stepping, am I? I realize that I told you I'd be more comfortable if you took the reins on the affection stuff, and then I've kind of . . . well, maybe I'm getting too comfortable. You've *gotta* let me know, Fee. Please."

He sounds tortured, and I hate it. I hate that it's become so difficult to say exactly what I'm feeling and what I want, to put thoughts to words. That it's seeping into everything, now, even into my work. Despite my never sharing my more repressed feelings with him, everything else was so easy before.

"My. . . ." I've had the chance before to lay it out there, with alcohol as an excuse, and even then I chickened out.

You can't keep doing the same things and hoping for different results, though. So, I won't let my friend feel this exposed or vulnerable, not when it's the last thing he deserves and he's all that I want.

I reach out for his hand, push my thumb along his palm and drag it, a place for my eyes to focus. "Meyer, I—I like it. I'm . . . I'm enjoying this. More than I should, I think. To the point of distraction. I think we just do what comes naturally and what feels good, now, yeah?"

I allow myself one more blink, a little pause when my lids close, before I hazard looking up at him again, hoping to see relief. But his face is held tighter, if that's possible.

"Can I kiss you again?" he asks, and I can't help the smile that pulls on my lips.

"Yes." And he does. And I know there are people around with their phones, but I somehow know this is for me and because he wanted to. Could just be lust-based, but I know it's not for show this time.

He holds himself with restraint, for which I'm thankful, because I don't trust myself not to do something embarrassing like try to burrow beneath his shirt just to feel his skin on me at this point, lobby or not.

His lips smile against mine and our tongues lightly bump into one another. A little happy sound pops out of me, a throaty chuckle in response from him. It's brief, but everything.

When he breaks away, he's trying and failing to repress a smile. The Uber honks from outside. "Go," I say, smiling back. Because I'm somehow calmer now, reassured. That edge taken off just enough, even as joy surges through my body, pushing beneath my skin and ready to break free.

"Alright. I'll call you later."

"Call me when you land?" Okay, that was ridiculous, but he smiles bigger at it.

He trips a little, walking backward to the doors, but catches himself and laughs. "Okay."

SEVENTEEN

18 MONTHS AGO

A day without sunshine is like . . . night.

—STEVE MARTIN

MEYER

I love drunk Fee. She's even more unhinged than normal. The man that still exists buried somewhere deep within me can't help but preen a bit at how her eyes linger a little more when she's this way, biting her lip occasionally. I let myself think that the drunk her is into me, only because I know I'll never do anything about it.

The rest of me rolls my eyes at myself, and is mildly disgusted at that pervert, though.

Being drunk together may have not been a wise choice, I'm realizing, but numbing my brain felt like the *only* choice tonight. After I couldn't even come through for her, after I embarrassed myself on stage.

I look down at the three-foot-long, neon, plastic drink cup

in my hand with the matching swirly straw. The thing blurs in and out of focus as I slurp loudly.

Ah. Bummer. Empty again.

I set it on top of a slot machine and blow a raspberry at it before I wander after Fee. Even in my state, she's easy to track with the balloon animal hat bobbing around. My hand flaps around my own head to make sure I still have mine.

Fee gasps, then, pointing to the twenty-four-hour restaurant sign. "I require a BURGER. Tallyho!"

I nod my agreement silently and follow behind, throwing glares at the dudes whose eyes peruse her too comfortably, or for too long.

Oh yeah, man. I'm sure you're menacing as fuck in the balloon hat.

TIME FADES AND GOES A bit blurry again, but I manage a cognizant moment when I look across the booth at her. She chews a supremely large bite of her burger with a moan, eyes closed, balloon hat askew, cheese and sauce on her chin.

That's mine, I think. *She's mine.*

It's as if I've said it out loud, because her eyes shoot open, and she swallows the bite audibly. "What? You can't hit me with the eyes like that, My."

"Like what?"

"They're like a weapon you wield when you look a certain way. You hit women with that stern gaze and it's like you're compelling them to take off their clothes."

I close them, then open them dramatically as far as they'll go, stretching them until she starts cackling. When it fades, she sets the burger down with intent, pats her mouth primly with a napkin. "Meyer—"

Raucous cheering and whooping explodes to my left, pulling our attention that way.

"I CAN'T BELIEVE WE'RE MARRIED!" the woman shouts.

"HEY, EVERYONE! THIS IS MY WIFE RIGHT HERE!" the man declares, puffing his chest out proudly. I make the mistake of catching his eye. "I've loved this woman for a decade, man," he declares shakily, his eyes unmistakably filling with tears.

"I've loved you longer, baby. As long as I can remember," the woman wails, before they begin making out violently.

"Je-sus." I wince when they almost topple over. I look back to see Fee wearing a sad expression as she watches them.

She raises a wobbly finger their way. "That's what I want," she says. And it catches me so off guard that I scoff at her.

"You want to have some shitty, drunken wedding in Vegas?"

"No. I want someone to love me enough to be completely stupid with me. To do something *stupid* like get married in Vegas. Or put it on one of those signs carried by a plane in the sky. Sing me a terrible song at a karaoke bar in front of a crowd. I want to be stupid, embarrassing with love." She swipes an eye and laughs hollowly. "I'm sure that sounds dumb to you. To someone who's so perfectly balanced and measured and smart, like you are." She rolls her eyes before she digs the heels of her palms under them and wipes angrily.

Her statement hits me like a sharp elbow to the side, expelling oxygen and the following words:

"You're the only person I've ever been stupid with, Fee."

Her eyes snap up to me in shock, searching.

The balloon hat jiggles, trembles. Slides further down before she readjusts it.

"We probably need to get back to my room. Early flight," she whispers, eyes darting between mine.

I sigh, nodding firmly. *You absolute idiot, Meyer.* "Okay. I'll walk you back."

We take care of the bill and ride up the elevator in silence, the only noise coming occasionally from the rubber of the balloon against the skin of my palm as I try not to crush the fucking thing.

I walk her to her room, help her with her key after her fifth failed try. It's obvious that I freaked her out with my comment.

We get inside and she tosses her hat before I slip into the bathroom, taking a moment to come up with the words to fix this. But, when I reemerge, I find her struggling with the strap of her heel, teetering dangerously. "Whoa, hang on there." I go to her, try to steady her by the shoulders. But my reflexes are off, so when she tries to slap a palm to my shoulder it ends up pushing me, our feet tangling. I feel myself going over, so on instinct I wrap her up and twist so I take the brunt of our weight. We flop onto the bed in a knot of limbs, chest to chest, every curve of her settled against me. Our eyes meet, wide and confused, as she pants out a quick breath that lands on my lips.

Her scent reminds me of those fucking s'mores bars she makes, and I lick my lips, starved. It's sweet, but there's something smoky, even under the alcohol, and my mouth waters. Her bourbon eyes blink slowly, long black lashes resting on her cheeks a moment before they sear into me again. And then, almost imperceptibly, she leans, tilting just so, just a click. And I'm being pulled to it, can't fight it as much as I could fight gravity in this moment, despite alarm bells blaring through my brain. Less than two inches away. So many oversized drinks . . .

POP

We jolt up and apart, her balloon hat deflating with a winded wail that goes on for hours.

She lets out a frustrated sound and starts fidgeting with her hands, kicking off her shoes angrily. One bounces off the nightstand. "Fucking salt and booze and planes. My fingers are swelling." She starts yanking on a ring. *"Dammit!"* she chokes out through a sob.

"Fee. Hang on okay? Just, shh." I try to soothe her, and myself, and de-escalate whatever this situation is that has left all our nerve endings exposed and frayed.

"I can't get it off—I can't!" She continues jerking with trembling hands.

"Fee. Take a deep breath."

"I. *Can't*." She digs her nails into a finger and starts to yank again until I grab her hands and pull them apart.

And then I do something that I can only attribute to alcohol, instinct, and sheer insanity. I take the finger she's been abusing and slip it into my mouth. I tuck my teeth around the ring and work it off her finger.

I've hinted at my feelings with a reckless statement that she kindly didn't push me on (that clearly wasn't reciprocated), almost kissed her, and now I've sucked her finger off like a lover. I pull the ring out of my mouth and slap it in her palm, her finger shining, the tang of metal and salt on my tongue. I close her fist around it before I mutter a throttled-sounding *"Good night,"* and turn to bolt.

"Meyer," she croaks when I open the door to leave. I pause, but can't bring myself to turn around.

"Meyer. I think you're the only person I've ever been—ever been *smart* with. You're the only relationship I've made the *smart* choices with. And . . . I don't want to ever lose that. I want to be smart with you."

I nod, hearing all that she means without saying, even as my heart deflates faster than the balloon hat.

I'M FEELING WAY TOO FUCKING sober again by the time I get back to the casino floor, and head back to the bar.

Not long after, when I've remedied this thoroughly, I stumble onto the strip, and the first thing my eyes see is a neon sign.

I'm feeling pretty fucking stupid.

EIGHTEEN

NOW

FARLEY

I get back to my room and flop onto my bed like a starfish, bringing one hand to touch my lips before I scream-squeal into my palm. I lose track of time, lying there like that, until dizzy thoughts become languid, and I remember that I need to get ready to meet up with Kara and Shauna.

I decide to head down to the hotel bar to fetch some shower-wine and a water, humming the whole way like an idiot. I think I twirl upon my exit.

But when I complete my pirouette off the elevator, the stupid grin plummets, because in steps Meyer, back through those revolving doors, looking *furious*. He stomps my way and I freeze to the spot.

"W-What? What are you doing here?" I look down at my invisible watch again—*really, I need to start wearing one.* "Aren't you on a plane?"

"I'm not." He's flushed and breathing hard. "On a plane, I mean."

"Then what—"

"Well, for one. I forgot my bag."

"Oh. Oh, okay. Well, don't forget it again," I say, trying to laugh. It comes out as a high-pitched *heh*.

"And two." Another step. "I want to kiss you again. And I want to do it well. I *want*—" He mutters a curse under his breath, runs a palm over his beard. "I want to stay. I wanted to tell you that. I just—wanted to say the words to you and tell you. I've stopped myself from saying shit before and—*fuck*—I just didn't want to do that again. You can tell me to go, and I'll go, and nothing will change, Fee."

My heart drums a leaping staccato. "Yes. I'm—I want that," is what I say back, even though there's so many more words in my mind, important things that I know I need to say but can't manage to push out.

"You want me to go?" he says, his voice clipping at the end, stating it more than asking.

"No—*No.* I want you to stay."

And the next moments don't go by in a flash: they go by painfully, awkwardly slow, because when you make big declarations without forethought, you don't think about having to wait for an elevator. Or seeing both of your reflections with their wide-eyed expressions in the shiny doors. You don't consider that you might hop onto that elevator before he remembers that he needs to grab his bag from the concierge, hopping out at the last second and leaving you to ride up to your room alone.

You don't think about the state of your hotel room or how you left the Do Not Disturb sign on it, which means that it still reflects what an utter pig you are the moment you walk in. And as you cover the bloody tampon trash in the garbage can with half a roll of toilet paper, as you shovel clothes into the closet like a dog digging for a bone, and as you hide the disturbing amount of skincare and makeup on the counter (which you fear will be the thing that ultimately reveals how you turn into a troll at night, thus destroying the only shred of feminine allure you *barely* maintain), you definitely don't think about keeping your phone on you because he might not actually know your room number.

I have no idea how long he's been calling by the time I hear it vibrating, but when I do I answer in a breathy panic, "Room 1148."

"Okay," he says before he hangs up.

I look at the bed, the last frontier, and scramble to make it.

I specifically avoid a mirror, knowing I'll obsess and spiral further, choosing instead to sit on the edge of the bed and study my hands; the rings I always wear that once belonged to my mom. A band of opals and one with two tiny diamonds on a skinny gold band. *"A square and a pear. They don't match, but they sure look good together,"* she'd say.

It reminds me of the last time Meyer and I were in a hotel room together. The feel of his teeth sliding up the flesh of my finger . . . the pinch-pull of it and the heat of his mouth. How angry and terrified I was with myself over how desperately I wanted to kiss him, how I wanted to tell him everything. Like how he's made me a better person, how he's given me the strength to do that for myself. How I don't even think lemon things are my favorite but that I order them because they make me think of him, in some small, silly way. How, after losing my mom, I'd been so miserably lonely until him and Hazel.

But when I could hardly stay upright, I didn't trust that it wasn't also the alcohol making me see what I wanted to see in his eyes that night. How just the thought of saying or doing something that could scare him away was enough to make me shove it all down again.

My head snaps up when the door opens; I'm happy I snuck the latch in there so he only had to push it, saving myself from further greeting awkwardness. I watch him as he flips it back and lets the door click shut before he returns it to lock, the sound ricocheting throughout the space. He braces his palms on the frame a moment before he turns around.

"My . . . ," I say when his eyes find mine and I register that glimpse of panic that matches my own.

But then he breathes into a smile, and I fall into it, my steady hammock, and my fear evaporates.

At least, all my other feelings overrule it for now.

He sets his bag down on the floor next to the desk before he crouches, pulling something out of it.

"Tums. For your reflux later," he says when he stands and gives the bottle a little shake.

It probably shouldn't have the effect on me that it does. Tums are hardly an aphrodisiac. But it's the fact that even among everything, he took my passing comment to heart and put my needs before his own, that he took the opportunity to do something small that he knew would make me laugh.

He's there, jacket sleeves pushed up on thickly built forearms, brows lifted, that bemused look on his flushed face. Pieced together in such a way that it's somehow obscene, him shaking that antacid my way.

I'm floating, filling with heat and this rising feeling in my chest. So much love and adoration for this man. So I stand and walk over to him, slide my palm up from his chest to his jaw. "Thank you," I say, before I weave my fingers in his hair and tug his face down to mine.

There's a desk and a bed, and yet we end up against the wall at first, his mouth devouring my own. "Shit—sorry, are you okay?" he asks when my head thuds against it.

"Yes," I manage through a small laugh before I dive back in, desperate for more of him. His hands splay out against my rib cage as he slides me up the wall, body pinning me there. And I can't help myself: my hips undulate, seeking friction against his thigh, sliding against an equally hard part of him in the movement. He hisses, and I let loose a gasp. "I'm sorry—sorry," I whisper, even though I'm anything but.

"What the fuck for?" he asks, his voice taking a gravelly edge. Deeper, commanding even in its quietness. A secret for me, another something new that I want for my own. His tongue slides across his lower lip before he tucks it behind his top teeth, biting. His eyes traverse my face, down the slope of my neck, to where our bodies meet.

"I'm—uh—I can't," I say. "I should've told you before. I can't right now . . . this week, I mean. I'm sorry."

He looks like he wants to laugh, but graciously refrains. "Why would you apologize about being on your period, Fee?"

"I don't want to, like, give you false expectations," I say, playing with the short strands of his hair at the base of his skull.

"I didn't *expect* anything. Kinda sounds like you do, though." He smirks. "I just wanted to kiss you again. What is it you think I expect?"

"I think most guys probably expect to have sex when they come up to a girl's hotel room, no?"

"*Boys*. Idiot, juvenile boys, Fee," he growls. "I plan to savor this. *You*. And maybe I like the idea of making you wait for the rest." He smiles at my little sound of protest. "Now shut up and let me keep kissing you." His mouth goes to my jaw, down my neck, tongue dipping to the hollow of my throat before he pulls the strap of my camisole aside and kisses just below my collarbone. I tug on his hair and bring his mouth back to mine, eating up his small grunt when I grind on him again.

He slides his thumb across my nipple before he dips down, nibbles it through the thin material of my top. "My—I want—" I don't know what I want, though. More? Less? To go back in time and slap the shit out of Eve for cursing us all with menstruation?

I finish the thought by showing him, digging my heels into the backs of his thighs and pressing that aching spot against him in reply. He doesn't hesitate, just scoops me off the wall, finding my lips again before he carries us over to the little armless chair in the corner and sits, pressing me into his lap and pumping my hips once. When I let out a small moan against his ear he tilts his chin up to me, rewards me with another searing kiss as he drags my hips back and forth again. Each movement ratchets up the sensations buzzing beneath my skin, closer and closer in spite of the clothing that still separates us. I slide the straps of my ratty tank top away, exposed and open to the frigid hotel air. And then I look down and realize that I've just whipped out my boobs to my best friend and it should absolutely feel weird, but the way he looks at me, like I'm some unexpected treasure, has me feeling impossibly confident and sexy. I smile, and his returning one starts out shy before it heats, before he leans forward and catches one pebbled nipple into his mouth and pulls. He works out a rhythm of sliding me against him while he lavishes me with tongue and teeth and lips. Until I'm frenzied, gyrating and circling, friction and sensation and heat, and so, so close. Until his head falls back against the chair and his brow furrows in concentration, as the pads of his fingertips spread down to my ass, kneading, squeezing and pressing through my leggings while he works my hips. His mouth falls open and his eyes meet mine, as he tilts his hips and presses up against me and I come completely undone.

NINETEEN

NOW

MEYER

She blushes when she comes. A watercolor pink that spreads across her chest. She does it quietly, with a breathy groan like that first stretch after waking. It's all I can do to not try and coax another one from her, to start collecting them, hoarding them. I want to build a library in my mind to store them in. With floor-to-ceiling shelves and a rolling ladder.

"God, you're pretty like this, Fee."

She opens heavy lids and smiles drowsily at me. "What? Topless and quiet?"

"No. Satisfied and on top of me." And a surge of pride rushes through me at the way her eyes dilate when I say it.

She adjusts a little and I hiss, still painfully hard.

"What if I want to know how you look? Satisfied, I mean?" she asks, palming me through the jeans before I grab her wrist to stop her.

"No, Fee. You don't have to."

"I think it's only fair. And I *want* to."

I choke on a groan. "Don't you have to meet—" Someone, though I can't call it to mind when all the blood in my body seems to be occupying one region. "—soon?" Though I know it won't take long. Embarrassingly quick at this point, I'm sure. Her eyes dart down to my watch.

"*Shit!* Yes, in ten minutes!" And she flies off my lap with a push that has me going cross-eyed in a grunt of pain. "Oh my god, I'm so sorry!" she cries. I wave her off while I try to catch my breath, balls in my stomach. She starts laughing and I attempt a glare that probably turns into a stupid-looking smile when I realize her top is still pulled down. "I'm so sorry, My." She puts a knee on the edge of the chair between my legs, far enough that I don't clutch myself or flinch harder. She leans over and puts her cheek to mine, whispers in my ear, "I'll make it better later, if you'll let me," before she pecks my cheek.

She swaggers away, biting the tip of her thumb in a smile as she turns and walks off to the bathroom. When she shuts the door I grab my phone as I cough, and change my flight again, before guilt makes me second-guess it.

WE MANAGE TO MAKE IT all the way into the elevator before I notice the calm starting to evaporate from Fee like steam. I stupidly assume it's about me. "What's up?" I ask, aiming for casual so she knows she can tell me if she's freaking out about things, so she knows that I myself am not freaking out about it despite the drumline that's taken up residence in my chest. She surprises me by stepping my way and wrapping herself around my side.

"Just nervous about my set and the tour. I feel guilty that

everything else is so . . . good. That I *want* to just go out and have a good time tonight and put it off some more. I normally *want* to work, you know? I'm distracted and I feel bad that I like it."

I slide my hand around her shoulders and up, touch her soft cheek while her other one presses into my chest. I don't know if I should feel good about her being distracted, even though she says she likes it. Because I certainly don't want to be a mere distraction. I also don't want her work to suffer, though, so I try not to complicate things further by demanding we put a name to this thing between us and define it. I put on my manager hat for the time being—or at least I try to. These various hats I've been wearing all suddenly seem too small.

"We'll work through it. It's probably all better than you realize, as usual. But I get it, and I know you've been putting extra pressure on yourself. Fun will probably do you some good." I don't want to brush it off; I want her to know her concerns are valid and that I'll help, while still making sure she allows herself a break tonight. We always work through it, and she always exceeds every expectation, including her own.

"...I AM TELLING YOU, the barometric pressure in the atmosphere changed when these women all met in a room. It wasn't some sloppy girls' night or frilly bachelorette party; I'm saying you could taste violence in the air. They went after it all, *hard*." Fee has everyone in stitches talking about the PTA night. "They truly didn't give a shit about anyone's attention. They were all completely different, with completely different lives, parenting philosophies, and struggles. Not all of them were even moms, either. Some were just members of the school administration.

And yet, they *all* needed an escape. I think that's the only thing those women had in common, actually." She peers off to the side with a frown, like it's a new fact she's absorbing.

"And yet I've never found anything more relatable," Kara says, tossing back a shot.

"Hear, hear." Shauna raises her own. "My question is, how did *you* get involved in this night?" she asks.

Fee looks my way with a shrug. "They wanted the scoop on Meyer. I go to a lot of Hazel's events and such, so they wanted to know what our story was and if he'd be interested in any of their sisters, or brothers."

The last time she brought this up comes back to me, along with her explanation to them. Something about telling them she was in unrequited, bittersweet love. . . . I snort. If only she knew.

I'm not naive enough to think that her feelings match the depth of my own, even if I know she's interested in a step further than friendship now. Even if I've had a thought or two cross my mind in the past, there's never been that hard evidence. And something tells me to stay guarded against thinking she might want more now, outside of this. The umbrella of this whole arrangement is what feels safe, for now. . . .

She jokingly tells them the same thing she told me, but I laugh a little too enthusiastically this time.

"Hey, let's FaceTime Hazel before it gets too late?" Fee says to me, and some part of me is grateful that she's not the least bit hesitant or awkward where Hazel is concerned, though I'm struggling to reconcile the dad in me with the guy that is vividly picturing Fee half naked and grinding her hips on my lap, head falling to the side when sensation took over.

"Meyer?"

"What?"

"Uh, did you want to call Hazel?"

Shit. "Oh—yeah, I would, but Marissa took her to a movie tonight."

She smiles and shrugs. "Alright. How's her state project going?"

I can't help but laugh, leaning in to her ear while Kara and Shauna are back at the bar. "Fee, you're in the city, in your twenties, in the prime of your life and career, with two of your idols. And you want to hear about a report on South Dakota?" She laughs back as the music gets louder, then slips into ASL.

"I'll save my voice this way. And yes, I want to hear about Hazel's South Dakota, because anything that kid does is funnier and better than any other stupid report on the place."

I blink when she finishes, shaking my head. *"How did we get so lucky with you? Who do I thank for you coming into her life?"* I sign. They're all the words that come to mind.

"You can thank a shitty umbrella!" she replies with a laugh.

Something catches the corner of my eye and I turn to see Kara and Shauna staring at us, both sipping from the little red straws in their drinks.

"That looked very intimate!" Shauna yells across the table in a decidedly un-intimate way.

"My nipples feel all tingly!" Kara shouts, the music dying in the latter half of the sentence and drawing the eyes of everyone else in the place.

A voice comes over the sound system then: "Alright, ladies and gentlemen! We've got a special surprise guest for you tonight. I need everyone in here to give a warm welcome to Shauna Cooper!"

And the magic begins.

TWENTY

NOW

Nobody knows what they're doing. Nobody does.
Everyone's winging it out there. Some people are
just better at pretending to be confident.

—KUMAIL NANJIANI

FARLEY

If I'd have known there was a surprise set tonight, I would have insisted it be mine.

When it's time to do something that terrifies you, always, *always* go first.

I learned this when Marissa and I decided to go skydiving in college. Each step felt more treacherous and scarier as the process progressed, anxiety building at each step. What began with the instructor dipping into a serious tone and making eye contact with everyone, demanding that we all be honest when it came to filling out our weight so that we could be paired with the appropriately sized tandem diver, graduated to a ride in a rickety tin can that masqueraded as a plane. The man whose lap I sat strapped to was an on-brand, terrifying Aussie named Timothy (not to be confused with Tim, Timmer, or Timmy, I was informed) with a curly gray ponytail and *zero* sense of humor.

The biggest moment of terror (emphasis on *error*) came when they asked who wanted to go first. Marissa looked over to my horror-stricken expression and volunteered. She and her partner rocked once, twice, and then *poof,* my friend dissolved into the atmosphere. I actually screamed, over and over, until they calmed me down and told me she was fine, that it was just the velocity that made it *look* like she evaporated. I eventually sucked it up and went, swallowing back bile and unable to enjoy the experience until halfway down. It wasn't until I went again, a year or so later, and was *first* to jump, that I found it to be the exhilarating thrill that so many claim.

So, as Shauna makes her way out onto the stage, and as people whip out their phones to make calls and take pictures, *my* anxiety begins to rev up. And it's justified when she absolutely *kills* it. The room does not stop laughing from start to finish. The jokes manage to be relatable even as she talks about mingling with celebrities. They manage to be moving and eye-opening on issues I've been clueless about. She's so naturally funny, so creative with her poignant takes, and so fucking brilliant.

It makes me suddenly wonder if I'm on some new messed-up game show. Like *Punk'd,* except they tell you you've accomplished a dream before they pop out and tell you they were kidding, you were only nominated for charity, you're actually not good enough. Cue laughter cards.

"Well, I think it's safe to say that stuff is staying!" she proclaims after dancing her way back to the table.

I try not to do this. This thing where I make everything about me. And, because I like Shauna, because I've worshipped her from a fan standpoint and I genuinely enjoy getting to know her as a friend, it *is* easy to be happy for her success. It's also easy to enjoy sharing the same atmosphere of that kind of talent. So I set aside my inner bullshit and focus on those parts.

Plus, I'm buzzing from the drinks and laughter and the high still lingering from . . . earlier. Those flashes of Meyer's face and hands and thoroughly coming apart above him. Not to mention anticipation of what's to come. The rightness, and the relief that rides alongside the longing. Relief that he wants me, too.

I'm aware that I should be worried about the iceberg of emotion that we are—so much to still address beneath the surface—but I'm flat-out floating on it for the time being.

"You fucking killed it," I cheer for Shauna.

"And now you're totally freaked out, aren't you?" Kara says with a laugh my way.

"How'd you know?"

"Because we've been there!" Shauna shouts, grabbing her drink. "I like to go first and get it out of my system before I sit on it too long, but I gotta say, *I* think you need to work with that PTA thing and play off of that. When you're just talking, it goes a bunch of directions and it's funny as hell."

"I will. For sure. I'll keep it worked in."

"Now what about you, Meyer Harrigan? What's in store for you?" Kara asks, as we start to shift on our seats to the beat.

"In between projects right now," he replies. "But I plan to write a new screenplay soon."

This is news to me. "About what?" I ask, smiling at this small secret he's managed to keep.

He shrugs as he stands, looking down at me in a downright flirtatious way, his eyes dipping. "Don't exactly know yet, but I've got a few ideas to play with. Another round of drinks for everyone?"

"Yes, please!" we say in unison, heads turning to watch him walk away.

"I *know* his dick is big," Shauna says.

"I bet he has no trouble finding *it,* either," Kara follows with a sigh. I laugh even as I level them with a look. He found it through two layers of pants and underwear.

"I know y'all have hooked up already," Shauna prods with a brow raise, waiting for me to confirm or deny.

"Ah—no, no, don't tell me, just let me picture it." Kara closes her eyes, gives a silent pump of her fist. "For female comics everywhere."

"What do you mean?" I ask with another laugh.

"I mean that female comedians never get the hot, silent type—definitely not the ones who are funny, too. Male comics, though—they can get whoever they want. They can be ugly and only moderately funny, and they'll still score models, singers, reality stars. Any male fanboys of ours tend to be inherently creepy. Finding a man, let alone a very successful man, as a female comic is a Herculean task."

"Valid point."

"No, *really,* Farley. I dated a clown for six months when I was starting out." Kara gives me a hard look.

"He wasn't even a good clown, either!" Shauna yells, and we all bust up. I'm tempted to ask for her to define what even determines a good one, but refrain as Kara pushes her face into her palms.

"Seriously, though. Just . . . be careful. Meyer seems like a good guy, and I know he's been out of the stand-up game for a bit, anyway, so there's no need for him to be threatened or anything. But there's a reason they say all funny men are insecure, right? Don't be too shocked if he starts distancing himself the more successful you become," Kara says gently, putting her hand on mine.

I slip it away with a frown. "If anything, he's the reason I've even gotten this far. And he'd never ice me out of his life. We've got too many other . . . ties," I say confidently. "The only thing I could see him distancing himself from is the media attention, and he's already throwing himself into that for me."

"Well, that only tends to increase with this kind of success, babe. It's not the same as being an actress or a singer or anything, but it's there," Shauna adds.

As if to highlight her point, a woman taps her shoulder and asks us all for a picture just as Meyer returns with the drinks.

"Will you take one of the four of us?" she then asks me, pushing her phone my direction. I look up in confusion, but it clicks when I see the looks of sympathy on all three of their faces.

"Of course!" I shout brightly. I nail the smile to my face while I take it.

"You're gonna want one with Farley Jones in it, too. Trust me," Kara says, yanking a guy over to take one of all of us. I appreciate the vote of confidence, even if it's embarrassing. Even if Meyer's stroke on my arm feels like it's trying to be reassuring.

Of course she knows their faces. I'm still more new—newer than all of them. It's not shocking and it shouldn't bother me. It shouldn't. It doesn't.

THE REMAINDER OF THE NIGHT is everything I could've hoped for. Tyson meets us at another bar, where he and Meyer hit it off, slipping into manly conversation as the three of us slide onto the dance floor.

It's pushing 3 A.M. by the time we make it back to the hotel. I flop onto the cloud of a bed and rapidly kick my shoes off, exhausted and exhilarated.

When I prop myself onto my elbows, Meyer has his bag on his shoulder and a tired smirk on his face. "Wait—where are you going?" I ask, wishing I could sound less needy.

"I had to get a spot on the 5 A.M. flight. So I gotta just head to the airport now. If I lay down, I'll crash."

"Why didn't you say anything? I would've come back way earlier." I stand up and approach him, already forlorn.

"Because we were having a good night," he says, brushing a strand of hair from my face with a sigh. "Your flight's later today, yeah?"

"Not until four." Too far away.

"Okay, good. Rest, then. Call me when you land?"

"Meyer—" I don't know what I want to say, though, without sounding truly desperate or dumb. *Thanks for forgoing sleep and a night with your daughter so that you could support me and my career and also give me an orgasm?* Jesus, what the hell am I doing?

"Hey—what's going on in your head?" he asks, eyes flicking to my forehead like he can read the thoughts there.

"I'm just . . . sorry you stayed away an extra night and lost sleep," is all I can bring myself to say.

"You're *sorry?*" He frowns, clears his throat a little. "Do you—I mean—are *you* sorry about earlier?" His tone is limned in careful restraint.

"God—no, not at all. I'm only sorry I didn't—couldn't—return the favor." My cheeks heat, not nearly as confident as I was in those moments after.

"Fee." He waits until I look at him. "No more apologies, please. Especially since I've been thinking about that, imagining it, for a very long time."

"You have?"

He nods. Once. His hand comes up to cup my jaw and he drags his thumb across each of my lips. "Let's just say it was more satisfying than you realize," he says, and then he leans down and kisses me. "Call me later."

He leaves the room and I watch him through the peephole, waiting until he's cleared the corner and is out of sight before I turn around and slide down the door, melting in a puddle of bliss.

TWENTY-ONE

NOW

FARLEY

I somehow manage a few hours of sleep, even as I'm counting down the hours and minutes until it's time to get back home.

I fling a little wink at my own reflection on my way out of the room, "Proud of you, girl." Proud that I have refrained from texting Meyer all day, proud of my killer impression of an "I've-got-my-shit-together-and-don't-lose-my-cool-over-a-man" woman. No matter how fucking sexy, sweet, intelligent, or impressive that man is. No matter that he is the best friend I've ever had and I can't wait to know how his flight was and who annoyed him on the plane and what he and Hazel had for breakfast. I wonder if he worries about Haze as a teenager, wonder what she would think of us together, if it would change things at all.

Aaannd, there it is. The anxiety. The worry that pulls me under for a second, a wave crashing over me.

A feeling that immediately synchronizes with the realization that Meyer himself has not texted, or called me at all.

The thoughts submerge me further.

By the time I pull into the airport, I've worked myself into a knotted wreck, and I decide to do my best impression of a mature adult with conflict resolution skills. I call him.

It goes right to voice mail.

I try again and the result is the same.

Try again when I get to my gate.

Storm clouds gather in my mind, hovering over the churning ocean of my thoughts.

IT'S ASTONISHING HOW QUICKLY MY brain can go from congratulating myself, proud of how I owned up to some of my feelings, even *celebrating* how that panned out, to borderline loathing and disgust in the same day.

He absolutely regrets hooking up. It was a result of too much forced affection, too much build up, so of course he got confused. That's the only reason he thought he wanted to come back. Watching you come on his lap probably forced reality back into his brain and now he's going to want some space. You're no seductress, Farley Jones. That's probably the impression you could pull off the least. You have farted in front of this man—an accident, but still. Not a lady toot, either, it was a "Brussels sprouts are my food hyperfixation at the moment" kind of rip. You are gross. Remember what your father always told you? Men don't want girls with foul mouths and bad manners. It's unbecoming. Men don't find your cavalier attitude attractive, let alone sexy. Men don't want a dirty, unorganized woman. Men don't want a woman who wants to be lazy for an entire day, then immediately wants to take on twelve projects, plus a hike and a new hobby on the following.

Men don't want a woman who spends a day in bed after having her soul ripped out by a book, or who gets choked up over a song.

Stop being so dramatic. Men don't want women who fill every silence with a joke or a "welp" just because they can't sit still or quiet for five minutes with people they can barely tolerate.

Meyer has been subjected to all of that, every side of the warped bouncy ball that I am. More than I've allowed any other man, really. And even to those other men who I've dated—the ones who've seen the bits and pieces . . . to them I've always been *charming* in my quirkiness, in my crassness. I'm a good-times gal, the friend, the jester. Not the kind of woman they fantasize about, who gets under their skin.

How could I expect his feelings to be like mine? I can't expect that of him. I need to give him space, to respect it when he inevitably tells me he's changed his mind about this and that it's gotten out of hand. This is why I had reservations.

Look at yourself! This man is doing this for your career, and yesterday only happened because there's been too much mixing. Maybe it was the football. The collective competitive energy caused a surge in testosterone and you happened to be there, clinging to him.

It's pathetic, really, how my brain jumped through portals and to a different reality, where we'd both be desperate for each other.

Even if this was going places, who wants *this* messy girl? The one who already needs constant reassurance. Who collapses this way in a matter of hours. Meyer deserves someone stable, someone who is funny but not in an attention-seeking way. Someone who doesn't accidentally fart in front of him or verbalize her gastric woes. Someone sexy, organized, and secure.

THE PLANE LANDS, THOUGH I'VE no memory of getting on it. I pull out my phone with trembling hands while I wait for my luggage and check my calendar, grateful when I see that my therapy appointment is tomorrow.

I'm so angry at myself for letting those thoughts take over, so shaken up at the mental whipping for which only I am to blame, that it takes me a minute to register the hand on my wrist.

When I look down to Hazel's face, and spot Meyer following behind, I collapse onto my knees and hug her. My people. My girl, whether or not I get my wish where Meyer is concerned.

I pull away, crying. Hazel's frightened face is comical. *"Fee, I saw you two days ago."*

"I know. I was listening to sad stuff again." Not exactly a lie. *"What are you guys doing here?"* I swipe at my eyes, shift my gaze over to Meyer, his expression agitated. I wonder if he wants to go to me even half as badly as I want to go to him.

He braces his stance and starts signing rapidly. *"I fell asleep when I got home and forgot to plug in my phone. Alarm never went off, then, and when I woke up it was time to grab Hazel, since I gave Marissa a couple days off. So I flew out the door to get her and then I"*—he corrects himself when Hazel smacks him—*"we wanted to pick you up. I didn't have time to get back to the house for my phone and get here to grab you."* Then, out loud, "I hope this is okay? Is it too much? I'm not smothering you, am I?" He scratches the back of his neck and an impossibly large bicep rolls.

I swallow the lump in my throat, laugh a short, hysterical little sound, but manage to shake my head. "Not too much. Believe me, I am too much." He looks a bit confused, but accepts it for the time being.

"Do you want to get pizza with us?" he asks then.

Hazel slap his leg. *"I can't read lips!"*

"Do you want to get pizza with us?" he signs, correcting himself again.

"*He says he'll take us to the place with the dance game,*" Hazel adds, as if I needed to be pitched.

"*Only if you get him to do it.*"

"*Deal,*" he agrees with a smile.

AND THAT'S WHAT IT TAKES to get my mind calm—albeit not quite fully right. To make me feel warm and soft with gratitude. It takes terrible arcade pizza and the sight of Meyer's too-big body trying to keep time with the rapid dance moves on the game, both of their faces scrunched in laughter among the neon lights. And it's not just because we found the laugh, either. It's because their love holds me up.

I recognize that Dr. Deb and I need to continue patching up my mental umbrella, so that love and confidence comes from within, so that I can protect myself from the thoughts that want to surge and drown me.

But these are my puddle people, the ones who will go splash around with me, even when I can't.

WHEN HE TAKES ME HOME after, I know I need to talk to him about my mental tailspin. The anxiety battles with just wanting to *be,* though. Just wanting to move on to this next good part, whatever that may be. But he can feel my hesitation. I know he can. I catch a furrowed, concerned look lingering on his face and I know he's onto me. How I'm on the verge of saying something but can't seem to spit it out. He walks me to my door as Hazel sleeps soundly in the car.

When we step around the corner to my little alcove, I feel the unease creep into every muscle fiber in my body. I feel him looking at me, but I stare at my toes, an utter coward.

"Fee," he sighs. "What's going on? What is it? Why were you crying earlier?"

"Meyer." I finally look up at him and the sight of his face, in its chiseled and rumpled perfection, the wrinkle between his eyebrows that never smoothes away anymore, even when he's relaxed. It's like my own private billboard that states: *You're safe.*

So I decide to try my best to be open again, to remember to trust my friend and myself. "I self-induced a meltdown earlier. About us. About this," I say. "I know . . . I know you came back to the hotel, and I know that you said you wanted me, too. But then I had myself completely convinced when I couldn't get ahold of you that you regretted it, that you were going to pull back. I mean, I went down a truly crazy spiral there, it was not sane . . . and, I'm not trying to fish here, but I reminded myself the entire plane ride home how impossible it is that you could want me as much as I want you."

He inhales sharply, brows nearly touching before his face relaxes into a smile. If it was an art piece it would be called "Tentative Relief." "Fee, I only didn't push a bigger conversation yesterday because I didn't want to distract or take away more from this time for you. I didn't want you to be tempted to miss out on any time with Kara or Shauna, either. And then we were literally out of time, last night and again this morning. Honestly, when you seemed fine afterward it made me think that *you* weren't as . . . affected as I am. I think the only reason I didn't have a similar spiral is because I didn't have the same amount of lucid time to *let* myself after the whole phone mishap." A hollow laugh fans out of him. "My time between getting Haze and driving to the airport was enough, though." He inhales when he registers my returning smile. "But now I gotta know—what would make you say that? About me not wanting you as much as you want me? How could you think that now?" He runs a knuckle down my cheek and I lean in to it.

"*Because,* Meyer," I groan. *Because it's embarrassing and I feel insane and hate putting my insecurities on blast almost as much as I hate having them.*

"I'm genuinely confused, Fee. I need you to help me out here."

I just shake my head silently, trying to summon the words. Why is this still so hard? This real part of life. Why do I feel like I'm always doing an impression of someone else? Someone funny who doesn't care about the disapproval. Someone sexy and confident. Someone who communicates, who goes after what she wants.

"Do you really have no idea how much I care about you?" he asks. "How beautiful you are? How much you mean to me? To us?"

"My, I do know that you care about me. I mean, you wouldn't have agreed to this if you didn't. I *do* know that but . . . I'm re-alizing what's at risk, here. If this blows up in our faces. I'm realizing how scary it is. And *God,* okay, fine. I'll just say it." I suck in a breath. "For the first time, I'm also *really* thinking of all the dumb shit I say and do on stage. I feel like I oblit-erated most of the sex appeal I may have had at some point," I admit, my hand flapping up before it slaps against the side of my thigh. I've admitted it and I'm angry at it. Angry at the honesty of it.

His response is to *laugh.* My face dives into a glare. "I'm sorry, I'm not laughing at you," he says. "Well, maybe a little, I am." I fold my arms and lift an eyebrow before he moves, backs me against my door and cages me in. I feel my eyes widen, hands clamping down to my sides. He smothers his laugh and sharp-ens his attention to my face. "When you're on stage, talking about fecal matter or awkward sex or even that bit about the time you developed a crush on your barista—which makes my blood actually *boil*, by the way—do you know what I see?" He doesn't wait for me to respond, his smile going tortured. "I see the way the lights make your eyes sparkle, the way you grin so big I feel it in my sternum. Your hair, Jesus, you have the most incredible hair. I couldn't give a shit less about hair until I started looking at yours. It's shiny and smooth, the prettiest color I've ever seen. I love it when you do it that one way, all wavy. You'll wear it in a ponytail and I imagine wrapping it around my wrist, letting it slip through my palm." He lets out a shaky breath and I feel it on my lips. His eyes dip to them. "I see the way your ass looks in whatever it is that you wear, and it kills me. Do you realize that every time you bend over on stage you stick it in whatever direction I am? It's agony. I don't care if you're yards away from me. It's like a homing beacon, and it's every single time, Farley Jones. And I try to be a decent guy, I swear I really do, but I'm not a fucking saint." He shakes his head ruefully. "I imagine you bare and bent over for me at least every single day. You could be up there talking about the various states of your underwear and all I get hung up on is picturing you in your underwear. You'll do some wacky voice and when you get extra animated, sometimes your hand will slip into a sign, and I'll think, 'Oh my god, that was just for me.' Even though it's only one word and it's unintentional, because no one else notices, I latch onto it and hoard it to myself. And later, I take those moments out and examine them. I obsess over them. I think about how you make a joke sometimes and it makes me want to write an entire movie or show based on it, because it's so goddamn intelligent and funny and yet it also has this extraordinary heart because it's *you*."

My palms press into my door as my chest rises and falls, my

heart twisting and pulling in my throat. I look at his mouth as he wets his lips.

His head tilts and he snags my eyes with his again. "So, if you're worried about me thinking about you in those terms, if you don't think I find you painfully sexy, the kind of sexy that haunts and colors my every thought, you're misinformed. You might be funny, but not even *you* are funny enough to distract me from all that, Fee."

And then he bends and leaves a peck on my open, dumbfounded mouth, before he pushes off the door and turns away, leaving me speechless.

He stops again before he turns the corner and says over his shoulder, "About that other stuff, Fee. I'm scared too. I'm so damn terrified that it's taken me years and this deal to work up the courage to risk it." He turns all the way, then, and meets my eyes. "But I figure if it means that much to us both, then we just can't let something bad happen. We take care of each other like we have from day one, and we'll be okay." He nods, like he's affirming this to himself, too. "Plus, we agreed in the beginning, and no matter what, that stands."

And he walks away. Just like that. He's said it out loud and it's there, an ever-present speech bubble hovering above us. And instead of letting it catapult me into thinking *What if you're no good for him, though, and he's just the only one who doesn't realize it yet?*—because that *is* the thought that rises, like my mind is some kind of backwards eight ball that's just been shaken up—I decide to toss it aside for what's real. I decide to trust my friend and his words, to let them wrap me up and hold me.

TWENTY-TWO

6 MONTHS AGO

FARLEY

I'm finally settling in for the night, top knot secured in a scrunchie, face cleared of all makeup along with signs of life, slathered in all my "slimes" (as Hazel calls them), when Meyer's face pops up on my phone screen.

"Yello," I greet, flopping loose-limbed onto the couch and scrolling for a new *Survivor* season.

"Fee. Do you have any more of those s'mores bars things?" he asks urgently, like they're an essential life-saving tool he needs, making me sit up straighter.

"No, why? I just gave you a tray of them two days ago! What's wrong?"

"Your house is on my way back, and I'm going to eat the goddamn hat floating around in my car if I don't eat something soon. I gotta eat!" he declares vehemently.

"Okay, sir, dial it back. I'll remind you that I have tried to give you the recipe for those bars many times. It's just one I found on the internet, not some generational memento passed down from my hillbilly camp-loving ancestors or something. It's s'mores, not exactly baked Alaska."

"I just need to eat something. And I'll remind *you*, again, mine didn't turn out the same!" he whines. Actually whines.

"*Jesus*, My. I'm about to start *Survivor*. These people get a bag of rice and are stoked. I think you're being dramatic." I hold the phone away from my face so I can smother an evil laugh.

"I'll be there in ten minutes." And then he hangs up.

In five, he Cosmo-Kramers through my door like a man possessed, his glare narrowing in on me before he stomps toward me in the kitchen.

"Why are you all dressed up?" I accuse. "Where did you just come from?"

"A dinner thing."

"A dinner for what?"

"For the finale of *Funnybones*."

"A dinner celebrating *you* and your show?! Why didn't you tell me?!"

"Fee, I'm dying here. What do you have as far as snacks?" He rips open the refrigerator. "Aha. *Yesss*, fuck me up with some mozzarella," he exclaims, grabbing the bag like a prize. "And it really wasn't a big deal."

It was a big-enough deal for him to get dressed up. A blue jacket-blazer thing over a crisp white button-down, with matching indigo dress pants that hug his truly spectacular ass.

"What're you making?" he asks around a mouthful.

"I'm making your stupid s'mores things," I grumble. They're a pain at every step and are incredibly messy, though I love how much he loves them. So much that I've long-conned him and made him dependent on me for them, only ever giving him the recipe sans one ingredient or two. I claim to not know which recipe I used originally, but I know. I blended a few of them.

"Good, I'm going to watch you make them," he says before he reaches into the cheese bag again and pinches a handful.

"Get your hands out of my cheese, you animal! At least get a bowl!" I demand. He dips his head back, showing off the column of his throat as he drops some in his mouth. "And no, I don't need you hovering while I make them."

"You mad at me or something?"

"I mean, I wish you would've told me about your dinner. I would've wanted to celebrate you, too," I admit.

"I was a cowriter. It wasn't about *me* at all, Fee. It was for everybody." His eyes widen when he realizes what he's said.

I carefully set down the rolling pin that I'm using to painstakingly fine-crush graham crackers and drag my eyes to him. "Does that mean the cast was there too?"

"Fee . . ."

"*Meyer.* Did you deny me my one chance to meet Dermot Mulroney?!"

"Fee . . ."

"And then you come here, begging me for treats?! Nah-ah." I set everything aside and go walk to the couch haughtily.

I hear him sigh behind me and zip up the cheese. "Jones, I'm sorry. Would you believe me if I told you it was because I don't want to share you?"

I scoff, even though the statement fills me with a frothy, bubbly feeling. "Meyer, I stand in front of hundreds of people for a living and wax poetic about my innermost thoughts. I quite literally share myself with whoever cares to listen." I glare at him over my shoulder.

"Exactly. Maybe I just don't want anyone *else* interested in you . . . or your s'mores bars," he says lightly, trying to pacify me, pouting his lips and lifting his eyebrows in a *forgive me I'm a cute man-baby* sort of way.

He's the first to relent with a sigh. "I'm sorry, Jones."

"I don't believe you, Harrigan."

He walks around to stand between me and the TV. He's ditched the jacket somewhere and starts rolling up the ends of his shirtsleeves, exposing miles of well-developed forearms, my eyelids peeling farther and farther apart with each inch. I bet I could swing from those if he'd let me. I swallow and try turning up the volume to distract myself. Remind myself to blink.

He thwarts my efforts when he steps in every direction I try to lean, blocking my view until I give up, turn it off, and lift an eyebrow his way. I catch the wisp of a smirk, but he smartly flattens it and puts on an earnest face, hands on his hips.

"I mean it. I didn't think. I didn't even want to stay long and I think I assume that everyone else is miserable at those things like I am. I should've invited you, and I promise I will next time. Maybe then I *won't* be so miserable. I'm sorry, Farley Amalie Jones."

I make a sound in the back of my throat. "Don't use my middle name, that's cheating." It makes me feel all feminine and lovely, which makes the reptilian part of my brain want to follow it up with a burp.

And then the avatar currently operating Meyer's body gets on all fours and begins to crawl toward me. I'm unable to look away. "W-what are you—?"

He folds his hands in front of him, sitting up on his knees. And then he juts out his lip in the saddest, most pathetic expression I have ever seen. "Please forgive me," he begs, fluttering his eyelashes.

I can't help it, I snort nervously. He's so ridiculous and unlike himself. "You must need food. You're acting loopy. Why didn't you eat at the party?"

"It's Hollywood, there's never enough food at those things," he replies before he resumes his phony lip-quivering.

"Fine." I move to get up and he wraps me in a hug from his knees, almost knocking me back over. My hands flap at my sides, his cheek against my belly button. And instead of patting his shoulders like a normal hug from any other normal human in this position, my hands both go to his head, cradling it, nails lightly scraping against his scalp. It's a lovers' embrace, not a friendly one. It's so at odds with how we normally are together, hovering like repelling magnets, unable to touch—actually *avoiding* it. He went and flipped on me sometime today and forgot to warn me. I feel myself cracking.

I grapple for a segue, *any* segue. "Uhhh, I'll only make the s'mores if you cut a deal, though," is what I come up with.

He's frozen, we're frozen like this, his arms crossed and resting just above my very clenched behind. Ovaries can't make sounds internally, right? Like how a stomach growls? His ear is pressed so close to them. I can practically feel my eggs screaming in tiny cartoon voices, *"We're in here, sweet virile man! Save us from this would-be spinster she-devil! Let us not waste in vain!"*

"Yeah?" he replies.

"You take a selfie with me, *and* you let me cut your hair," I say. Maybe that will cover me as far as why my hands seem to be touching it in such a proprietary manner. Hazel hates his hair in this longer, scruffier style anyway. *I* personally think he could pull off a bowl cut if he wanted to, so it makes no difference to me.

"Are you plotting shaving my head or any other nefarious act of revenge?" he asks warily, his deep timbre vibrating through my core. I swallow.

"No." I feign a laugh, my own voice coming out a full octave higher. "Just clean it up a bit."

"Alright, I can do that." He takes a deep breath and I panic-part away from him, shuffling back to the kitchen.

He follows me, continuing to hover while he inspects every ingredient and measurement that I combine. He's clearly suspicious, stopping midsentence to say things like, "Okay wait, how much of that?" and "How long did you mix that, then? And that went in first?" He leans back onto the counter on his palms, head angled my way while he continues to watch me work, as he shares anecdotes from the party, some of the drama from the show that he's neglected to apprise me of. Tales about entitled celebs and their insane demands. I'm more interested in the smaller, pettier gossip, though. The set designers clashing over a wallpaper, the sabotage and food-stealing wars. He nods to the bowl with a frown when I've stopped working, when I turn my full attention to him in shock after hearing how one sound tech paid for Ubers for a week just so he could leave his car in the designated spot reserved for his work nemesis. "Alright, alright. Patience, my guy."

I distract him just enough to maintain my secrets. I ask him to go move my clothes to the dryer for me so I can quickly add the browned butter I've discreetly made. And when I pull them out of the oven finally, I ask him to open a bottle of wine so I can grab the flaky salt. I grab a healthy-sized pinch before I close the cupboard and start to sprinkle.

"What the hell is that?" his voice sounds, inches from my ear. In my panic, I throw the salt over my shoulder. "Fee?" he growls. I turn around slowly. There're flakes of salt stuck in his beard and the front of his hair. "What. Is. That?" My jig is up.

"It's just salt, okay?"

"You *never* included that on the ingredients list."

"No?"

"*No!*" he parrots.

"Well you'd think you would have seen it on the bars themselves, Meyer, it's not exactly hidden," I say with an undignified eye roll.

"You've been keeping this from me!"

"It's salt, Meyer! Not exactly groundbreaking." When I meet his eyes they're crinkled, suppressing a laugh.

"You didn't want me to have the secrets, did you?" he teases, squinting at me. "You wanted me needy, *begging* for it, didn't you? You're high on power."

Sweet salmonella, why does *that* idea make my stomach drop to my toes? I shove a bite of the dough I'd reserved into my mouth to hide my shock.

"Aww, Fee. Don't worry, I'll still be desperate for your treats, whether or not I have your secrets." I go white-hot and cold in an instant.

"Y-You don't need to. You can absolutely make them on your own now. Save me the trouble. It was an honest mistake, Meyer." I try to convince him with a shrug, all false bravado.

"Sure," he replies playfully.

"For real, have you checked your blood sugar? You've been especially weird all night." I point the spoon at him accusingly and he laughs, taking a massive, gooey bite.

"Yeah, yeah. We taking this selfie before or after my grooming appointment?"

"After. And really, though, what's gotten into you?"

He shrugs once, a quick toss of his shoulders. "Maybe it *is* my blood sugar." He frowns.

"You know what, maybe it's me. Maybe I'm finally having an effect on you. Maybe I just make you feel younger." I smile with all my teeth and mime tossing my hair.

He feigns a gag, but then replies, considering. "Maybe?" He cants his head to the side with a squint, leans a hip on the counter next to mine. "I know you have some kind of influence on me and how I feel, that's for sure. I don't know if I'd describe it as *younger*, exactly. Maybe lighter. You make me feel a little less weary."

Blood flees my head in centrifugal motion and I stand there, mouth suspended in a little "o" . . . because isn't that the dream? To have a heart that's less burdened simply because of who you share it with?

"Anyway." He propels himself off of the counter, clearly not suffering the same profound moment that I am. "Let's get this cut done."

THIS WAS A MISTAKE OF epic proportions. Cutting his hair has my fingers on it, in it, and on *him*. It's wickedly intimate. It's his eyes cataloging me as I circle him. It's me bending, leaning forward into him to keep the lines straight. His breath ghosting against my wrists or my face.

"Meyer, do you ever think . . ." I *can* ask. I *should* ask. "Do you ever think about meeting someone? Do you try? I realize I'm kind of a selfish friend, that I never ask."

He looks down, considering again as he folds his arms across his broad chest. Jesus, he's getting broader, somehow.

"I guess, sure. But I feel like I'm just now starting to get ahold of my life again and of myself. Like I'm just starting to break the surface, reaching calmer shores, sun breaking through the clouds, whatever kind of analogy you want to throw at it. So, I'm not putting pressure on it. I'm feeling . . ." He pauses, sighs. ". . . happy, with life. Anything else is an added bonus. And dating when you have any kind of fame is . . . complicated, believe it or not."

"Of course. That makes sense." *That's why he hasn't dated, not because he harbors something for you.*

"Thank you for this." He gestures up to his hair as he takes off the sheet. "Want to watch *Survivor*? Maybe it'll motivate me not to eat the entire tray."

"Okay. Good idea."

I end up falling asleep during the show, and don't remember to take that picture.

When I remind him the next day, I get a photo message back of him leaning over and grinning toothily next to an open-mouthed and passed out me. The photo is from the couch, though I woke up in bed this morning with no memory of walking myself there.

TWENTY-THREE

NOW

Ego is hilarious—especially the vanity of a comedian. As soon as you see one start worrying about how cool he is or about how many stadiums he can fill, he stops being funny.

—RICKY GERVAIS

MEYER

"Strip it down," I say.

"Gladly, but Lance and Bob are, like, right around the corner," she replies.

"*Jesus,*" I mutter under my breath when the mental image of her stripping is immediately conjured, my abs going tight. *Point, Fee.* My eyes dart over to her satisfied expression as she leans back in her chair.

Backstage is quiet for the most part tonight, just the low sound of the television in the distance from where Bob and Lance are sitting in the break room.

"I meant the set," I clarify. "You're trying to layer it too much. Take it apart and get it back to the basics." I cross my arms and sit on the counter behind me, let it be obvious as I look down the length of her. The look aims to seduce, but lazily perusing her body ratchets up the tension in *my* gut, too. I cross a foot over the other to give my jeans some room.

In the week since San Francisco, we've fallen back into our tit for tat, but it's graduated to teasing glances and touches, abrupt remarks to test how the other's eyes dilate.

Now that we both know we want each other, it's how we pass this waiting period. I'm not sure what we're waiting for, exactly, because since we've officially given ourselves permission, it's all I seem to think about. Where we so often avoided contact before, it's crossed over into being harder *not* to.

But I'm still trying to focus on spending as much time as I can with Hazel before she goes to Ohio, and I know Fee needs both the room and support to work on her material.

Which is why we decided to try Lance's and wing it tonight, without Kara or Shauna and that added pressure, just to see what happens. And our game is the thing that's keeping her distracted, keeping her from stressing. We always do some form of this before a show to warm up. A game of wit and banter, challenging and rising, but tonight's improv has rapidly turned downright heated. While it feels a bit like hydroplaning—rudderless and potentially dangerous—I can't bring myself to tap on the brakes or steer out of it, either.

She groans, and maybe I'm just imagining things now, but it sounds a little like a moan. "I'm trying, but everything just feels . . . disingenuous."

"Then make it about your life. What takes up space in that brain these days?" I chew my lip to stop the smile.

Her cheeks lift only briefly before they drop. "Jesus, I have to go out there and talk completely out of my ass. This is going to be a disaster." She blasts out of her seat and scrambles around, snatching her notepad and a pencil. "I probably shouldn't be letting you distract me with your vampire eyes and your body right now, Meyer. I'm flustered and tense enough as it is."

I chuckle. Time to double down. "*Letting* me, huh? And do share with me how my body's involved?" Her cheeks redden immediately. "I'm here for tension relief, if needed?" I add, and she chuffs out a choked sound.

She's not one to be outdone, though, so I see it happen when the gears in her mind turn over and land on her next words.

"You'd just let me take what I want, then?" The huskiness in her tone has warmth crawling up my neck.

"Jones, I'm happy to follow your lead in most things. All things, really, up to a point." I watch her chest rise and fall quickly, trace her collarbones with my eyes. "But past that point, I'd be certain to give you what you need."

"Awful full of yourself, aren't you?" she breathes, eyes lighting.

"I could help you out with that, too?"

She gasp-laughs and her eyes go wide. "I doubt even you could wind me down right now, My."

"When have you known me to be unjustifiably conceited?" I ask, clamping down my jaw as I mentally shuffle the ways I've imagined working her body, wringing her out. How her skin would feel on mine, the fit of her in my lap.

She inhales through her nose, and the red in her cheeks spreads down her neck. I imagine the color bleeding to her chest the way it did in the hotel and *shit,* okay. *Now* it's time to walk this back, immediately, before I go full mast.

Her eyes grow bigger, though, color shifting beneath the surface again. "Meyer," she says, the words bursting from her lips in a panic, "I can't remember anything, not any of the old stuff either. I can't remember it. I'll freeze. I'll die out there." Her lips go completely ashen in an instant that has me diving for her.

"Whoa, whoa, whoa." I snag her eyes and hold them. "You've gotta breathe, Fee. It's just another regular day. You—You're sharper than everyone out there in that room. Go out there and tell them whatever it is going on in that insane brain of yours, literally, whatever it is that you're thinking, and you'll make them fall in love with you, I promise. They're going to hang on to your every word. You're safe here. It's Lance's." I suck in a slow breath, blow out. "Breathe with me for a second here, angel."

She's never, ever spun out like this, but she gets her bearings and matches my breathing.

In, two, three, four; out, two, three, four. We repeat it countless times, the minutes slipping away.

Her face and lips start to regain their color eventually, but my eyes remain glued to her until she sighs through her nose. My thumbs stroke back and forth on her shoulders rapidly, like I'm seeking my own comfort. Because damn if her panic didn't just throw me into my own a bit. . . .

"Fee, I didn't know you were on the edge like that. I'm sorry. I wouldn't have teased."

"I don't think I really knew either." She inhales and shudders. And then her eyes meet mine, her tongue darting across her lips. "Kiss me?" she asks.

I search her face, unsure if this is actually a good or healthy diversion, but when her teeth sink into her lip hesitantly, self-consciously, I break.

More like I keep my foot on the gas and hope we don't spin out.

With a groan, I grab the lapels of her little vest and yank her to me.

It's fucking, what our mouths do. Tongues and teeth and lips, biting and sliding and pressing. It's warm and heavy. Then there's that fruity mint-flavored gum that I plan to buy a whole damn pallet of. I moan into her mouth when her cool fingertips graze beneath my shirt, and I feel her lips curl into a smile in return. I'm immediately relieved that the distraction is working, despite my warring emotions. My hands skate down her waist to her ass and squeeze as her hips arch into me, the jut of them pressing to my thighs. The recesses of my mind prompt me to check the clock, so I eye it when I tilt her head and kiss her neck below her ear, her warm scent invading my senses like a drug. Under twelve minutes until showtime. My hands trace the soft skin of her lower back and around to her front, just above her jeans button, my heart thundering in my chest because it's been at least four—maybe five—years since I truly touched a woman, and this is *Fee, my* Fee. I look down at her and she's already nodding, eyes heavy-lidded. She tries to undo her button with shaky hands, movements jerky. I grab her hands and kiss a palm before I link them around my neck. "Let me."

A breath winds out of me as I do, my rough and clumsy hands so at odds with the delicate scrap of yellow lace I uncover. The heels of her palms press into the base of my skull at either side and I have to stifle a groan, feeling the heat of her before my hand even reaches its destination. And then when I do, *fuck*, my own eyes roll back in my head, and I clench my molars together to stop my teeth from chattering because I'm *dying* to be here. Right here. I press my forehead to hers as she hitches on a sound. I think I could come just like this, I realize. Swallowing her gasps, watching her expression knit tighter and tighter, eyes closed and lost in feeling. I circle and slide and I *feel* every tiny noise she makes from high in her throat, feel like it's me being tugged with each filthy little wet sound. She pulls tighter when I stay right here, not pressing hard, just lightly swiping at a steady pace. The steadier I am, the more frantically her breaths drum against the shell of my ear. Until she stops breathing altogether, holding it just a beat before she begins pulsing rapidly on my fingers, her lids cracking open and whispering my name through a pant, melting all around me. On and on and on.

I rest my head against the wall for a brief moment, trying to collect myself before I lean back and steady her on her feet.

I zip and button her back up, hands trembling much harder than when they started, my voice even more so when I say, "Fee?" She smiles hazily up at me as I start walking her in the intended direction, shaking my head a little to clear it. "I want you to go out there and tell everyone what makes you angry, sad, happy, horny, whatever pops into your head, you say it. You go out there and start talking to them and tell them every funny feeling. It's showtime." And then I spin her around, give her a nudge with a swat on the ass before she steps out onto the stage.

TWENTY-FOUR

NOW

Comedy is defiance—a snort of contempt in the face
of fear and anxiety. It's laughter that allows room
for hope to creep back on the inhale.

—WILL DURST

FARLEY

"So on that note, I'd like you all to give a warm welcome to
Miss Farley Jones!" Lance calls into the mic.

The applause roars as I turn and look back over my shoulder
at a smug Meyer, though I'm not sure how someone can pull
off "smug" while adjusting his pants like he is. The corner of
his mouth flicks up and he blows a bubble my way—a bubble
with *my* gum, I now realize.

I look around with a smile, immediately recognizing a few
faces as I take stock of how I feel.

Somehow, making me thoroughly fall apart on his hand,
detonating me into shimmering little fragments of light that

rival the ones shining down on me now, has wiped my head clean of the anxiety and the panic.

A little road map forms in my mind, one with no street names or distances but a guide for how this thing is going to go. I lengthen my strides, my smile curving genuinely.

The mic is a friend, a comfortable weight in my hand. Their claps are little bursts of energy that shoot straight into my veins.

"Hello hello, everyone!" I smile and wave at the faces I recognize, Marissa at a front-row table. "First, and foremost, I have some announcements to make. To declare. To decree, if you will . . . ," I sigh happily. "Fuck it, I'm smug, you guys. I. Am. Smug. And I don't care who knows it! Because things are *good*. They're really good. They're so good that I'm actually *more* anxious. Like, how bad things happen in threes, good things only happen in singles, so around the corner, any minute now, I think I'm going to trip over my own feet on the sidewalk and snap my neck on the curb before a bus comes and squishes my head like a grape—that kind of anxious." A swell of laughter lifts me. "Sidebar here: I no longer allow stools in my house since watching *Million Dollar Baby*." The laughter rolls, accelerating.

"But back to business. I am smug, and yes, anxious about *why* I'm so smug, so I'm here to talk it out with you all and unpack this baggage because this just seems like a great place to air out all my shit, you know?

"First announcement: I am no longer single. You may have heard, but *I* am in a relationship. Yes, me, okay? And I get it, yes, go ahead and clap because it's a feat worth celebrating. . . .

"It's a feat worth celebrating because we all know it's not this kinda girl"—I jab a thumb at myself—"that gets the guy. Not

the loud, crass girl who knows she's damaged and high maintenance and makes jokes about it. No, no. It's always two types
of women who get the man." I hold up two fingers to elucidate.
"It's either the subtle wallflowers, or the ones who *know* they're
sexy and confident. It seems like you either have to have no idea
how appealing you are, or you have to be fully aware of it and
proud to embrace your power. It's not us weird in-betweeners.
Not the *truly* unhinged." I open my eyes as wide and crazily as
I can. "The ones who get dressed to the nines in the sexiest get-
ups they own, and then get drunk and aggressively convince all
the other girls on the dance floor to take off their foot-prisons,
build a shrine with them in the middle of a ceremonial circle,
while you get them all to perform a weird-girl tribal dance to
Beyoncé." I mime a little dance, hopping around the mic stand
in a circle as I cackle maniacally. People start jostling around in
their seats with the laughter, like they're all on an off-roading
adventure down a bumpy mountain road.

Well, buckle up, motherfuckers.

"No. It's not the ones who incite chaos and riots and bring
down the collective sexiness in the atmosphere, the ones who
dial up the crazy.

"And yet, I've somehow managed to land a man, so of
course I now feel qualified to give pointers on what I can only
guess has worked for me."

"First and foremost, I'm here to tell you that bonding over
a shared love of things is overrated. I mean it. Fuck your hob-
bies, Andrew, I don't care about what you love, what brings you
contentment. No, give me the things you *hate*. Bonding over
things you hate?" I clutch my chest and let my eyes roll back in
mock ecstasy with a moan. "If there isn't a dating app centered
around that yet, there needs to be. Because you can learn to

craft your own home-brewed IPA by yourself, leave me out of it, that's fine. But if we go somewhere together and you don't share my hatred for the bicyclists who are pedaling away *on* the goddamn line and not in their lane, then already our night is off to a bad start. And if you won't talk shit with me about that other couple we know who created a joint Facebook page, then I don't want it. I mean that wholeheartedly."

The minutes pass in a flash that flows, and I continue to surf along the rising and falling waves. It's like all the bits of material that have been stored in the corners of my brain finally reveal themselves, and they all stick the landing. It's all good; it's exactly how I wanted it to be.

I never say Meyer's name, but I know they all know who he is, which is what makes it work extra well when I start centering the jokes around him.

"It's almost disgusting, really, how great he is. He's so out of my league, you guys. He's hot, and he's funny . . . ugh, I know right? I hate me, too." I pop a hip and smile demurely. "And he's *older.* So he just gets it, you know? He's so together, so scheduled and organized and sure of himself. Sometimes he'll do something and I just—" I make a fawning noise, start rocking side to side and hum-sing Salt-N-Pepa's "Whatta Man," before I bring a hand out again to count on my fingers. "He's always got Tums or Advil on him." One. "He never wants to stay out too late." Two. *"He goes to therapy."* Three Four Five Six Seven Eight Infinity . . . I put the mic between my thighs so I can count on all my fingers, then pause long enough to let the energy settle, let the appreciation sink in before I flip the script.

"Now, I want you to think about everything I've just said, and apply it to a woman." The laughs start to rumble again. "Yeah, not *quite* the same impact, is there? 'She's so together, scheduled, organized, sure of herself.' ... Makes her sound like she's not all that much fun, huh? 'She's older.' Don't lie, your brain went 'Ew.' 'She's always got Tums and Advil on her, never wants to stay out too late, goes to therapy'—Jesus, what is wrong with this bitch?" Laughter rises to a rolling boil.

I indulge myself in a laugh with them to close that section out. "I mean, it really makes you think, doesn't it? It made me think, at least. I actually got invited out with a group of women who were all on the PTA once, and let me tell you, I learned some shit that night, too. I learned that the pressure and the double standards placed on us have not *really* changed, not where they've been ingrained into us, truly. And consequently, the way that those women cut loose was closer to a horror movie than some funny, silly romcom. That night escalated to something dark and sinister, quickly, and I have a few theories as to why. . . ."

AT SOME POINT LATER IN the set, I branch off because I use the term "sure as shit," which prompts me to veer into a discussion on how bowel movements are anything but a sure thing for me. "If I travel, change my coffee brand, look at my phone a second too long in the morning, or if a butterfly flaps its wings on the other side of the world, it *will* affect my digestive system."

I steer things back on track at some point, to what it's like to be constantly aware of how we are perceived, constantly asking questions of ourselves that would never even occur to men.

It splinters a bit more than my normal stuff, has a sting to it. But it comes together as I take apart arguments and thoughts, piecing them back together in new collages.

For once, when I find Meyer as soon as I exit the stage, it's not his frown that ropes me in. It's a lopsided smile with a little shake of his head. And it doesn't occur to me to be self-conscious in that moment, either. I hop into his arms, lay an obnoxious, smacking kiss on his lips, and say, "Tell me some-one got some of that on video so I can memorize it!"

"Yes, camera was set up for the entire thing," he says with a laugh.

"I think our new warm-up routine stays, too."

"I think I'll allow it," he replies, sealing the deal with one more kiss.

TWENTY-FIVE

NOW

MEYER

Me: Do you think my daughter hates me?

Fee: When you picked her up from school in JNCOs and the sideways Flexfit, yes, 100% she hated you.

Me: That was YOUR idea.

Fee: Please don't ever tell her. I've never seen that shade of red on a human before. The chain wallet was your touch, I'll remind you.

Fee: Why do you ask?

I pull my phone up and send her a picture of the movie. I've kept it on mute since I actively try to avoid watching the first five minutes.

Fee: Lolololololol Fly Away Home again?! You have it on mute right now don't you?

Me: . . .

Me: She LIKES to make me cry with the fucking song, I swear. I get that the geese are cute but it feels like she just wants to torture me at this point.

Fee: Lol. You know that's not really it, right?

Me: ?

Fee: Meyer . . .

Me: ???

Fee: Jeez. Even you are clueless, I swear . . .

Fee: Fly Away Home is about a little girl who loses her mother. She then goes on to live with her dad, who struggles to connect with her. She's angry and lonely and feels isolated. They start to establish trust when her dad lets her keep the geese and supports her caring for them. He builds her her own plane so she can fly with them, My . . . It's a movie about a dad who goes above and beyond to support his girl's dreams, even when it's dangerous/crazy and makes no sense to anyone else.

Me: Oh . . .

Me: You don't think she thinks we're struggling to connect though, right?

Fee: You're such a dude sometimes. Even if you do cry every single time you watch it. (Which is adorable, by the way)

The way I feel my face pull into a grin at being called adorable is fucking ridiculous.

Me: So?

Me: . . . ?

Fee: *Sigh* No, Meyer. I don't think she feels like you are struggling to connect. I think she just likes the part about the girl getting to do amazing stuff with the support of her dad. And the cute geese.

HAZEL ELBOWS ME. "*THE BEGINNING is over, you big baby*," she signs with a smile. "*Did you invite Fee over?*"

"No, not tonight."

"Why not?"

I sigh. "*I think I've been a bit distracted lately and wanted to make sure we got family time before you go to Grandma and Grandpa's for three weeks.*"

"*Fee is family too, though.*"

I pause at that and stare at her for a second, at her determined, serious face. I wonder if she gets it from me, that intensity. . . . Maybe she does, but that wide-open heart was just something she was born with. If being a dad has taught me anything, it's that so much of the good stuff isn't a product of my parenting at all: it's pure dumb luck.

"She is family, isn't she?"

She throws a "duh" face my way before turning back to the TV. I nudge her again, feeling bold.

"What would you think of it if Fee became"—I struggle to find the right wording and translate it in my mind—*"more? More to me?"*

She frowns a little, considering. *"It would be mostly the same, though?"*

"Yes. Just . . . more."

"More what?" Her face changes as it dawns on her. *"Like Olive's mom and Mr. Prestley?"*

My heart trips over a beat. *"Yes."*

She cocks her head with a blink, the gesture making her look so much older for a moment that I feel an instant wave of panic, like I need to make grabby hands at her and wrap her closer to my side, to demand she stop growing. *"I think I would like that. But maybe don't kiss with tongue in front of me. Olive says it's disgusting."* Her lips curl downward in a shudder at the thought.

I bark out a laugh. *"I can do that."*

She scoots over on the couch and curls up against me then. No grabby hands required.

TWENTY-SIX

NOW

FARLEY

Days roll into weeks that fill up with busy. Meyer and I find ourselves together a bit less, texting a bit more, as I attempt to use my personal time to carve, sharpen, and smooth out my set.

Even Christmas comes and goes. We manage to fit in our normal traditions, like visiting our local tree farm. Despite me telling them every year that they can, he and Hazel no longer cut down a real tree since I let slip how allergic I am to them. It's a flaw that I'm strangely self-conscious about since I love and crave those kinds of traditions. Instead, we created our own a few years back. We pack a thermos of hot cocoa and still go to the farm to spy on the other families and couples arguing over finding "the one," laughing with them whenever they find it and light up with joy. And we always snag a real wreath and a new ornament for the faux tree.

But . . . as time passes, it starts to feel like we're in limbo in regard to us. As if not so much has happened that it couldn't be blamed on adrenaline and need. An itch scratched that we could still step back from. And since I'm the only one that's been properly "scratched," I don't want to push him too hard, happy to slow down for the time being, and not force the pace. It settles that fitful feeling in me to know that regardless of those lines getting blurrier and blurrier, we're still able to laugh and go about life together like we do. There's no strangeness in our friendship, even if he's had his hand down my pants . . . inside me.

Still, since I want to confirm my interest without pressuring him, I'm trying to walk that line, allowing little indulgences here and there, happily surprised each time he reciprocates heartily. Like when I intertwined our fingers while we watched a family with three little girls clap and squeal over their tree. He immediately swept me to his front, our hands clasped together on my shoulder. I looked over at Hazel nervously, only to find her on his other side, smiling up at me. We watched as the dad convinced mom to go with a ten-footer. He was all flirty downward glances, lip biting and hip squeezing, a chubby baby drooling happily from the carrier strapped to his chest, until mom eventually rolled her eyes with a smile and caved. We all laughed at the sight of their loaded-down SUV teetering out of the lot.

Meyer and Hazel leave on the twenty-ninth for Ohio, where they'll spend the week together until Meyer comes back, and Haze stays behind with her grandparents for another two. It works out that her school is off track for the month, and she'll get to visit with cousins and relatives she doesn't normally get much time with, but I still feel a nagging, hollow guilt over Meyer being away from her for that long. And, truthfully, I feel guilt over my anticipation of that much time together, alone. It's one of those small things that reminds me just how much

I am *not* a parent, and can't quite empathize with all the planning that goes into everything, or the constant duplicitousness of the emotions that go along with it.

I love her with something fierce and frightening; I get almost angry over any hypothetical thing in the world that might get in her way. And I miss her every time we aren't with her. Yet my mind constantly wanders to being alone with Meyer. Regular daydreaming that is swiftly followed by guilt. Guilt that can't be dissuaded with logic. It's fucking exhausting.

IT'S 6 P.M. ON NEW YEAR'S EVE, and the only buzz I'm feeling is from a cocktail composed of boredom, anxiety, and a splash of bravery.

I have the message typed out. The one I've deleted and rewritten at least a hundred times:

Me: Do you ever think about Vegas?

There are two ways his response could go.

First, he could say, "What about Vegas?" He might be completely oblivious as to how close I was to kissing him. How much I wanted to. He drank a lot that night; maybe he forgot how he slid my finger into his hot mouth and stripped off my ring with his teeth. Lust clenches its way through me and I shiver at the memory even still.

Maybe he forgot what he said to me; maybe he only said it because of alcohol and the high emotions of the whole evening. Maybe he didn't even mean it the way I interpreted it.

Or, what if he says, "Yes, I think about Vegas." What if he says, "Yes, I think about how I said one thing while under the influence of many overpriced drinks and you immediately wanted to go back to the room together. I think about how you got so worked up that you panicked and I had to be the better, more sensible person as always and walk away. I think about how you told me you wanted to be smart with me, even though you were so ready—just moments before—to be stupid. I knew that was your way of apologizing and I forgave you for it and went on with our friendship to spare you that embarrassment."

Obviously, I know he'd put it in a much kinder way. Maybe he'd act like it was no big deal at all to him. But that night was the first time I thought, *I love him. I love him so much that I'd be stupid with him the moment he asked me. I'd run to a chapel now and marry him, consequences be damned.* And then he said, "You're the only person I've ever been stupid with." He echoed my thoughts, in simpler terms.

And then I suggested going back to the room . . . where everything proceeded to fall apart.

I've never been embarrassed, exactly. Because he's never made me feel like I should be, never changed how he treated me. But part of me just wants to tell him, to lay myself at his feet so that he knows what this is for me. "Dating" has already exposed a lot of us both, but I think he deserves to know how long this has been going on, really.

If someone's carrying your heart, shouldn't you do them the courtesy of warning them? Like catching someone driving with a mug on top of their car. *Hey, there! You probably need to stop, pull over, and take care of that! At least slow down.*

I'M DELETING THE MESSAGE AGAIN when I see the little dots pop up on the screen.

Meyer: Time change didn't matter, Hazel fell asleep before 9pm.

A laugh honks out of me, abrupt and overloud.

Me: I love that girl's lack of FOMO. She's my hero.

The dots pop up and disappear. Appear and go away once more.

Meyer: We miss you.

I do a yoga worthy inhale-exhale.

Me: I miss you too. Wish we were together.

I hit send and feel my heart beating through the top of my head. And then something occurs to me . . .

Me: Why don't we ever spend New Year's together? We never have, I realize.

The dots appear enough times that I lose track then. I set my phone facedown and tell myself to go to the bathroom, force myself to get a glass of water. When I get back, there's finally a reply.

Meyer: Hard to go out and do much for New Year's with a kid who loves her beauty sleep.

And then another text appears.

Meyer: And because all I ever needed was an excuse to kiss you, I think. So, maybe I thought I had to avoid it.

Is this what fainting feels like? A chorus of something rushes through me.

Me: Would me wanting you to have been enough of an excuse? If that's the case, you've executed amazing restraint.

Meyer: Have I, though?

I think about the way his hand slid against me, the pads of his fingers and their steady, relentless rhythm.

Me: You have.

Meyer: Guess I'll stop holding back, then.

I'm still trying to retrieve my eyes and put them back in my skull when he follows it up with:

Meyer: Can I call you or FaceTime you at midnight, here?

Something has me feeling shy over seeing his face, but I would kill to hear his voice.

Me: Call me. I'm doing the Darth mask tonight.

I slap my palm to my forehead after I hit send. *He sends you something that manages to come off as hot and your response is to remind him about your red-light mask. Fucking hopeless, Farley.*

I'm surprised when, not fifteen minutes later, he ends up texting me again. Meyer isn't exactly . . . chatty. Perhaps this is easier for him this way, too. A buffer.

Meyer: How's the force healing going, then?

I send him a photo in the terrifying mask because who are we kidding at this point, anyway.

Me: Strong, with this one.

Meyer: How are you feeling about the set? Did you end up meeting with Clay?

Me: Better every day. Some parts I love, and I know they're going to kill. Other parts feel a little lackluster.

Meyer: They're not, I promise.

Me: Thank you. And yes, I met with Clay. He wants me to start posting videos now, of everyday "funny" things. He claims people will be intrigued by my personality. Barf emoji.

Meyer: You can't just type barf emoji. You have to change it to the emoji. Come on. I expect more from a youngster like you.

Me: I was being ironic. Also I was speak texting. It's hard to look at my phone through the glare of the red light.

Meyer: You're probably slowly blinding yourself with the red light from that combined with the blue light from . . . every other piece of tech.

Me: I'll be able to see just enough to appreciate my glowing complexion, though.

Meyer: Just call me when you're done and don't burn your retinas anymore, Jones.

I groan on the tail end of a snicker. I'm *giggling* over the notion that he wants to talk to me so much that he wants to continue on without a lapse.

Where are my flower petals? *He loves me, he loves me not.*

The mask times out and I put it away with slow, determined movements. I definitely do not speed-shuffle back to my phone . . . with a glass of wine, prop myself up with a stack of pillows, or do any other nonsensical preparations to have a *conversation on the damn phone.*

This is ridiculous.

I hit call on his number before I start scribbling our names together in a notebook or bring any additional embarrassment upon myself.

"Hey," he answers in a ring.

I seize up on that syllable. His voice is low, quiet . . . a burr on the edge of it through the phone. It's not his typical phone voice I hear, anymore—the one he uses when he calls to ask me if I want to do a show at a certain venue, or to ask for my help making Valentines for Hazel's class. It's now the one that told me how he's *not a fucking saint;* that he imagines me bent over and bare for him. "Hi." I swallow.

"Give me a sec? I need to move Haze to her bed."

"Yeah—okay." My voice is high and tight.

"Alright, back." He sighs. "I realized I asked if I could call you at midnight here but forgot to ask if you had plans already, so I figured I'd better try earlier."

I smile. "No plans. Just doing all my maintenance and chipping away at the set. How's your sister and everyone?" I immediately ask, trying to avoid the gaps in conversation.

"Good. The boys picked up quite a bit of ASL, too, so Hazel's having a great time."

"Good."

"So . . ."

"So—"

"So, I miss you, Jones. I know I said we miss you, earlier. And we do. But I miss you."

"I miss you too, My."

"Tell me more about your meeting with Clay?"

"Not much more to tell, really. I need to get a little more active with the social media stuff, so I will. He seems excited for the tour."

"You feel good about him, then?"

"Sure. He seems like a good guy."

"He's knowledgeable and has a good reputation," he says, his tone seeking validation.

"Sounds like someone has a crush," I tease.

"Did he talk to you about Shauna's premiere?" he pivots.

"Oh—that's right! Yeah. That's exciting. Maybe I'll finally meet Dermot."

He scoffs, and I laugh lightly.

I hear his intake of breath before he quickly asks, "Will you be my date for that? I mean, I know you would be anyway with the publicity stuff, but—"

"Yes. I'll be your date," I breathe. And somehow, in the proceeding pause, I know that we're both smiling.

"Then I'll apologize now, because no fucking way am I letting Dermot near you."

* * *

WE STAY ON THE PHONE until midnight his time, and his phone voice grows huskier with fatigue.

At 11:59 P.M. my time, the phone rings again, waking me.

"—Meyer?" I say, half muffled by my pillow.

"Wanted to spend New Year's together twice. Make up for the ones we didn't." His own voice sounds muffled.

I love you runs through my brain, addled as it is. Like it has a hundred times in a hundred daydreams before, so crystal clear I'm not positive I didn't actually verbalize it. "Okay."

He must have a countdown on in the background, because eventually I hear it get to ten. "Jones, I hope this year is the best year yet," he says over the sound.

. . . *Five, four, three, two, one.*

"Happy New Year, Meyer. It already is."

"I think so, too. Goodnight, Fee."

"'Night."

TWENTY-SEVEN

NOW

MEYER

"Tell me something I don't know about you," Fee says.

It's day two of the new year and it already feels like we're catching up to the rhythm in this new dance. Where we both know that this has traveled across borderlines into something new; excited, but checking our pace against each other with every step, too. We talk or text throughout the day, sharing trivial details with one another, funny videos or observations. Things that aren't out of the ordinary for us, but have increased in frequency and morphed in tone. Somehow, via phone, I think we're . . . flirting?

Yeah, I'd call it flirting.

"What do you mean?" A thread of worry tugs at me when I think of the conversation I know we'll need to have at some point about our work partnership.

"I mean tell me something I don't already know about you. An embarrassing dating story, an irrational fear, an oddly specific dream or some niche thing that will be the measure of success and happiness for you."

"As in . . . ?" I'm struggling not to laugh at the budding annoyance in her voice.

"*As in* . . . as in did you know that I've been practicing yoga for the last year?"

"Really?"

"Yep. Dr. Deb recommended it. She told me I needed to be able to 'sit quietly with myself, with my own thoughts and feelings.'" She sighs through a laugh. "It took me an entire month to be able to sit through a whole session without laughing, crying, or leaving. But now I practice daily."

"Fee, that's . . . that's incredible." I smile as I picture her sitting peacefully in deference. My pants tighten when that image melts into one of her stretching into a pose, bending and pushing, holding and pulling—concentration laced with bliss. Sweat and breath and . . . leggings.

"It is, actually. I love it now. . . . Okay, your turn."

I shift in my seat. "Um. I work out a lot."

"No shit, Meyer. Tell me something I'm not *extremely* aware of."

"*Extremely* aware, huh? Alright, alright." I think. "Honestly, my story isn't exactly 'ha-ha that's embarrassing but cute,' more like, 'oof, I don't know how to respond now.'"

"You can tell me, and I can respond with a really bizarre noise if you want?"

"Uh, why?"

"Because then whenever it pops into your mind, instead of cringing, you'll remember that noise and you'll laugh instead. It's like electroshock therapy but with laughter."

God, she's cute. "I don't think that's how that works, Fee."

"I don't want to brag or make this about me, My, but I *am* an expert on handling embarrassment."

I snort. "Alright, then. Here goes. . . . When I went on a date for the first time after Hazel was born, I, uh . . . cried."

The responding sound is a combination of a cartoon villain's laugh and a trombone, and I tell her as much.

"You know, I've often thought of myself as, like, the love child of Pee-Wee Herman and Jessica Rabbit."

That makes me choke on my water. "Nah. Smaller boobs," I say through a cough.

Laughter tumbles out of her and my grip tightens on the phone, fingertips denting. I'm anxious for that sound in person again.

"Meyer," she says softly, "I'm sorry that happened."

"That sound, or—?"

"No, My. The crying. Dating is miserable in general, and you'd just gone through a lot and I'm sure it was terrifying getting out there again. Especially with new emotional baggage in tow."

"It's alright. I think I just got overwhelmed. I was anxious, drank too much, and blubbered," I groan, remembering against my will.

"I can't imagine you blubbering." She sounds mildly delighted by it, though. "But I'm sorry. Did she make up a family emergency and bail, or was she nice? If she was mean I'll key her car for you."

"Uh. . . ."

A stilted pause before a laugh blasts out of her. "Wait . . . she didn't . . . did she *sleep* with you?"

"Um."

"You've got to be kidding me."

"What's so unfathomable about someone wanting to sleep with me?"

She scoffs. "It's that you cried on a first date and her response was to want to fuck you, Meyer. If I did that it would send any man running."

I wish I could tell her she's wrong. Instead I try for a subject change.

"What were the other prompts? Irrational fear?"

"Yeah. Like, how I shudder at cotton balls, though, not my fear of inadequacy or daddy issues. Not a deep-seated fear; hit me with something light that makes you illogically anxious," she replies.

"Bangs."

"Bangs . . . as in . . . hair?"

"Specifically, long bangs. When they catch on someone's eyelashes and they're just constantly in someone's eyes it fills me with unnatural dread."

"Okay?" Her voice tilts up at the end, trying, and failing, to sound nonjudgmental.

"I just don't know how that wouldn't drive you insane. Having the blunt ends of a hundred hairs stabbing you in the eyeball."

"While I do think that's extreme, I suppose I kinda get it."

"Also, Hazel cut her own bangs when she was three or four, but they were nowhere near even. She looked like Froggy from *Little Rascals*. I had to learn to do these antennae pigtails at the front of her head for, like, six months. Bangs and I have a complicated history."

"Oh, god, *that's* what's happening in those pictures," she cackles. "And you know what, most women and bangs have a complicated history, too."

"I did my best, Fee," I sigh, before I admit, "I feel like this question game is counterproductive and with each answer I'm revealing something that makes you like me less."

"Not possible. And in a way, revealing your minuscule, arguably nonexistent faults—let's call them *quirks*, actually— makes me feel like we're closer to even footing and makes me like you even more. Which I know you're not supposed to admit as a well-adjusted adult trying to practice good relationship skills—or just general mental stability—but I like being transparent with you."

I laugh through my nose. "You're not as unstable as you think. I believe you're just more honest than most people are brave enough to be. Especially at your own expense, Fee."

A wistful sound leaves her. "I haven't . . . I haven't always been."

"Yeah, me either," I say. "Jones, I think I should—"

Hazel and my nephew Liam burst in then. They're nudging each other with elbows and excited glances when Hazel sees I'm on the phone.

"Is that Fee? Can we FaceTime her?"

"Fee, Hazel wants to know if we can FaceTime?"

"Yes! I miss her face!" She hangs up immediately and I nod with a grin to Hazel when the call comes through.

Hazel's bouncing on her toes when I set the phone up next to me so Fee can see both kids.

"Do you want to hear a joke?" Haze asks, looking back and forth between me and the phone, Liam barely containing a laugh at her side.

"Sure," I sign, and Fee likely does the same.

Hazel's smile drops in a dramatic, practiced kind of way. *"Me too."*

Liam howls. Fee wheezes a laugh that I peek around to see. She's got a palm to her forehead, shaking her head merrily before she looks up and our gazes clash. Her teeth sink into her full bottom lip.

"Uncle Meyer, I have one too, I have one too!" Liam interjects.

"Your mom is getting pretty liberal with letting you use the iPad again, isn't she?"

"Why did God make farts smell?" Liam's brow furrows determinedly as he signs it after.

I know this one, but I play along anyway. *"Why?"*

"So Deaf people can enjoy them too!" he signs back, polishing it off with an actual fart that Hazel follows with a perfectly timed plug of her nose.

Honestly, the laughter that ensues would make you think we just witnessed something revolutionary, rather than the polite chuckle these internet jokes deserve. But all their hysterical expressions manage to drag me into it, too. I'm holding my ribs by the time I'm through.

"Alright, Liam. Now that you've managed to hotbox my room, why don't you go see if Nana needs help with dinner."

"Alright. What's hotboxing?"

"Ask your mom. Also ask her where babies come from, and how the garage door really got that dent in it while you're at it." He throws me a quizzical look before he shuffles away.

"You want to talk to Fee for a bit, Haze?" I ask.

"Yes. You can stay though."

"Thanks for your permission." I laugh as she grabs Fee off of the nightstand and slides next to me against the headboard. She props the phone up on the lap desk.

"Are you having fun?" Fee asks.

"*Yes, Aunt Melody let me do her makeup and I baked snicker-doodle cookies with Nana. Watched all the* Mighty Ducks *movies with Liam and Connor and they taught me some hockey stuff.*"

"*Is there still a lot of snow there?*"

"*Yes. But there's a storm coming on Wednesday and Thursday so we'll get even more!*"

Fee's brow furrows. "*Aren't you supposed to fly back home Wednesday?*" she asks, looking my way now.

"*Yes. I'm sure it'll be okay.*"

"*The bus leaves on Thursday,*" she reminds me, concern still tight in her expression.

"*I know. It'll be okay.*" It has to be. I hope it is. Fee's first performance is on Friday in Sacramento. "*I'll get there.*"

And then I recall a memory from the day before when, after a long day of ice hockey, baking, snow shoveling, and a home full of people and noise, my dad doggedly promised Hazel to play Yahtzee for the hundredth time after dinner, despite appearing to be asleep on his feet already.

I'd warned him, then, because I know how it feels to be desperate for bed, only to be reminded of one of those earlier deals. The guilt of reneging when you can't bring yourself to come through.

"I'd be a little stingier with your promises, Pop," I'd said.

"*What's WHAT?!*" I hear my sister yelp from downstairs. "MEYER! WHAT THE HELL DID YOU TELL HIM TO ASK ME?!!"

TWENTY-EIGHT

NOW

FARLEY

"So what can I get you? Do you need an energy drink, a snack, a water? What's your typical preshow routine?" Clay asks. And I have the same desolate thought that I've been having for the past twelve hours. Since the last of my hope disappeared.

More specifically, since my hope got stuck in Phoenix after miraculously making it out of both Cincinnati and Chicago in spite of the midwestern snowstorm, but still.

Fucking Phoenix. Two states away. But after all flights were grounded until this morning, it's the closest they could get Meyer to Sacramento, today, with the last leg tomorrow morning.

This cannot be happening.

Clay's fine. Nice. Attentive. A little pedantic with the way he speaks about everything. But this is the prequel to the biggest career opportunity I've ever had, and his persistent efforts are having the opposite of their intended effect.

"Farley?"

"What?!" I snipe. And now I'm more irritated that I have to apologize for *that,* as well.

"Sorry, Clay."

"It's alright. I get it. I won't hover. I'll just give you your time." He nods graciously and leaves the greenroom.

I lurch up from the sofa and begin pacing, taking stock of my feelings.

I'm tired and wired. My first night on the tour bus, in the tiny single bunk, was far from peaceful. I don't know why I thought the bus would have a room with a normal-sized bed. We're comedians, not pop stars, after all. There's only a hallway lined with four bunks, plus a fold-out sofa, and a single bathroom at the rear. It won't be too uncomfortable to manage, since it's only in between towns and then we'll have hotels lined up.

But up until we all scattered for bed, I'd simply not allowed myself to consider the worst. I'd stayed distracted; laughing with Kara, Shauna, Clay, and our driver, Sven, assuming Meyer would make it and meet us here.

Now that it's here and he's not, I feel wholly unprepared again.

"But you're not," I say out loud, turning to my reflection in the vanity. "Oh, *you* again," I laugh on a breath before I let my face harden.

"You are prepared. You love this shit *because* it scares you. Because you're damn good on your toes and you're even better when you work from your mind. You defied every ounce of logic getting here. You've made it because you're not afraid to do scary, uncomfortable things so that you can take part in something that you *love.* You are fucking funny, Farley. *Fuck,* that's a lot of F's. What they lack in knowing, you make up for in showing. Just wait until you blow their minds."

I shove open the door and march out into the hallway.

I didn't grow up playing sports—at least not very competitively—but this hallway is my stadium tunnel tonight. This isn't some big arena—it's a small club, so there's no walk-out song to announce me aside from the roaring sound in my brain and the echoes of my thoughts. Thoughts that are shaded in angry defiance: for every time someone made me feel strange, crazy, overly emotional, or too much of too many things. Even more so for all the times I was made to feel insignificant and unimportant. For anyone who ever felt they were too good for me, or better than me. For the ones who made me feel less than.

I'll take this microphone and I'll shout into it, into their fucking faces. And I'll get them. Because they *will* laugh. They won't be able to stop themselves. Because I will shirk my pride, my self-esteem, and every ounce of self-preservation down to my marrow, and I'll lay it all at their feet until they laugh in utter disbelief.

I don't want to just entertain tonight. I want to evoke emotion. I want my jokes circulating through their thoughts, making them laugh into their coffee tomorrow.

I want to channel my inner Hazel. I want to be someone who can dance without music. Someone who can make art with *my* frame of understanding.

"You ready?" Clay looks up from his phone, his eyes shifting and going wide when they meet mine.

"I'll kick ass, Dad."

"What?"

I walk out onto the stage with a smile.

*   *   *

MY SET BECOMES A SINGEING, burning thing.

It's not the largest club I've gigged at—it might even be on the smaller end of the spectrum. But people are yelping in laughter. Kara and Shauna more loudly than anyone. There are tears being wiped. Drinks being choked on. I see it when someone's beverage shoots out of their nose, their friends crying in agonized fits for minutes after.

Every single face in the room that I can see is losing it, and when they're not clutching their middles, they've got astonished smiles tacked onto the corners of their lips.

All those faces, except for *one*.

It started when I went offtrack with a lead-up story I've been playing with that crosses over into the PTA bit. It's based on another true tale that only Meyer has heard. It's one he begged me not to tell on stage, simply because of the punch line But I'm fearless tonight, because I have given myself no choice otherwise, and I *want* their gasps and I *crave* the sight of them hiding their expressions in their palms, embarrassed for how hard they laugh at such an inappropriate line.

I begin by telling them that I fear becoming a parent one day, because the pressure put on parenting as a whole, nowadays, seems insurmountable. The only real goal I'd have is to raise someone *not* terrible to other people. Yet, I can only imagine that this is harder than I understand, and I use *this* story to explain why.

I change the kids' names, but I tell everyone about a mean-girl (*sic*) in Hazel's class that I had interactions with while I covered Meyer's volunteer hours at school (a gift for his birthday that he was more stoked for than when his show got an Emmy nod). I explain to them how this little girl pretended to be Hazel's friend: volunteering to help or making sure to smile and sign happily when the teacher was looking; how she'd pretend not to see Hazel sign or attempt to communicate with her when the teacher wasn't. How condescending the girl was when she *would* interact. I watched her eye Hazel's artwork patronizingly, and then rearrange their art displays so that her own work was *only* next to her hearing friends', as if she didn't want to be associated with Hazel or something. I share how Hazel would excitedly show her a beautiful drawing or a perfect spelling test score and her response was something like "That's . . . exciting for you," or just "Wow." She would never actually tell her anything she did was *good,* never would pay her a true compliment or show support. She was only eight, yet she knew how to be so intentional as to manipulate her words so that she was withholding.

And then, the pièce de résistance: At recess one day, while Hazel happily jumped rope on her own, minding her own business, I heard it. I *heard* this little girl mimic a Deaf voice. Heard her snickering to some other little sweater-toothed, snot-licking gremlins, mocking some of the Deaf students' sounds.

Now, in stand-up, you have to be willing to offend people at times. You have to make your peace with it and draw your personal boundaries, but ultimately you *will* get under someone's skin occasionally if you're pushing the conversation correctly. I don't mess with race or say anything that will promote ableism, and I keep it light when it comes to religion. I try not to take up space where I don't need to.

Myself and my own lunacy, the patriarchy, and asshole kids, though? All free game.

I don't think this joke breaks my vow.

So, I distinctly register when this particular woman's expression pinches into one of disgust and loathing tonight, because it's also the moment that I tell everyone how I completely snapped to Meyer (in the joke, to a teacher) later and called this little girl "—an evil little cunt creature who will grow up into some equally mean-spirited boss babe twat who produces another crotch goblin that she acts like is Jesus incarnate."

The woman in the audience refuses to crack at any of the stuff that follows, too, and I become hung up on it. I find myself growing louder when I near her side of the stage. Looking directly at her, over and over again.

When I finish the portion of the set focused on sex stuff and the things that really blow my dress up these days, I find her again, only to see her scowl clenching harder. It drives me crazy, because all I've done here is joke about a mean-spirited little girl and *myself*. And yet, her nasty looks are all I can focus on. Her eye rolls. Every other face in here is having a beautiful night and all I see is this one.

So, I decide to do something I've never once done in my stand-up career. I call her out.

"I have got to tell everyone. There's a woman right over there who just is getting more and more visibly angry with each word that comes out of my mouth. And I have to tell *you*, ma'am"—I locate her eyes—"the more angry you get, the *funnier* I find it." I smile cruelly.

The place roars as she kicks up out of her chair and storms away.

It's *victorious*.

I might feel a twinge of guilt later, but for now, on this stage, there is something violent within me, clawing layer through layer with everything I say. I'm swinging from my own wrecking ball and screaming *weeeeeeeeee*, practically gleeful with it.

The audience in this overheated, dingy club gives me a

standing ovation when I finish, and I tear up like it's The Greek on a summer night. Like it's a packed stadium under a sky full of stars.

And yes, it's not as if I don't easily cry as it is. But I think I've often felt like my success is held up by Meyer. That he somehow justifies it, I suppose. So I'm proud that I didn't actually need my steady, respectable man as my foundation to feel confident or worthy tonight.

Still, my walk to the side stage feels a little more unsteady, my legs wobbling down the stairs to go meet Kara and Shauna. I feel a bit out of control, trying to remind myself that even though that was a little outside my brand, I've seen and heard so much worse. It is—I'm okay. The joke was not bad. Singling out that woman was not something I'd ever thought of myself doing, but . . . it's not as if she was having a good time anyway. . . .

I don't fully register the movement in my peripheral before hot, liquid pain cascades down the side of my face, sears against my collarbone, my hand, another splash against my shoulder on the same side.

A guttural screech wrenches its way through me before I gasp, trying to paw it off my face.

"Farley?!" "Security!" I think Kara and Shauna yell.

The seconds come into focus along with the face in front of me. The woman I dismissed, and what appears to be an empty coffee cup in her hand. Red, bloodshot eyes and a constellation of popped blood vessels on each of her cheeks. The same putrid scowl. She jabs a trembling finger at me.

"I'll tell you one thing you have right. The idea of *you* ever becoming someone's mother is terrifying. I pray it never happens."

A security guard smacks the cup out of her hand and a high laugh whistles out of me. *Too late, I've been burned,* I think idly. The other guard wraps her up and hauls her out of view as Kara and Shauna swoop my way.

Did I walk down these steps ten seconds ago or ten hours ago? The moments balloon together.

"Are you okay?"

"I'll get a cool towel."

Shauna is helping wipe and cool down my arm and my face, while Kara presumably talks to security elsewhere. The skin is hot and bruised, bright pink, like when Hazel and I tried to dye Easter eggs red last year but could only ever get them to turn pinker. It's nothing I need to have seen at a hospital. Still, I can't stop staring at it.

No one says anything for a long while. I'm asked if I wish to press charges, and I don't. Then, they argue with me. I don't care.

I meet Shauna's sympathetic gaze. "You can't tell Meyer," I say.

"Can't tell me what?"

Shauna whips around and Meyer's there, looking harried and exhausted and confused. Perfect.

My chin begins to tremble and I clench my jaw as firmly as I can to halt it.

His gaze roams over me as he steps closer, before the hint of his grin flattens and his eyes harden.

I have the odd memory of being taught in school that it takes more muscles to frown than to smile. It makes me marvel at the strength of his.

But then, *there.* A small flare of his nose, eyebrows twitching up and in to one another. I think again, if this expression was art: "Helpless Anger."

"*Who?*" he grits out, helplessness fading.

I make the mistake of stopping my eyes from dancing along the other parts of his face and meet his own, and the trembling starts anew.

"How? How did you get here?" I ask.

"I rented a car in Phoenix. Now you answer mine."

I shake my head, and it jostles a tear loose. I do not want to lose it, not here.

"Hotel?" Meyer asks Shauna.

She passes him my backpack. "Already checked in earlier."

He scoops me up and tucks me against him as we walk toward the exit, him practically carrying me. When we emerge into the parking lot I notice a 7-Eleven across the street and recall that the woman's coffee was from there—per the paper cup, at least. Piping hot and fresh. I wonder if she had it before the show or if she got it when she left and came back. It must've been the latter.

Meyer slides me into my seat and shuts me into the safety of the car, chin bouncing erratically as fat tears begin to roll down my cheeks. He slips into his seat and immediately starts the engine when I reach for the sports drink in his cupholder, trying to occupy my hands.

"*No.* Not . . ." He gentles his voice. "That's a pee bottle, Fee, not a Gatorade."

"But . . . you're a guy. You can just pee anywhere on the side of the road." Two more tears splatter on the center console between us. So at odds with the stupid sentence I just uttered.

"Didn't want to stop at all," he says, pulling away from the curb. He grabs my hand and I hold his in both my palms. I laugh a little hysterically when I picture Meyer trying to drive and trying to pee into a Gatorade bottle simultaneously.

"Jones. Fee. I'm sorry I didn't make it in time. I really wanted to." His voice catches on *really* and the lump in my throat seems to calcify.

I nod, but I want to tell him that he didn't need to, that I don't even know if I'm crying over the happiness at seeing him, the success of the show, or the confusion over what took place after. Did I take something too far? I bullied a paying patron, in a way. Even if she wasn't justified in attacking me back, I struck first. I know I did.

And for the first time, in as long as I remember, I question whether I want to go forward with this. I think I might not be getting it right. My *why*, or my *how*.

"I'd like you to tell me everything, Fee. I need you to, please. Let's get up to your room and get you cleaned up and then I need you to talk to me. Okay?" Meyer says, snatching me from the flushing whirlpool of my thoughts. It's now that I notice we've stopped in front of the hotel; I notice the tight lines of his expression, and the white knuckles on both of our hands.

"Okay," I croak.

He loads himself down with his luggage before retrieving my hand again and leading me straight through the lobby and to the elevators. Another hysterical laugh flaps out of me when I think about the stark contrast between this hotel visit together versus our previous one. He, again, doesn't question it, just asks for my room number.

And then I continue to crack. The fluttering wings in my chest materialize in the form of laughter. The frothing, bubbling, uncontainable kind. Meyer speed walks us down the hallway when we make it to my floor. He shoves through the door as soon as it unlocks, me in front of him, and in one swift motion tosses his bags into the closet before he strides determinedly toward me and crushes me to him. My arms crash around his middle, gripping each other.

"I'm sorry I can't stop laughing," I say through the maniacal sound, sucking down a breath through a hiccup.

"Angel, I hate to break it to you, but you're not laughing. You're crying."

He tips my chin up with two fingers and heartbreaking gentleness, cradling the back of my head in his free palm.

Sure enough, I feel the tight wetness around my eyes, already swollen to anaphylactic proportions, I'm certain. I give in to the urge to sniffle, and a litany of emotions cross his beautiful face: anger, sadness, an attempt at a reassuring lift of his lips that dies out in the same second it starts. And as the last of the adrenaline leaves my system, my teeth begin to chatter.

"Are you cold?" he asks.

I shake my head even as I note how hot the latest tear feels on my face. He walks me to the bathroom and wraps me up in a couple of towels before he sits me on the toilet and starts the bath.

"P-P-Please don't make it t-too hot?"

His head turns up to me and he searches my face with a scowl I know isn't reserved for me. "Of course."

I stick my tender arm out of my towel cocoon and look it over. Not very red anymore, which somehow seems to fit the situation since the burn did more internal damage than anything.

"I j-just want to w-wash the coffee smell out of my hair," I whisper. He nods.

And even though this could not be further from the warm and sticky daydream I've often had of being fully naked in a hotel room with Meyer, I strip down and climb into the bath with my back to him without much preamble. Maybe it's because this was what my mom always did when I got hurt or had a terrible day. Perhaps it's because I want to be taken care of right now and some part of me knows that Meyer wants to care for me, and this is a comfort that I don't have the strength to fight.

The water is a degree above tepid. Warm enough to slow the shivering, cool enough that it doesn't sting the more raw parts of my skin. I keep my back to him as he takes down the shower head and directs its spray to blanket me. And I tell him about the entire night, beginning to end, every high note and low.

I lean my head back when he lathers shampoo in my hair, his fingers stilling against my scalp when I get to the part about the woman.

"I felt like I had something to prove tonight. I think . . . I think I wanted to prove that I was okay, that I was good even without you. I went out there and was *burning* with it. And that entire room was with me, they were all loving it. And instead of enjoying it, I became fixated on one person's negativity, Meyer. Why did I let one person get to me that way?"

I keep my eyes fixed on the ceiling while he rinses the shampoo out. I tell him he was right, that I never should've told that joke, and a few fresh tears spill down my temples.

He punches the faucet to off with a fist. "Fee . . . it would not have mattered if you didn't utter a single bad word or had an entirely G-rated show. People like that will always find a way to be unhappy. All the warnings were there for them to look up. She knew what she was getting into. She had absolutely *no* right to physically assault you even if you had called *her* a nasty cunt to her face and told her to light herself on fire. No one. *No one* has the right to lay a hand on you."

His tone turns to a growl at the end and I hear him huff out a breath in agitation. I nod once in acknowledgment.

"I'll grab you something to wear to bed," he mutters softly.

When I hear him return, I stand up and turn around, stepping into the towel he has up and waiting. I feel his gaze on my face like a brand, but can only bring mine to his throat, just as I see it stall on a swallow.

"I'll give you a minute," he says before he leaves. I look down at the shirt he's handed me. One of his. Impossibly soft and large. A dog in a Hawaiian-print shirt on the front of it. I put it to my face and inhale as best I can through my stuffy nose. I don't think I'll ever return it.

When I emerge he lifts his head from his hands. He's sitting on the foot of the bed, hunched over with elbows planted on his thighs. I can trace the exhaustion in every line of his posture.

"My. I'm sorry, I'm sure you're tired. You"—I swallow—"you can s-stay. Or you can go to your room if you don't think you'll be able to sleep."

Something flickers across his face while his eyes stay transfixed near the hem of the shirt against my thighs. Something desperate.

"Fee. It makes me sick that I wasn't there. I'm so sorry."

"Meyer, don't. It's fine. It was . . . shocking. It sucked. I'm not trying to downplay it. But it did not kill me. It didn't even seriously injure me. I just—" I cross my arms and tuck my hands against my sides. "I just need to keep it in perspective. Take a day or two. We have a few days before the next show, anyway." I smile weakly at him. "Maybe this will be the thing to finally help me kick the caffeine addiction."

He groans. "Don't, Fee. Please don't fucking reduce this shit to a joke right now."

"This is what I do, Meyer. It's quite literally what I do. And I should be able to do it for myself sometimes if it's what I can give other people, too. I was attacked. I'm not fucking stupid, I know what it was. I also know that I struck first using my own weapon and I don't know what the fuck is going on in that woman's life. I know that I purposefully worded things all for that shock-value laugh, and I knew it was a risk. I took it even further by pointing her out. I handed every ounce of my power over to one person tonight, instead of doing my thing." I blow out a breath. "It does not make it okay. But I'm standing here just fine. And I'll dismantle this whole thing as much as I want until I reduce it to some story that I can make into a bit or use at parties. If I want to."

He looks at me then, and stands. "What aren't you telling me?"

I scoff. "What do you mean?"

"I mean I can tell that you *are* shaken up, but I don't think it's just to do with the coffee if you're already joking about it. I know you, Fee. Was there something else? Did she threaten you?"

I turn away from him.

"Tell me, Fee. Please."

I sigh, but don't turn back around. "She said that the one thing I got right was that the idea of me ever being anyone's mother was terrifying," I choke out, throat burning.

I feel him approaching me, so I continue in a rush. "Maybe she has a kid at home with some behavioral stuff and I struck a nerve. I don't know."

"And with someone else, your joke might have been the thing to help them realize that they need to check in on their kid. Maybe that little shit's parent will take the teacher comments seriously and stop thinking the sun shines out of their ass. Or, at minimum, take a closer look just in case. It's a good bit, Fee. The only reason I didn't want you to do it was because I assume the worst of people and didn't want anyone complaining to the school. And sure, calling a kid a cunt is bound to upset someone. Not everyone has the same superior sense of humor."

He tries to make the last part sound light, but I still feel defensive.

"I changed it so it was referencing when I used to work as an aide," I say, turning around and looking up at him now.

"Oh." He blinks. "Well. That was smart."

I nod meekly.

"At the end of the day, Fee, you're telling *jokes*. It's in the job description. No one knows what's true or not. No one knows that you're giving them . . . *you,* when you're up there. Sure, sometimes you put on a caricature of yourself, but you get what I'm saying, right? Don't let them have *you* all the way."

I nod again. "I know. I won't . . . I won't tell it again, either. I don't need to."

He inhales, his chest rising. "If *you* don't want to, then don't. If you do, then fuck them. It's a good bit about how kids can bring out the best along with the worst in us. Do what feels true to you, though, don't let me or anyone else persuade you otherwise."

"Okay," I whisper.

"I'm sorry that happened, Fee."

I shrug. "Me too."

"Do you want to rest?"

"Yes."

"Do you want me to go?"

"No. Please stay," I respond, probably too firmly.

He nods silently, and I move past him to crawl into bed.

I watch him as he takes himself apart, then, piece by piece. First, with his shirt. I can't help but smile at how he carefully folds it and slips it into a bag I assume is for dirty laundry. So precise and measured. So much forethought. I certainly didn't think to pack a separate bag for my dirty things even though I'll need to do laundry occasionally over the next couple weeks. My travel clothes are still strewn over the nearest chair from when I changed earlier.

His shoulders are miles wide, the well-defined valley of his spine between them. Shadows play on the dips and swells, and I chew my lip wondering how many pens he might be able to store between those two blades. The sound of his belt slipping through the loops zips through me, my breath hitching. He turns and smirks when he catches my eye.

"Jonesy, I'm gonna need you to stop looking at me that way."

"What way?"

He ignores my feigned ignorance. "Because this isn't a night that calls for a distraction. I don't want . . . I don't want *us* overshadowed by the other events of the night."

"Okay," I whisper, hoping the pout isn't obvious. But he's right. I'm depleted. I'm sad. And ashamed and angry and confused. I don't want to be . . . *this* version of myself with him. Not in that way, tonight. I just want to find my rest with him tonight.

But then he slides his jeans off, folds them just as deliberately as his shirt before slipping them into the bag, and stands to his full height.

My gulp echoes in my ears.

He's a god underneath those unassuming layers. Absolute

honed perfection. And the juxtaposition of the tiny, self-conscious tug he gives to the right side of his briefs somehow makes him that much more to me.

Mine, mine, mine, I think.

I don't know how I ever thought I could stand him being anything less. He's awash in the cool gray-green of the night shining through the window; marble-like, if not for the twitch of his hands at his sides, and the roll of his jaw when my eyes make their way back up to his.

I slam my eyes shut when he makes his first stride my way, not trusting myself to not stare at more inappropriate places, effectively ruining any thoughts of rest I could hope to have, now or in the foreseeable future.

I feel him slide under the covers, his warmth caressing the backs of my thighs and making me grit my teeth against the urge to scoot closer.

"Can I hold you?" he asks, and I nod, my face making a quiet *swish* against the pillow.

He wraps me up against him from head to toe, my back to his front.

God is not a woman, I think. At least not a sympathetic one tonight. Because the feel of his warm, hard body against mine is almost enough to make me forget my better judgment.

He smoothes some of my hair down before tucking my head under his chin.

"I wanted you in my arms when I said this to you so you couldn't turn away from it, Fee," he whispers gruffly, his hold on me tightening. "But you will make an amazing, incredible mother one day." I choke on an instantly thick inhale. "You might not always have to deal with some of the less fun parts of it, but you've already played a mothering role in Hazel's life from the moment you slammed through the doors at Lance's. You protect her, even when you're pushing her. You care. You teach. You're generous with your time and you're a fierce advocate for her in everything. No matter what happens with you and me ever, I want you to know, again, that you've earned your place in her life. I think . . . I think her mother would have been okay with me telling you that."

"Thank you," I say through a sob, relief flooding through me at his words. I didn't realize how much I needed them. I close my eyes, a final few tears spilling through my lashes, before sleep takes me.

TWENTY-NINE

NOW

MEYER

I've technically spent the night with Fee numerous times. There's always been a hallway, a guest bathroom, or a floor or two between us, though.

So when I wake up at five with morning wood and a dead arm, I react to the sight and scent of her by panic-flailing my body out of the bed with all the grace of a reanimated corpse. I have no idea how it doesn't rouse her, but it's a testament to how tired she is that she manages to stay asleep through the shuffling.

I take care of my business and change into gym clothes before I look back at her one last time, still sleeping soundly. I clock the steady rise and fall of her chest, body curled tightly into itself. So quiet and delicate and unnervingly different from herself. It does nothing to quell the rage still floating through my system.

She rolls and her shirt rides up in the same movement that

pushes the duvet down, revealing the slope of her bare hip. I smother a groan.

I scrape a palm across my jaw before I leave, closing the door as quietly as I can before I stomp my way to the elevator. I slap the button as I'm hitting call on Clay's name.

"Meyer?" he answers groggily.

"Meet me at the lobby Starbucks in ten." I hang up, too agitated for niceties.

HE HAS THE GOOD SENSE not to look annoyed when he strolls through the elevator doors. He looks like he's been expecting it.

He holds up a placating hand my way. "Meyer—"

"No. Clay, there's no fucking excuse. You said you were up for being the sole acting tour manager for the real thing and on night one—*night one*—of the pre-tour you didn't make sure security was arranged?"

"I didn't think we needed security arranged for stage exit in a club that size. Obviously for bigger venues that will not be the case."

"You fucking thought wrong, didn't you?"

"Apparently yes. I suppose I did." He flops into the chair adjacent to mine. I level him with a glare.

"How was she? Before that, I mean. Did she have fun?"

He shrugs with a frown. "From what I could tell, she was having a fucking blast. She was reveling in it, man. She did seem off before the show, so I just gave her space, like you said. She accidentally called me 'Dad.'"

"What?"

"Before she went on stage. She got this real determined look and said to me, 'I'll kick ass, Dad.' *That* was a bit off."

I start to chuckle. My god, that woman will never cease to amaze me. Inspire me. Drive me insane.

I look up to his confused expression. "Don't worry about it. It was an inside joke."

He sighs with a lift of his brow. "Look, Meyer. You know I respect you. And last night was a freak thing. It will not happen again. But I hope you can relax on some of the helicoptering. I actually have more management experience—"

"Let me stop you right there, Clay. You might have more management-specific experience. But I have *years* on you when it comes to this business. On multiple sides of it. I know what it means to put yourself out there for public consumption and how that makes people think they're entitled to *consume* every bit of you. I also know how to be more protective of myself and the people I love."

"Is that why you agreed to put yourself back out there, too? All so you can stay protective?" Clay asks knowingly.

I snort. "It's part of it, yeah. I'm sure it's obvious that that's not the only reason."

He sighs. "Can I ask you, then, why were you so against it when I first suggested it— god, what was it, seven or eight months ago now? When I brought it up at the *Funnybones* party. And then again when Kara wanted to do the tour? You still acted irritated."

"Because it shouldn't have taken an excuse for me to act, I guess. And for the same reasons I told you again. She was good enough on her own. She didn't need me, I'm hardly relevant."

"It was just good business, Meyer. You came off of a really successful show and she—"

"She's a fucking good comedian, Clay. That's all there is to it. I don't even see how your whole scheme has played a role at all." I get up to leave. "Tighten up your security plan for the rest of this mini tour, okay?"

He looks like he wants to say more, but refrains. "Okay. We don't have to leave for a few days. Kara has some local places to pop into the next couple of nights. You guys don't need to go to a game. She doesn't need to go on again anywhere until after Shauna's premiere, really."

"Perfect." I stand, already putting my headphones in for the gym.

"Uh, Meyer?"

I turn back to him, a headphone suspended midair.

"Should I cancel your room?" He shrinks in his seat.

I cough. "Sure. Yeah. I think. I'll, uh, let you know later today," I reply, before I jettison in the direction of the gym.

I PUSH MYSELF THROUGH THE weights, thinking about that night all those months ago when I ran into Clay, someone who'd just been a friend of a friend of a friend in the business at the time. He'd tossed a stuffed mushroom in his mouth and told me everything he knew about Farley Jones, about how his biggest client, Kara Wu, *loved* her stuff. That she was planning an all-female tour at some point and expressed an interest in her.

"You know how you could give yourself, and Farley, a leg up?" he asked, then proceeded to answer before I could reply. *"Stir up publicity. You're just coming off of this show. You should start dating. Capitalize on people's nosiness. I could help you with the social media stuff. . . ."*

I'd dismissed him, simply excited for the confirmation that Fee was making it. I'd felt more successful that night than I ever had for any of my own achievements, had felt fucking *glory* on her behalf.

I'd also felt hungry when I left early, those goddamn s'mores blondies stuck in my mind for the better half of a week after yet another failed attempt. I'd polished off an additional tray the night before.

So I called Fee and went over there. Had one of our most carefree, simple nights to date. Caught her in her blondie, salty lies. Carried her snoring, beautiful body to bed that night.

She'd smiled when I tucked her in and had murmured "Love you" with her eyes closed. I'd stood there and stared, longer than I should have. Wanting to hear it again, just to be certain that I'd heard it in the first place.

Logically, I know it was just nonsense muttered in her sleep, but sometimes my mind wanders back to it. Like that Saturday last fall when she taught Haze how to make an omelet and, for my benefit, a pot of coffee . . . or like the time they picked out flowers to plant along the side yard during the latest drought, against my grumbling. When they swung around in circles with their hands clasped and faces to the sky when it finally rained. In those moments, I pretend it was real and I whisper it back to her under my breath. Sometimes I mouth it to her when she's on stage.

I never told her what I heard from Clay, because I never had any doubts that she'd make it this far. On her own. I wanted her to have that full experience for herself, without wondering when, or even if, it would come to fruition.

I SLIDE THE KEY I'D swiped from the dresser into the door, opening it carefully, shutting it as quietly as I can manage.

I'll need to grab clean clothes from my bag before I can slip into the shower so I can avoid too much more opening and closing of doors, since Fee gets petulant when she's up before seven.

I step into the end of the hallway where my bag still lies, only halfway in the closet.

And then, I freeze.

The moment pulses, my eyes devouring the little recoil in the curve of her ass as Fee whips around to the side, wet hair scattering around her bare shoulders. She clutches the towel loosely at her naked front, unabashedly. Not trying to hide. She holds my gaze before she continues toweling off. A droplet of water trickles down the ends of her long hair, sliding a slow path around a rosy brown nipple—one that tightens as I watch, transfixed. It slips under the swell before she swipes at it with the towel.

I should move. I should turn around. My temples throb with too-long banked lust that sears through me. My palms heat with it, a frantic gathering at every endpoint of my body screaming at me to take three more strides and fall to my knees before her.

"It's a new day, Meyer," she says before she tosses the towel aside and steps my way.

FARLEY

I didn't plan it.

I'd hopped into the shower, thinking that maybe Meyer slipped out to go get some better rest in his own room. I've been told I snore. Sometimes I thrash.

But then he walked back in, skin beaded with sweat. A faint waft of that petrichor smell of his hit me, stronger now. Hair still unkempt and fluffy atop his beautiful, stern face.

His eyes immediately clung onto me and heated, going hazy

like the time he had that fever for days on end. His cheeks flush now, as he sways a little on his feet.

I see when he gives in to it, throws the key card and whatever else he has in his clenched fist to the ground, meeting me halfway and crashing his lips against mine.

I lick into his mouth, desperate to taste him, to absorb him. I slide my tongue up along the salty column of his throat, reaching up onto my toes. He makes a helpless, ragged sound, lifts me and grinds into me clumsily. His desperation heightens mine, and I claw and press and pant. He walks me to the dresser and drops me onto it, my wet skin making an indecent noise that has us laughing breathily into each other's mouths. His big palms squeeze my ribs, thumbs tracing the skin beneath my breasts.

"Dying to taste you." He dips and rolls a nipple between his teeth and I gasp.

"My—" I suck in another gasp when he plants a sucking kiss to my inner thigh. Tug roughly on his hair when he bites the other.

"*Meyer.*" I try for firm. "I need—I need to touch you. I want to make you feel good."

"I know what you need, angel. I'll take care of you. I just need to slow this down a little, seeing as you tried to kill me when I walked in here."

I grin. "I'll be more mindful of your aging, frail heart in the future." I put the hand not gripping his hair against his chest. He swats the side of my ass lightly, shaking his head and flexing his jaw when I gasp sharply on that bit of contact.

Then, in one smooth, swift movement, he falls to his knees and buries his face between my thighs.

His first kiss is a hungry, hot swipe before a satisfied hum vibrates through him. A delicate pull that has my head falling back against the wall with a thump, has my hands clambering behind me to grip the edge of the dresser for purchase. A tight whimper peals through me when I catch sight of our reflection in the full-length mirror across the room, ankles crossed between his shoulder blades. He works me over with a steady rhythm, a battering ram to my senses, until my breaths start to puff out in time with it. Every muscle coils tighter and higher until I'm teetering on the edge, holding onto it by my fingernails.

And then he *stops*.

I wrench my eyelids open in frustration with an undignified, needy sound. He smiles knowingly, seeing the full scope of the blissful agony he's putting me through. Punishes me mercifully not a second later when he returns his mouth to me and takes me thoroughly apart.

A garbled string of colorful expletives unspools from my lips, mixed in with the chant of his name as the orgasm tears through me, one thigh trembling against his temple while the other slips down his sweaty shoulder.

He plants a kiss below my belly button, my hands finding their way through his hair, to his jaw when he kisses between my ribs, to his neck when he plants a last one at the base of my throat. I laugh a satisfied, giddy sound and pull his face to mine, kiss him with long, drugging kisses until I know my legs are steady enough to slide onto. My fists clench in his shirt and pull. "Need this off." We part only long enough for him to pull it over his head and kick off his shoes.

I use the little moment of surprise to switch places and push him against the dresser before I dip to my knees.

The corners of his lips stretch up as my palms do the same

along his legs, fingertips slipping under the hem of his shorts before I pull them back out and reach up to the waistband, biting my lip, anxious to hear his sounds and see his expressions.

I want my calm, stoic Meyer thoroughly undone and unhinged. Want to torture him and soothe him in the same breath.

My knuckles slide against the warm skin at his hips, pressing into a vein along the V of his torso, before he snatches my wrists and pulls them away.

When I look at him in (slightly annoyed) confusion, I expect to see a teasing smile again. Instead he looks sheepish, struggles around a swallow. I default to light humor.

"Listen, I'm sure it's not as weird as you think it is," I offer.

"What?" He asks, brows flicking down.

"Whatever's going on with your dick that has you shy. It could be S-shaped and have a tooth for all I care and I'll work with it."

It works. He barks out a laugh, abs flexing gloriously before he drops my wrists and slides a thumb along my jaw.

"Can I?" I ask. He nods.

"Fee," he grits out. "I won't last long. It's been a long, long time."

"Perfect, because I'm getting hungry and would like you to take me to breakfast soon." And I pull down his pants.

There's absolutely *nothing* weird.

I'm just . . . very happy for me. It feels good to be happy for myself.

But something catches my eye, right there along his upper thigh.

"A tattoo?" I smile. "You're certainly packing surprises, aren't you?"

But then I realize what I'm looking at.

An umbrella. Watercolor splatters in the ink, bright flowers raining from its canopy.

"Meyer—"

"It's the tattoo you gave Hazel the first time we met. That little temporary one? I only had a picture of it on my phone, so I don't know if it's exact or not. I got it in . . . Vegas. I got it for you." He swipes his thumb across my bottom lip. "Fee, I was so fucking lonely before you found us."

I plant my lips against it and close my eyes, gather my nerves before I stand and kiss him, not knowing how to express everything, no words for these feelings fizzing their way from my chest into my throat. So I show him instead. Pull him with me, walking backward in the direction of the bed.

"You already know that I'm on birth control. It's been well over a year and I've been tested. Nothing to report," I say.

He laughs shakily. "Fee, it's been about four, at least, for me."

"Four months?"

"Four *years.*"

My mouth pops open before I think to shut it, not wanting to embarrass him, but he catches it and laughs.

I appreciate that again. The fact that we can stand here naked in front of one another, keyed up and turned on, and still laugh with each other.

"Why the fuck do you think I work out so much? Had to work off the tension somehow. It got worse when this pain-in-the-ass, beautiful, *funny* redhead came traipsing into my life."

And then he corrals me to the bed with his big body. Digs his knee into the mattress and crawls over me as I slide up the bed on my elbows, his smiling eyes never leaving mine. He drapes my hair around his forearm, letting it fan out around my head when I lay down fully.

He settles between my legs, eyes roaming over me tenderly even as he trembles.

"Fee," he says, a hollow whisper. "I meant it. I don't think I can last long." A gust of a laugh.

I dance my fingertips along the skin pulsing at his throat. "Good. Because I don't plan on this being the last time I get you naked, Meyer Harrigan."

Because you're mine. And I'm yours. Yours, yours, yours, I think.

He lines himself up with me and I start to shake, too, despite my efforts to stay collected. I was hoping one of us could keep it together, hoping for it to be me for a change.

He works himself into me, and my breath escapes. His eyes stutter closed and he groans. I'm impossibly full of him, of desire and happiness and this swelling in my chest. Love. He moves, and it's just a perfect degree above too much. I sigh in nirvana.

I'm reduced to sensations, loops of them with no beginning or end. The sight of the flush in his skin and the haze in his eyes, the vein in his forehead that grows prominent in concentration.

The taste of the skin on his thick wrist. The one planted just above my shoulder that I hook my hand around and kiss when my head falls to the side mindlessly on a moan.

The sound of his gruff voice as it touches against me everywhere. When he tells me I'm beautiful, tells me it's better than he dreamed. I tell him the same, that I'm so happy that umbrella broke that day.

The way his palm kneads my thigh as he holds it, wraps it around his hip, the little indents of his fingertips bruising.

The way his muscles contract beneath his skin with each push and roll of his hips into me.

I relish the feel of the coarse hairs on his thighs against the underside of mine when he lifts us, kneeling and pressing me everywhere to him, holding me closer with each decadent upward thrust. His big hand as it presses against my lower back, the other as it slides up the back of my neck and curls into my hair.

It's an ache that pulls and thrums until every inch of skin between us grows heated and damp. Until he lays us back down and lightly picks up speed, relentlessly stroking an angle, steady and deliberate, until I start to grow wild with need. Our breathing mingles, a medley of groans and sighs. Until he gently pushes his palm against my stomach and thumbs just above where we're joined.

I shatter. A million pieces in a million directions, brighter than the sunrise shining through the windows. All other thought escapes me, leaving only him. The weight of him as his hips drive me into the bed, his control loosening when I sob out his name, his grip on my thigh tightening as he pushes up my knee, bringing him impossibly deeper. His other palm goes to the headboard, that leverage the only thing keeping me from sliding up into it. He chokes on a growled *"Fuck, Fee"* when his restraint finally snaps, my nails scraping along his ass, my lips sliding clumsily up and down his face while our bodies smack together. I don't want to tear my eyes away for a second, the sight and sound and feel of him unraveling more than my imagination could ever live up to. Until he breaks, biting into my shoulder before he collapses into a boneless heap on top of me.

We both dissolve and laugh like loons, high on one another, our hands sliding along each other's faces, kissing sweetly between more laughing. *This,* this is joy.

"God. How did we wait so long to do that?" I say, digging and pressing into his calves with my heels.

"I don't know, but I have a feeling we need fuel. Before we just keep at it some more."

"Mm. That sounds good."

"The food? Bagels? Pancakes? What do you want?"

"To keep at it some more." And I reach up and drag against his bottom lip with my teeth.

THIRTY

NOW

FARLEY

We never make it out for breakfast.

We eventually peel apart to order something to be *delivered* for breakfast, though, which goes cold outside our door when we forget about it.

Then we order in again for lunch. Again for a second lunch.

I wake up from an evening nap on Meyer's chest to find him smiling down at me, hair wild. The sunset casts an orange and blue glow through the room as he traces a circle around one of my nipples.

"You're going to end me," he mutters.

"Me? You're the one who wanted that fourth helping," I say, even as my thigh creeps up his, even though I'm content down to my bones.

"Are you sore?" he asks with a little frown, his hand coming up to trace a knuckle down my cheek. The sensitive one that's just barely swollen.

"Perfectly." I grin.

He suppresses a satisfied grin, lifts a brow archly. "I didn't mean like that."

"I know. But no, I'm fine. More than fine." Every muscle in my body wants to sing in happiness.

"Are you hungry?"

I shake my head. "Did you sleep?" I ask.

He shakes his head. "Do you want to go out anywhere?"

"Not tonight, if that's okay. I want to play a game."

He smiles lopsidedly. "Alright."

"Roll over," I command. His brow lifts but he obeys, pinching a tender nipple playfully before he slides out from under me.

He lies on his stomach, tucking a pillow and his forearms under his head and treating me to an unobstructed view of his strong back, the perfect mound of his ass. I indulge myself with something I've thought about doing countless times and bite the apple, drawing a quick yelp out of him. "Sorry, sorry. Had to be done. For science."

"I'll get you back later," he says, side-eyeing me with a wicked smile.

I straddle his hips, planting myself against the curve of his lower back. He sucks in a breath through his teeth. "I don't know how long I can play this," he says darkly.

"Why? Am I hurting you?"

"I can feel *everything*, Fee. All of you."

I laugh, but won't be distracted. "I'm going to trace things on your back and you have to guess what I'm drawing, okay?"

He grunts.

I trace a circle with spiked rays around it.

"The sun," he immediately says.

"Okay, that was too easy. Try this." I trace another shape, curling down at the handle.

"Fee, I literally have an umbrella tattooed on my body already, of course I know what that is."

"*Fine.* How about this?" I trace a series of clouds, poking my fingers all around to indicate raindrops.

"Rain and clouds. Now can I roll over and sit you on my face?"

"One more thing."

I hold my hand in the shape and press it against a spot on his skin. If I could sink it through him it would push directly into his heart.

I see the side of his brow twitch, an unsure look passing across it. He curls his neck up as much as the angle allows and searches my face.

When he notes the tears in my eyes he flips around and sits up, gathers me to his lap before he snatches the hand that still holds its sign. He presses it to his lips.

"I love you, Meyer. I think I knew I was going to love you from that first day I watched you stomp in puddles with a gaggle of seven-year-old girls. I love you for the man you are, the father you are, and the friend you've been to me. I was so lonely before I found you guys, too."

His eyes grow misty and he presses his own sign into my chest.

"I love you, too, Fee."

THIRTY-ONE

NOW

MEYER

Our hotel room looks like a deserted island that we've been marooned on. Two days later a sheet hangs draped from the corner of the TV, across the desk and a nearby chair. There's a makeshift shelter littered with discarded clothes and towels underneath, washed up from rounds of crashing into each other.

I think I threw the sheet during a particularly enthusiastic tumble, when we got tangled and twisted up in it until we fell off the bed, finishing on the floor as soon as I freed us from the obstruction. I'm pretty sure that's also when I earned the little rug burn souvenirs that adorn my knees, come to think of it.

Sometimes I feel desperate. Like each satiated moment makes the next one feel more urgent. Like if I don't get inside her again and tell her, press my lips between her delicate shoulder blades with her hair wrapped snugly around my fist, she might slip through my fingers. I think it must be the same for her, too. Like yesterday, when we left for the gym and made it ten minutes working out across from each other in the tiny hotel exercise room before we bolted back upstairs. Or later that afternoon when she came back from doing yoga on her own—having learned our lesson as far as that's concerned. I couldn't stop myself from tidying up a bit while she was gone; made the bed, showered. Sat down with a book that I got lost in until she walked through the door, tossed her key on the dresser, and planted a hand on her hip.

"This is going to be a problem for us, My," she'd declared, sounding exasperated.

I looked around the room in a mild panic. Was she irritated at me for tidying? Annoyed that I was sitting naked on the chair? I *had* showered. . . . "What?"

"I was unaware that you wore glasses," she said, and I moved to take them off with a laugh, assuming she was about to give me shit for my age. "*No,*" she shook her head slowly, eyes heating. "Keep them on." And then she peeled off every stitch of her clothes before she strutted my way, my clean-up work undone soon after.

I make the bed again now while Fee gets ready for dinner, but don't bother with the sheet this time. It weirdly embellishes the room and makes it feel more homey, I decide.

I spy on her reflection in the mirrored closet doors while she bops around the bathroom. She spins herself up in her hair dryer cord precariously while she sings along to some happy tune playing through the speaker, smiling to herself.

"Hey, My!" she calls out. "I was looking at the tour schedule and Hazel's off track again when we're in Florida! I was thinking we could bring her to Universal and Disney World!"

An oily feeling slicks through my gut, but I call back, "Yeah!"

She flicks off the hair dryer and pops her head into the hall-way. "What? I couldn't hear," she asks, smiling.

"I said yeah. I'd love that. She will, too."

"Okay, good."

"Good." I smile, but it feels wooden. And then, "Fee?" Her head tilts back out again, chin resting on the door frame. "I love you."

Her returning smile beams. It's my own ray of goddamn sunshine burning through me. We're not in each other's arms, we're just exchanging small words in a nondescript hotel room in a nondescript city. And I've probably told her I love her a hundred times in the last two days, but by the way she looks at me you'd think it was the first time all over again. "I love you, too."

She goes back to getting ready, and I dive inward and start contemplating. I know I need to talk to her about the tour, about not being her manager going forward. What started as a choice I thought I'd need to make for my own self-preservation has turned into something else entirely, though.

I don't know how to explain to her that she's inspired me to want to fall back in love with my career. That I've realized that the only thing I really love about managing her is . . . *her*.

That I'm already so protective of this thing we've got. That I don't want to put any potential strain on it with working to-gether. Because I don't ever want to resent it.

I groan inwardly at the idea, disgusted that I can't just *be*. That I feel I have to put every protection in place from the jump.

But after the events of the other night, when I *wasn't* there for her . . . I think—I think that all it would do right now is hurt her.

She's already working through everything that happened, has continued to talk with me openly about how she feels she abandoned herself a bit—not with that joke, but by singling out that woman and being harsh.

Her confidence is shaken, but not lost. And mentioning the tour and making plans is another good sign that she's going to be fine. I think bringing this up now would only throw another unexpected hurdle at her, and the last thing I want to do is make any damn thing more difficult for her in any way.

"Ready?" she asks.

I glance up and take her in, so much relief blooming its way through me at the notion that I *can*. That I *can* look her up and down so openly. That I can stand up and press her to me, such a contrast in our layers now to all the times we've been pressed skin to skin these last few days.

I kiss her lips and she hums her approval.

"Oh wait, do we have time to call Haze before we go?" she asks, amber eyes rounding. *Christ, how did I wait so long to tell this woman I love her?*

I check my watch. "Plenty."

We shuffle some of the debris out of the sightline of the phone before perching it on the desk. Fee sits on my lap, but immediately checks, "Is this okay?"

"Yes. I, uh . . . I actually already talked to her about us. I asked her if she would be okay with you becoming more to me."

"And?" she asks, eyes searching. As if it was really ever a question.

"Of course she was okay with it." I shake my head, chuckling softly. "She said she would like that. Her only request was that we not kiss with tongue in front of her."

A laugh bubbles out of her, eyes filling. "That's a big ask. I can handle it, though." She scratches her nails lightly down my jaw. "Thank you for talking to her. You have no idea how happy that makes me."

"You have no idea how happy *you* make me. She loves you, too, Fee."

"We should call her before I start trying to take off your clothes again."

I swallow, wondering how I'm so damn tempted again. "You do it."

She blows out a breath, but manages for us both.

Hazel answers with a chaotic wave into the screen, setting us up at what looks like my parents' kitchen table after some juggling.

"Hi! I miss you guys!" I grin at her bright expression. She's clearly not missing us too badly. It eases something in me to see it, though.

"We miss you too," Fee replies.

"Are you sitting on my dad's lap?" she asks, smiling conspiratorially.

"I am. Is that okay?"

"Yes! He told you the rule, though, right?"

"No tongue kissing. Got it."

"And s'mores blondies once a month."

Fee turns back to me, *"Why do I think that was your addition?"*

I shrug innocently.

Hazel tells us about a new book she's reading, seeing a movie with my nephews at the new theater, the one with the new electric recliners. She talks about bowling with my parents, who also squeeze in to get on the phone. My mom looks near tears seeing us together, cooing over everything Fee says. Even my dad sits up straighter in his chair, repeatedly pushing his glasses back up the bridge of his nose and booming out laughter. She charms the pants off them, to absolutely no one's surprise.

"You can stay in my dad's room when you want to stay with us now, Fee," Hazel says enthusiastically when we start wrapping up the call. I'm grateful when there's no awkward laughter from Fee's end.

"Thank you. I'll take you up on that."

"He's got enough of that bath stuff you like to last forever. He gets it every single time we go past that store," Hazel says, rolling her eyes. I groan sheepishly, utterly called out. Fee's hand finds mine and squeezes.

We say our I love yous and our goodbyes, something so settled and natural about it that my mind cartwheels into the future. Straight into thinking about keeping Fee forever—something I'd intended to do no matter how she'd have me, but with a new color added to that thought, a new angle.

The January night is cool, but not exactly cold. Just like the too-warm fall we just had, it seems like we're going to have a too-short winter, with spring already trying to pepper the air here. We walk along the river, over a yellow bridge, where we eat fancy food on a patio under string lights and vines, next to an outdoor fireplace. And then we follow it up with candy from the lobby vending machine that we eat in our bed, in our messy hotel room oasis, before we strip back out of our clothes and rock against each other slowly from beginning to end, falling asleep with our limbs still tied up together.

THIRTY-TWO

NOW

FARLEY

"Three days of near-constant sex immediately followed by try-ing to sleep on a tour bus, plus a plane ride, has indeed made me feel my age, Fee," Meyer grumbles, one fist shoved into the small of his back.

"Poor, poor man. I'll work on your knots later." I practically skip at his side and he grunts. "Need me to get your bags?" I ask him, and *oh, if looks could kill.*

We're back in L.A. for Shauna's premiere, the tour bus still up north, waiting for us to return to San Francisco.

Meyer retrieves our bags from the belt with a stilted grunt and we head to the exit. "Um. So should I just head back to my place? Let you rest your weary bones?" I ask.

"Absolutely not. Come home with me. I want you in my bed."

"For rest?"

"You know what, woman? Yes!" he says, laughing. "Probably

for some rest. Maybe an Epsom salt bath. Perhaps a few milligrams of ibuprofen, but then I'll rock your fucking world." He grins and chuffs down at me, a combination that delights me more and more.

In the end, his king-sized bed sings its siren's call to my own fatigue and I relent, toeing off my shoes and collapsing into it even before he does. We slumber deeply, this time only our pinkies finding each other across the expanse of the bed. Until my alarm blares through the house and I have to drag myself out from the sheets, hurling my body across acres of mattress and into his shower before I head out to have my hair and makeup done.

I have to scrounge for him, buried in the pillows and a marshmallow comforter, before I plant a kiss against Meyer's beard. He smoothes a palm up my arm, thumb pushing into the crook of my elbow as he pulls me back down, cracking open an eye.

"Mm. My body wash smells good on you," he says huskily, half his smile obscured in a fluffy down cushion. I cover his sleep-rumpled face in a smattering of kisses.

"I have to go. I'll be back for the car to pick us up from here at five, though."

"Hmmkay. I love you."

I'll be sad when the somersault my stomach performs every time I hear that fades one day.

"I love you, too."

I'M SITTING IN THE SALON chair, a dazed smile molded to my face, mind wandering to what it would be like to *live* this way. I weave a fantasy from the mundane, the simple ordinaries. From waking up in the same bed every day, in our own cloud. To cooking side by side in the kitchen, Meyer circumspectly trying to tidy up behind me as I go. To playing board games around the coffee table, Hazel snacking on her favorite lemon cookies, me with my mug of wine, Meyer with his beer.

I think about spring, the annual field trip Hazel's class takes to a farm just outside of town. How maybe this year I'll have enough power to convince Meyer to let us take home a few of the downy chicks. His yard is big enough for a few hens, I'm sure of it. We could build them a perfect coop over in the corner. Make a silly sign for it and call it the Chick Inn.

I want to take her up to Abel's farm this fall, too. Go fishing in the pond that they stock while we eat apple donuts.

I imagine Meyer and I together, on a plane, in various cities throughout the country. Him waiting for me at the side of the stages in every place we go.

My phone vibrates on the counter in front of me and I lean over abruptly to get it, my stylist laughing as she's forced to chase me with the iron.

> **Meyer:** I get it now. Why people say they're so happy they
> can't stand it, or something's so great it's disgusting. I feel
> like I might need to be tranquilized.

My feet flutter-kick against the footrest as a terrible squeal-sigh pinwheels through me.

> **Me:** I was just thinking the same.

WHEN I WALK THROUGH HIS front door later to him in a pale gray tux, the lapels a navy velvet blue, my dress draped over the couch and waiting for me, it's too much to resist.

"Okay, we can't fuck up this." I gesture to my face and hair even as I'm sliding down his zipper. He smiles and laughs before he spins around a dining chair and falls into it, slacks pooling at his ankles. I strip off my pants all the way as he loses his jacket. He eyes me hungrily as he loosens his tie, braces his hands on his thighs, and watches me quickly undress. He doesn't bother with removing my underwear, just mutters a low curse when he sees the lingerie and reaches for me, hooks them to the side as I straddle his lap and sink down onto him.

It's torturous, the not kissing. Not tugging into each other's hair, simply watching each other's expressions, watching where our bodies meet and slide. Trying to come undone while staying so very put together adds a sharp edge to it that rapidly gets difficult to skate. My feet won't reach the ground, so he's forced to bear the brunt of the work as he pumps and pistons me against him, working out a hypnotic rhythm. His chin dips as he slows, lifting me with a wicked, leisurely curl. "Touch yourself," he quietly commands. And so I do, while he gazes at me intently. There's heat in it, and wonder, and agony, and love. A tear leaks out of my eye when I find my release; his lashes fan against his flushed cheeks when he does immediately after.

I make a note to remember how many times I feel beautiful with him tonight. Not only when he tells me that I am, repeatedly, but all the other moments in between. From fucking on that dining chair, to him zipping me into my silvery dress, sweeping the curtain of my hair over a shoulder and kissing the nape of my neck before we leave hand in hand.

When we smile easily and pose for photographs. Some together, others with Kara and Shauna. When we slip up the carpeted stairs inside the venue to our balcony seats where we watch Shauna's movie, me snort-laughing, Meyer letting out the occasional chuckle through his nose and shaking his head.

There's the moment he surprises a delighted shriek out of me when he hops gingerly onto the banister on our way out, sliding sideways with his arms in the air, feet kicked out for balance.

When we speed walk down the remaining stairs and out the doors, back to the car where we take turns pouring champagne directly into each other's mouths, spilling it, and licking over the spots that grow sticky on our skin.

Later, in the bath together, with his chest pressed to my back and his beard scraping against the crook of my neck, forearms shifting across my middle while I grip the edges of the tub in ecstasy, his ministrations hidden beneath the bubbles. Afterward, when he makes us pizza-dillas with pepperoni and mozzarella in tortillas. While I sit on the island in his tie and a fluffy robe, telling him stories about when Marissa and I first moved to L.A., him contributing his own ramen-noodle-day tales in turn.

We almost miss our plane the next morning. Neither of us remembers to charge our phones, which means we oversleep and I hold us up even more as I shove everything back into my suitcase in a palpable panic. Meyer nearly gives himself an aneurysm over not saying *I told you so* since he tried to pack for me last night. I think he might be really angry with me, and I mentally draw out all my apologies while we jog through all the jog-able parts of the airport.

But then, when we finally manage to scramble into our seats, the last two passengers to board, I notice that he's wearing mismatched shoes at the same time he finds a false eyelash stuck to the side of my neck, and we laugh until we cry and gasp, and a flight attendant has to come calmly ask us to *please* try to *quiet down*. We spend the short flight avoiding eye contact so we don't burst into any more giggle fits.

The next week passes in this special brand of domestic bliss. Our own version of it; between a plane, a tour bus, and more hotel rooms.

It feels exactly like you'd think. Like being at overnight camp with your best friend who also happens to supply you with mind-bending orgasms.

I go out on stage two more times, and I feel . . . fearless about it. Relaxed. It feels as good and as fulfilling as the high I remember, and I have no doubt that this is because he's by my side.

There is only one more show for me on this mini tour, though, and it's also the same day that Meyer leaves to retrieve Hazel from Ohio. I promise him that I'm fine, and I think I truly mean it. It feels like all my pieces have settled into place, and I've got the set memorized down to each word and facial expression now, honed to sharp perfection.

Meyer's hovering, though. Worried. There's a weird, melancholy layer in his words, like his mind is elsewhere or churning on different words, no matter how I reassure him.

"Jonesy?" he calls to me now from somewhere inside the room.

"Out here!"

I smile up at him in his towel when he walks through the door. "Jesus, aren't you cold?!"

"Not for long." He smirks before he slips behind me on the lounge chair and cradles me against him.

We sit together quietly this way for a while, sharing the same glass of wine as we look out at the Golden Gate Bridge from a hotel balcony in Nob Hill. And I don't know why, but my brain can't seem to help it: I start to think that maybe this is all too good to be true. How does one person get this lucky in life? To do something big that fills them with such incredibly overwhelming feelings, with their best friend—best *love*—alongside. Something that takes them so many places in front of so many faces. And yet, the view that far outshines them, the faces that I love more than anything, that fill me with the biggest feelings of all, also exist with me the most quietly. I pull Meyer's arms tighter around me.

"Are you packed? You know, you shouldn't put that off until the last second. Just a pro tip for you." I knock on his forearm with my knuckles.

"Ha. You don't say? Yes, I'm packed." He kisses my temple.

"Are you—are you okay?" I ask after a bit.

He sighs. "Yes. I just need to talk to you about something and I'm being an idiot about it."

"Really?" I whip around, but I can barely make out his eyes even with the city lights shining. "Let's go inside."

HE SHUFFLES AROUND THE ROOM a bit, picking up odds and ends. Plugs in his phone with a meaningful look and a halfhearted grin my way.

"Meyer. You're scaring me. Come talk to me, please." I flip over the corner of the comforter and pat the empty spot at my side.

He nods and removes his towel, the dim lighting making the umbrella appear black and white. He slides in beside me and I start to trace it with my fingertips.

"Fee"—more sighs—"I was thinking . . . I know the tour is

going to be great. I *know* it." I still my fingers and frown up at him.

"I know that, too," I say, and *that* makes him blow out a breath with a nod. "We've got each other's backs. Just like we have from day one, yeah?" I add with what I hope is a reassuring smile. His eyes round for the blip of a second, and I almost think I've said the wrong thing . . . but then he smiles back, his fullest one.

"Yes. Of course."

"Is that what you wanted to talk to me about? *Again?*" I nudge him with my elbow.

He shakes his head and his brow furrows. "Move in with me? Would you—would you want to live with Hazel and me?"

It feels a bit like ascending the stairs in the dark. You think you have another step, but then experience that swooping, bottoming out feeling when you realize you're already on the top floor. Hearing that his mind is on the same plane as mine is a happy surprise, even if it's also a little jarring.

I slide my knee around to bracket his hips, cup his face in my hands. "I'd love to live with you guys," I say, swiping along his beard with my thumbs. "But make sure you get Hazel's approval, first, okay?"

He nods solemnly before he cups the back of my head and brings my lips to his.

THE NEXT MORNING I OPT to ride with him to the airport after a small internal debate. I still feel like he needs something from me, like I need to ease his spirit somehow. It makes me wonder if I should act nonchalant about being separated from him, even if it's for two days. It *should* probably feel nonchalant, but

I've never been great at modulating my happier feelings, only ever mastered reducing some of the sadder ones.

So we ride to the airport in hushed conversation, taking turns kissing our clasped hands. And when we pull up to the curb to drop him off, I focus on imagining the next time he'll be on an airport curb, in L.A., when I get to pick him up with Hazel, our trio reunited.

"In Vegas—" bursts from him just before my lips make their way to his. "In Vegas. I tried to tell you. I know I was drunk, but it only let loose what was already there. When you said you wanted to be stupid with love, I tried to tell you how I felt. That you were the only person I've ever been stupid with."

I search his expression, not sure what I'm supposed to find. "And I immediately tried to get in your pants, Meyer," I laugh. "I thought I scared you off."

His face crumples in confusion. "When did you try to get in my pants?"

"Uh, when I immediately invited you back to my room?"

"You said . . ." He tilts his head to the side, trying to remember. "You said we had an early morning and should get back to the room."

"That was just my attempt at being smooth about it."

"I said I would walk you back."

"Which one *would* do if one was going to go join the other in their room for some coital revelry."

"*Fee.* I thought I scared you off by saying that. I thought I was just walking you back to be polite and say goodnight," he replies.

And now I'm laughing full-out. "I thought I scared *you* off when I had a mini meltdown. I thought I scared you off with my obvious panic! And then when you left I told myself I'd misinterpreted the whole thing." We're both laughing, eyes shining.

"I guess we're both pretty stupid after all, huh?" I say.

"No. Becoming your friend was—*is*—the smartest thing I've ever done," he says, laugh fading. "I got the tattoo because I wanted to remember that feeling that you gave me the first time I met you. When you burst inside and demanded to make a connection. I wanted to remember to not be afraid of that anymore. Even if it doesn't look the same for everyone. Even if some people speak with their hands, some use a mic, or art, whatever. You did it with your friendship with us."

"So you don't regret it, then? I couldn't help but wonder, since you did put it in such a discreet area." I laugh because if I don't, I'll cry.

"I mean, I was drunk, but even in my state I knew if I showed up with something permanently inked on my skin to show you how I felt, it might feel a little manipulative." He quirks a brow down at me.

"Nah. I liked it better how it played out, anyway. Like double the reward."

He nods, brushing against my nose with his. "I know." His palm slips to the base of my throat, shifting into the sign against my chest as he smiles into my lips. "I'll see you in a few days."

I kiss him like it'll be a few years. Hold out my hand in the sign when he steps away from me.

THIRTY-THREE

NOW

Cynicism masquerades as wisdom, but it is the farthest thing from it. Because cynics don't learn anything. Because cynicism is a self-imposed blindness: a rejection of the world because we are afraid it will hurt us or disappoint us. Cynics always say "no." But saying "yes" begins things. Saying "yes" is how things grow.

—STEPHEN COLBERT

FARLEY

Kara and Shauna distract me backstage by sharing some of their favorite pre-show routines. Shauna has symphony music blaring at full volume because she likes to imagine her favorite raunchy songs against their rhythms. We end up composing our own operetta between the group using the lyrics from the classical "My Neck, My Back" over the musical stylings of "La donna è mobile." Even Clay joins in, though I'm pretty sure he only lip-syncs.

And even though I'm aware that it's a distraction, it works. I don't think I'll ever *not* be reduced to tears when I imagine the largest of security guards breaking out into an operatic soprano of "then you roll your tongue from the crack back to the front," for as long as I live.

By the time I make it out onto the stage, I'm as happy and as confident as I typically am, even without Meyer. It's a little louder inside my head, and my heart drums a bit more rapidly, but it's nothing I can't handle for the time being.

The material goes over without a hitch. It hits at every climax, the timing rolls through smoothly. I tell the joke where I call a kid a bad, bad name again, because that's all it is: a joke. It's *funny*, this time.

When it's over, some people stand and clap, others hold up their drinks in salute. I feel connected and wonderful, and am reminded again that *this* is what I am meant to do, and I am not ashamed of any part of it.

I refuse to be, ever again.

As long as I remain true to myself, I know that my silly streams of words have the power to make someone's day brighter.

When I exit the stage, I'm surrounded by six security guards, and I can't help but laugh when we make it onto the bus.

"Meyer's doing, I take it? I think *maybe* that was a little overkill," I say to Clay.

"Well, you make sure you tell Meyer that. I panicked at the last second and didn't know if four would be enough. The last thing I need is him calling me twenty-two times before *every* show and asking for every detail. I've had heartburn for forty-eight hours." He pops an antacid for emphasis.

I pat him on the shoulder. "Don't worry. He won't be as bad once he's here and sees it for himself," I reply. His eyes round and he coughs. I feel Shauna and Kara's laughter die down and their eyes turn our way.

"What? I mean, I know he won't be at *every* show, but he's not crazy or anything. He knows what happened before was a weird, freak thing. I'll make sure he doesn't drive you guys insane when he's gone." I huff out a laugh that goes unreciprocated.

"It's my understanding that he won't be at *most* of the shows, though, right, Clay?" Shauna asks, looking between Clay and me.

"What do you mean?" I shake my head, lost.

"I thought he would have talked to you by now," Clay responds, and I feel my eyebrows shoot up.

"What are you talking about?" They all look silently among one another.

It's Kara who speaks up finally. "Farley, Meyer withdrew from his management contract for the tour. He told us he wasn't planning on managing . . . at all, going forward."

"He appointed me as sole tour manager, and left a clause in there for you to be able to find your own, should you want it," Clay says, swiping at his forehead.

I sit at the same time that my phone rings.

I ignore it.

THIRTY-FOUR

NOW

My life needs editing.

—MORT SAHL

MEYER

When I don't hear from Fee after the fifth call this morning or the tenth text, I know I fucked up. And I know she must've found out about the management contract. That's the only thing it could be.

I put on a brave face for Hazel, because I am excited and feel almost whole having her back with me, but . . . it's a bit like that time last summer when I set out super early, before anyone else was awake, in order to set our stuff up on the beach and reserve us a spot. I'd thought I was doing something considerate—smart, even. But I'd forgotten that the tide was rolling in.

"I thought Fee would be picking us up?" Hazel asks when the Uber arrives.

"She just had something come up. Don't worry, the bus gets back tonight," I say after I load the luggage.

But she doesn't come by that night, and I outright lie to Hazel and say that it got delayed.

I feel sick.

Sicker when I go to my bathroom and find her toothbrush still at my sink. On my side, even though there are two vanities. She'd forgotten it in her panic the morning we sprinted to the airport, and we had to pull the tour bus over to a San Jose Target for her to get a new one.

She, Shauna, and Kara ended up spending three hours in there while the rest of us set up camp chairs in the parking lot and grilled hot dogs when we got hungry.

I know it's a low blow, but I have to try one more time, and come at it a new way.

I type out the text in Notes. Edit, delete, and rewrite it five times before I finally settle on the words.

Me: Fee, I'm sorry for not talking to you first. There's no excuse. But I hope you'll let me explain myself, please. We promised that we wouldn't lose each other and that we wouldn't let this hurt Hazel. Please.

The three dots finally pop up and the lurch in my chest has me thinking that I need to make an appointment to have my blood pressure and cholesterol checked.

But then they disappear.

They don't come back up.

I PACE AROUND MY HOUSE and find all the places that she's touched. Where she's already made it her home. I rub at a spot on my chest when I think about how I asked her to live here, how happily shocked she'd looked. How, barring a miracle, that won't be happening now.

I find my tie from the premiere slung over one of the stools at the counter, wrap it around my fist like a tourniquet, the skin above it fading to a bloodless pale.

I end up lying down on the couch eventually. The bed is still unmade in my room, and I can't bear to look at it. Each time that I do I see her through blurry eyes, woken by her kissing a path up my leg, swiping her sweet tongue over my tattoo. I think of her smiling over her shoulder at me after she slung a leg across my middle, planted her hands on my thighs and rode me in reverse, my thumbs pressing into the dimples on her back, the ends of her hair swaying against her waist with every grind and roll of her hips.

I look at the dirty pan still in the sink and don't want to wash it, remembering her and Hazel decorating Easter eggs. Pasting valentines together for Hazel's class, signing made difficult by glue-covered fingers.

I let myself imagine the things I never dared before, too, punishing myself with them.

Fee with a rounded belly and a smile, putting Hazel's hand in a spot to feel the baby kick. Hazel guiding her sister around the pool in a floatie, one of those ridiculous infant sun hats strapped to her head. I imagine us taking Hazel to Europe, maybe to see that play we never got to see. I imagine popping out of my office to ask for her thoughts on whatever it is I want to write, her opinions and feedback critical to me always.

I slice at my mind, my heart, over and over again until I exhaust myself with it, until my burning eyes finally close.

WHACK.

I startle awake when Hazel slaps my arm. I blink the bright lights away. Hold up a hand to ask for a minute, sit up, and manage to open one eye with a wince.

"Fee is here!" Hazel signs.

"What?" I say out loud, turning toward the door.

"I tried to call. I rang the doorbell, too, so when no one an-swered I let myself in," Fee says. She won't even look at me.

"I don't—" I start to say before I slip into sign. *"I don't know where my phone is."*

"Okay. I thought I could take Hazel to breakfast?" she replies, eyes barely darting my way, focused on Hazel's retreating form instead.

I can practically see the tension vibrating through her when I slowly step her way. She looks at me, now, expression cool. "I want to talk, I do. I just want to focus on Hazel this morning first, if that's okay? We'll talk after?" she says.

I manage a nod, and Hazel skips past me toward the door.

"You don't want to come?" she signs, looking at me quizzi-cally.

"I'll get everything caught up here. You guys go have fun."

I DO GET EVERYTHING DONE. Busy myself, my hands, my head with any menial task I can. I even make the bed, but don't wash the sheets.

When my girls return, the first thing Hazel does is tip her chin up at me in an angry scowl. The depth of discomfort I feel at this is irrational. If I were wearing boots I'd be shaking in them.

"Did you have a good breakfast?" I ask.

Hazel replies quickly. *"The best ever. You really missed out."* The corner of Fee's mouth ticks up as she smoothes a hand over Hazel's head.

"I'm going to my room and watching YouTube, don't try and stop me. I brought you leftover biscuits." She tosses a box onto the counter unceremoniously before she stalks off to her room.

"I take it you told her I'm not your manager anymore, then?" I say to Fee, and immediately wish I could take it back when she flinches.

"I hope you don't blame me. I didn't know if *you* would," she replies, making me wince in return. She folds her arms.

"Fee, I—" I wait for her eyes to meet mine. "I'm so sorry for not talking about this with you. I owed you that much, at least. I got scared."

"Of hurting my pathetic feelings. I get it, Meyer. I really do. I was sitting there yammering on about being together on all these things, being so fucking dependent on you that you didn't want to be the bad guy and let me down, I get it." She swipes angrily at a tear.

"That's not—Fee, you're not dependent on me."

"Obviously, Meyer, I am. I mean, I even needed you to publicly be interested in me in order to secure this job, right?"

"Jesus, no, that's why I didn't even want to at first. Stop, please."

"And then, when I go against your advice, it bites me in the ass. Or the face, more like."

"Are you mad at me for not talking to you first, or are you mad that I made this decision, Fee?"

"Both!"

"Well, can you let me explain to you where I'm coming from first, dammit?"

Her nostrils flare. "How long were you planning it—or I guess, more importantly, how long were you feeling this way? I want to know."

"When they came to us in October and I agreed to the dating, I knew that I wouldn't be able to continue working together after."

Her mouth falls open in shocked hurt. "Why didn't you—? What? I would have never—"

"Never what? Never told me your feelings for me? Gone on that way forever? You'd have been fine like that?"

"That's not—"

"I thought I'd have to pull back because I thought your feelings wouldn't be the same as mine, Fee. I thought that I'd get a taste of what it would be like to be with you, that way, and then it would end and I'd be even more ripped apart."

"And now, what? You got a taste and want to pull back because you realize you feel *less* than me? Why did you ask me to live with you? Out of sympathy?"

"Goddamn it, Fee, no. Being with you makes me want *more*. Of everything. Of *you,* more than anything else, but also, out of my career. I want to do something that I *love* again. It might not be stand-up, but there's something else for me, okay? I don't know what it is, but I know that if I want it to connect, I have to actually put myself into it again. Not just some writing here and there; I have to work at it."

Her face softens at that, hands falling to her sides. "Oh."

"It doesn't excuse not talking to you. I just—I wanted to find the right way. The right time. I don't know."

She nods with a shrug, looking down at her feet.

"I also . . ." I swallow, mouth dry. "I also know that in the long run, working that closely together can't be good for a relationship. I want to be smart with us."

She snorts. "So we're back to being smart, huh?"

"You know what I mean."

"It feels like . . ." She looks up at the ceiling, trying to hold back tears. "It feels like you're taking a step back. I know what the good, smart choice is, and I understand why you want to make it. I get that I should be happy that you want to do the right thing, and I know I should want that, too. But can I just admit that . . ." She growls in frustration. "Never mind."

"No." I reach for her hand and she slides it away from mine. I look down at it like it's been burned, until she takes it again. Such a small concession, and I could fucking weep with it. "Tell me," I plead.

"Can I just admit the wrong thing? That I know we'll be okay, that I know that it's smart, but that it fucking sucks in the meantime, Meyer?" Her floodgates open and I feel tears prick their way into my own eyes. "I moved here when I was nineteen, away from a dad who spent *years* telling me how wrong I was for everything. Who made this dream of mine seem shallow and stupid. I'd already lost my person, you know? I'd lost the one person who accepted and loved me for all the crazy, too." She slides the heel of her palm across her face before she clutches her chest with it. "And then I found you. And you just . . . volunteered to help me. *You,* who made comedy look easy, who always had some cutting remark, some brilliant, superior way of putting things. And *you* wanted to help me and my fart jokes and my foul mouth. It made me feel . . . *right.* Like, even if nothing big ever happened for me, I had the right to do it."

I will myself not to look away, to take in every hiccupping, sobbing inhale she makes even though I think I might be dying. I fold my free arm around my middle like I can physically hold myself together. This is so much more, so much worse than I imagined. I thought about finding that fucking woman who threw hot coffee on her, thought awful things. Now I wonder if I'll want to toss a vat of acid on myself when I look in the mirror. I cannot stand that I've made her cry. I'll make it up to her, forever, somehow.

"But Meyer, I love you. I can't fucking help it. I wish I had the ability to be smart or conservative with my heart, but I don't. I just don't. I get . . . I get why you don't want to be my manager anymore, and I'll be okay with it. *We'll* be okay. I have to do this stuff because I want to do it and not just because it feels safe or justified when I have you at my side. I do know this. But I also think that maybe we shouldn't move in together just yet. And I'm still going to mourn the loss of what I'd already built up and pictured, okay?"

I look at the spots on my arms that are wet. "I can . . . I'll support you, however I can. I won't push you to move in if you want to take that back right now."

"I'm only trying to stay on even footing, Meyer. Maybe—maybe it's petty of me, maybe I only want to take that back because you took something away, too. I don't really even know. But it's how I feel."

I nod, feeling like I might splinter bone from grinding my jaw so hard. "I'm sorry for hurting you, Fee. I should have . . . I mean, I would . . . you know that if you want me to I will stay on. I only thought I was doing the right thing."

She laughs darkly. "Oh yeah, that would be *great* for us, at this point. You staying on and sacrificing yourself just to spare my feelings." She wipes her nose on her sleeve. "No, that is *not* what I want. I want everything for you too. You deserve *everything*, Meyer. Of course I'm sad that that doesn't include some of what I pictured for us together, but I'd rather your honesty than your sympathy, always. And I would love to support every single dream you have. I want you to share that with me." She offers me a sad smile, her eyes bright gold and puffy.

"Please," my voice cracks. "Please let me hold you?"

She nods, and we hold each other there by my front door for a while, rocking, rubbing circles on each other's backs. "This is just a blip," she says. "And I'll get over it and I'm going to be so happy for you in everything else you do." She sniffs. "Everything we do together, too."

When she leaves, she lets me kiss her goodbye, but doesn't let it linger.

I know my job is far from over with Fee, but I have some more explaining to do with Hazel, too.

I walk into her room, and she immediately turns off the mute on the TV so that I jump at the blaring volume on some weird, eye-twitch-inducing YouTube show. I give her a stern look and she mutes it again. Give her another look and she turns it off.

"Why don't you want to manage Fee anymore? Why does she look so sad?"

I sigh and sit at the foot of her bed. I wish someone would write a parenting book on how to explain this kind of shit. Something full of perfect analogies and comparisons.

Reducing being with Fee to some kind of food overindulgence or activity feels cheap. I can't seem to scrounge up any applicable comparisons in the corners of my brain, so I default to the truth, without overexplaining, and hope she understands it.

"Because, Haze. I love her. I want her to live with us, and be a family with us, more than she already is. I want that for a long time. And sometimes, when you want something to last, and want something to still feel special, you have to let it be its own thing. You have to protect it, not stretch it and force it into too many other things. It might seem like I care less, but really it's because I care more."

She blinks, considering me. *"I don't think she knows, though. I don't think you've shown her enough. Fee is the one who comes to us all the time, who does all our life stuff with us. She's the one who makes things fun. She makes me try new things, and you, too. So if you don't help her with her work anymore, you're going to have to show her in other ways, Dad. What they lack in knowing, we make up for in showing."*

I squint. *"What was that?"*

"It's what Fee and I say before dance. 'What I don't hear, I feel. What they lack in knowing, I make up for in showing.' You have to do your best to show her, and if she doesn't get it still, then that's her problem. But you have to do your best to show her."

I blink. Astonished at the emotional intelligence of a ten-year-old girl. If adults were to get more of their advice from kids, I wonder if we'd fuck things up as much as we do. Somehow, I think we'd simplify a lot.

I shake her hand in agreement.

THIRTY-FIVE

ONE MONTH LATER

Laughter is the shortest distance between two
people.

—VICTOR BORGE

FARLEY

Marissa pulls into the parking garage after we give the guy
manning the gate our appropriate paperwork. I didn't want to
make a big deal out of arriving at this venue for our first official
show on the Wet 'n Mild Tour, since it's here in L.A. anyway.

"You sure you don't want to just have him come, Fee?" Miss
asks for what feels like the hundredth time.

"I'm sure, Marissa," I laugh.

Meyer and I are good. Every day we get a little closer to great,
as the sting of his decision dulls with time. Do I wish he'd have
included me in making it? Yes. But he continues to be my hammock, my support, and I've always had to come upon and fight
for my confidence on my own. It should never have been his

responsibility, even if he played a role in me finding it in the first place.

I stay with him more nights than I don't, even though we haven't moved forward with the living together thing, officially.

I stay because he and Hazel feel like home. From their quiet bantering hands and the way they both twirl a finger around in their hair while they read, to our soft weeknights snuggled up on the couch and our bright day trips on the weekends. It feels like we're living the life we already built together, with new discoveries along the way.

Plus, Meyer wears his glasses a *lot* at home.

After a surprisingly rainy winter this year, one we needed after too many droughts, the tulip bulbs we planted shot up and bloomed, along with the honeysuckle plants I helped them choose for their fragrance.

Still, I didn't want to ask him to come today. Perhaps it's pride.

It's probably because I just would rather rip the Band-Aid off. I think I'm healed under it, anyway.

Also, he didn't ask or push to, so maybe it's the same for him.

Marissa gives me a squeeze before she leaves the back room, and I sneak my head out of the curtain to watch the VIPs start to trickle into their front row seats. Miss is here, of course, then there's Lance and his wife. I laugh in astonishment when I spot Abel and Betty, plus a few of their kids from the farm, ambling down the aisle.

Someone flips a switch and the stage is illuminated, drawing my eyes up.

"Thought you might want to see this," Clay says beside me. "Meyer was adamant about the stage design elements."

Countless white umbrellas hang suspended from the ceiling. Some upside down, others right side up, strands of lights strung in and around them. It's breathtakingly beautiful, silly, and whimsical.

I suck in a shaky breath and beg my tears not to fall. I didn't bring an ounce of makeup for touch-ups. "Clay, when did he do this?" I ask.

"Oh, months ago. Before he even pulled out. He had it added to the contract so that I had to work it out with every venue beforehand. Let me tell you, some of them were not so stoked about it: there's a hundred and seventy-five umbrellas up there!"

I start to laugh and a tear escapes. That fucking man. He's here for me even when he's not here.

Suddenly, I have to call him. I have to tell him I love him, more vehemently than I did when I kissed him entirely too mildly before I left tonight. I need him to know that I'm more than okay, that I'm happy and excited and I love him and that I'm just as grateful for him as ever.

He doesn't answer, though, and I force myself to shake it off. I know he and Hazel had plans to go to the movies, so they must already be in the theater, or something. I fire off a text and hope there are enough exclamations to drive the point home.

We end up going with Shauna's pre-show ritual again. End up laughing just as much and passing time just as quickly. I swear I can feel the energy from the crowd creeping in, like dry ice slipping under the curtains and doors. It's a sold-out show, a sold-out arena for Christ's sake, and I don't feel a lick of nerves. I feel transcendent, feel like I could power an engine battery.

"Ladies and gentlemen," sounds from behind the still-closed curtain.

My neck snaps up and I see him.

Meyer, with Hazel at his side, both beaming at me.

The curtain opens and I have a distinct moment of terror grip me on his behalf. I can't stand the thought of him torturing himself for me. His stage fright is far from cured: I can see it in the way his shoulders inch toward his ears and hear it when he blows a breath into the mic.

"I'm sorry I can't speak this into this mic for you, loud enough for everyone in this room to hear," he signs. *"But Fee, I love you. I love you, you foolish, insane, beautiful, kind, intelligent, completely stupid woman."*

I laugh as another tear slips free.

"You want to get married in Vegas? I'll buy us plane tickets right now."

"I'll be your maid of honor!" Hazel adds.

"You want me to spell out my love for you on a banner and fly it through the sky? I'll start working on a pilot's license so I can do it myself. I'd tattoo your name on my forehead if it meant you wanted to wake up next to me and look at it every day."

He doesn't look away from me, but starts speaking into the mic. "It is my distinct pleasure to introduce you to the first Wet 'n Mild lady of the night, someone whom I've had the honor to watch grow from mimicking a bumblebee in a dumpy, low-ceiling bar—sorry, Lance—to the incredibly funny comic you'll get to experience tonight.

"I don't know what I believe in as far as a higher power, Fee, but I know that I now believe that rainstorms always precede something amazing, because you came into our lives on the tail end of one.

"I know that I believe in being stupid with love, in always looking for the laugh because of you. I believe that you've made me a better man and, by extension, a better father. I believe that you're

the kind of woman I hope my daughter wants to emulate one day. That's right, angel—foul mouth, bad manners, and all. Because your spirit is immeasurably kind.

"I believe that jumping in puddles is better than any fancy party, and I believe that I'll fight for your love, for the honor of loving you, every day, for the rest of our lives. Let me do that, Farley Jones, and I promise to make you the happiest woman for as long as you'll have me.

"Everybody, please give a warm welcome to Farley Jones!"

EPILOGUE

ENTERTAINMENT MAGAZINE, SPRING 2028
BY LUCY WADE

Farley Jones-Harrigan walks into the diner and greets me like a longtime friend. It's often been stated that she does the same to a microphone.

It's impossible to find comedy's darling unlikable, between her disarming, cavalier nature and her warm, self-deprecating grin.

Even now, when our omelettes arrive, she discreetly pulls a pile of Taco Bell hot sauce packets out of her purse and distributes them heavily across her $22 breakfast.

"Sorry," she tells me with a wince. "I've been addicted since I was pregnant, and nothing else quite measures up. I'm pretty sure my local Taco Bell added a tip jar on my behalf so I can shower them in guilt money every time I hit the place."

Like most young mothers, we fall into an easy back-and-forth over the parts of infancy and toddlerhood that we're more ambivalent about. We share pictures of our daughters—exactly one month apart from each other. We *ooh* and *ahh* over videos.

We even fall into sharing the graphic nature of our birth stories, growing louder and louder with each horrific anecdote.

It's almost easy to forget that the woman across from me
isn't just a girlfriend meeting me for a quick brunch, but a
household name in the world of stand-up. She's also married
to comedy icon Meyer Harrigan, with whom she co-wrote *PTA*,
a film that's already abuzz in awards talk.

L: Farley, critics are saying that your film is like *Bad Moms*
meets *Crash* meets *Silver Linings Playbook*.

F: All masterpieces, in my humble opinion.

L: What inspired *PTA*?

F: A whole combination of things, really. There was one specific night, when I was invited out with a group of moms, and
things got . . . wild. The same night that inspired a bit in my
first big tour. But, when it came to writing the screenplay, we
were more interested in everyone's stories. Why a simple night
out maybe wasn't so simple for all of them. I think being comedians always made us curious about what makes people tick.
What might be going on behind the scenes. Maybe the woman
who harps on school lunches is recovering from an eating dis-
order. Maybe the woman obsessed with fixing up the single dad
in the class feels like she's failing in her marriage at home.

L: Well, I know it resonated with a lot of people. How was it
working with your husband again?

F: Oof! I really wish I had some funny fight stories to share.
Believe me, I had a pen and paper ready. But sadly, it was a

dream. I don't know if it was because I was pregnant at the time and he took it easy on me or what, but he was wonderful to work with. Seeing him in his element is incredibly humbling. He was never afraid to dig deeper, to contrast the breast milk scene against the one of her character crying through her struggles, leaking through her bra in the middle of Target while in the throes of postpartum. He's got many gifts, and getting to share in this one with him was something I'll never forget.

L: It sounds like that love and care really translated into the film.

F: Thank you, I certainly hope so.

It's not long after that Meyer and their two girls show up to breakfast, the chubby-legged toddler teetering between them. "She refuses to let us carry her anywhere right now. I thought our backs were getting ruined by hauling her sturdy weight around, but it turns out it's not much better being bent over to hold her hand," Farley tells me with a laugh. There are rounds of kisses and greetings. Meyer asks Farley if she's proud of the whale spout pigtails adorning Georgie's head. Farley celebrates him accordingly. Farley signs to Hazel (age 16), who is Deaf, and turns to me when she sees my curiosity. "Just telling her I love her dress. She says I can borrow it. Having a teenager has its perks, honestly. Don't let anyone scare you about those years to come."

They're a happy, unassuming family, which is somehow what makes them extraordinary.

BONUS EPILOGUE

(4 YEARS AFTER WET 'N MILD TOUR)

PLAYLIST:
- "All I Want Is You," Vitamin String Quartet
- "The Book of Love," Gavin James

FARLEY

It's supremely satisfying to be a cliché, for once. Because it's my wedding day, and I *should* get to feel more beautiful than I ever have. And *I do.*

Even if I'm so damn tempted to make a joke in the face of every compliment.

"You're exquisite. Absolutely radiant," Marissa says to me, swiping at a few stray tears. And the reply nearly slides off of my tongue—*that's just the $65 highlighter you made me buy*—but I manage to roll it back. Because regardless of how much money I spent on professional makeup, on this dress, it's the contentment in every fiber of my being that makes me feel lit from within.

I sign to Hazel, *"Will you do my buttons?"* She nods, her eyes flickering, blinking back tears.

I summon her gaze back to mine. *"Hey, you okay?"*

"Yes." She gives me a watery smile as the photographer snaps photos in my peripheral and Marissa lets out a quiet sob.

"Just love you," she says to me in the mirror with a shrug. Then darts her gaze back down to the dress. I'm immediately hit with the overwhelming urge to stop all of this and push to talk with her more, to make her tell me everything in that beautiful fourteen-year-old mind. She's become so much more like Meyer in recent years, more contemplative and careful, a little more reserved with her laughs and smiles like any of us at that age. She doesn't love to be pushed, though, and always opens up when she's ready.

She finishes the last button and I turn to face her, taking her in. Meyer's going to lose his shit the moment he sees this beautiful young woman—his little girl—walking me down the aisle in her dusty blue dress.

But for now, I'm anxious to see him myself for a first look. I want a moment to ourselves before all of this, however small and intimate this whole thing may be.

I press my forehead into Hazel's—a gesture made marginally awkward since she just recently surpassed me in height. *"I love you too."* I hold the sign against her collarbone. When she pulls away, she replies, *"Want to practice your vows one more time?"*

"My vows to you or to him?" I reply with a laugh and she rolls her eyes in teenage perfection.

"I didn't demand vows. I politely requested a sibling as soon as possible. I've waited long enough."

I hand over her bouquet to hinder any further retorts. *"I'll do my best, as quickly as possible."*

Betty pops into the room she's graciously set up for us then. "It's time. You ready?"

Betty and Abel got far more into the wedding planning than I ever could've anticipated when we asked them if we could have it here at their farm. They were full of ideas of their own for the ceremony site; offered up the pond, a barn, their courtyard. . . . But we both agreed we wanted something simple, out in the trees where we first kissed.

That being said, the jaunt from the house, over the little ridge and into the orchard, is a bit long for my liking at the moment. Each step brings with it an increased awareness and the reminder of where exactly I'm headed and who I'm headed toward. It's almost shameful how tempted I am to start running, how fucking insatiable I am for that man.

There are about twenty-five more yards to the ridge, the path across the expansive lawn before me lined with the perfect mix of fallen leaves and white rose petals. I smile at the poetic contrast. Seasons changing, life and death, new beginnings while we celebrate what's already come to pass, all of it beautiful in its messy contradiction.

The moment I step onto the edge of the hill, I see him. He's concentrating on a tree, his broad back to me. That place there between his shoulders is my favorite place to rest. To come up behind him when he's making fried eggs in the mornings, loop my hands and slide them up his chest and burrow my face in that nook. Love to feel his hum of approval every time, vibrating in my palms and against my cheek. Love swatting his (perfect, tight, round, endlessly tempting) ass, too.

I bite my lip through a smile, remembering the night before . . . how we were supposed to stay apart—Abel and Betty were adamant about it and I blame them for making it more alluring—only to end up sneaking him in through my cottage window. . . .

"Jones—" he'd said, capturing my mouth in a kiss as soon as his feet touched the ground, even as he began pulling off his shirt. "I can't be sneaking in windows. I'm almost forty years old."

"You still planning on calling me *Jones* after tomorrow?" I asked him, my teeth tugging at his lip, trying to drag him further into the room. I palmed him through his sweats and he sighed out a low groan.

"I'll call you whatever you want," he said, smiling wickedly. "As long as I get to call you my wife."

That balloon in my chest inflated again, so fast I thought it might just pop and flow out as tears. I whimpered into his mouth when he lowered us to the ground, kicking off the rest of our clothes in a frenzy.

"Are you sure?" he asked, hovering above me on flexed arms, one ankle already hooked over his shoulder. I gripped his ass and tried to haul him into me. "How long have you been off, now? We can wait." He tilted his head to kiss that ankle.

"Are you changing your mind?" I asked, a twinge of panic stinging its way through my throat.

"*God,* no." He smiled, already flushed. Moonlight shone from behind him.

I laughed, relieved. As much as I love his careful, steady consideration, something about how worked up he gets any-time I mention getting pregnant only gets me worked up, too.

It was hot and hungry and slick, the carpet rough against my back. I nearly cried out when he slid out of me abruptly, tipped my knees wider and brought his mouth down onto me.

He took me apart with his tongue before he came back over me, drove himself into me until I was mindless with bliss.

"God, that was—"

"I know," he said through a pant and a kiss, his hand lovingly stroking my face. "Where are Marissa and the girls? Haze in bed already?"

"I told them I was tired and pulled the bride card. But they're all back at the big house with Abel and Bet playing cards." I worked to slow my breathing as he rolled onto an elbow to hover over me, swept a strand of hair behind my ear.

"You know, I'm not having second thoughts about trying. I just wanted to check in and make sure you weren't. With the movie halfway wrapped and everything, it's okay if you want to wait—at all."

I sighed through my nose. "Yeah, My. I don't think I want to try anymore," I said. And he was *so* good—nearly perfect—at hiding the little flutter of disappointment. No one but me would've caught it.

"That's completely okay, Fee," he urged with a kiss. "I wish you would've said something earlier just now, but that's okay, too. I can go to the store—"

"Actually, I already went to the store, My."

He blinked at me in confusion. "You? . . . I'm confused."

"I went to the store yesterday. And I think we need to tell Hazel tomorrow."

"You know that I try to be pretty open, but I don't know that Haze needs to know *everything* about our sex life, and—" He shook his head with a frown. "And I'm still not quite following, Fee."

"I went to the store and got this."

I reached over my head and into my bag, rifling around until I found what I needed. Handed it to him.

He cocked his head, studying the test for a moment.

And even lying on some aged, vaguely musty carpet in the dim October light, I don't think I'd ever seen his eyes shine brighter. I don't know if two friends turned lovers turned family have ever felt so much joy.

We laugh-cried against each other's lips until we heard the crunch of gravel outside. Until I was hustling him back out the window, him stealing kisses even after I shooed him away. I watched that broad back in the moonlight as he strutted off in his underwear, and saw his fist pump the air—his sweats in one hand—in pride.

I SEE THE AWARENESS SKETCH itself in his shoulders now, my dress swishing and rattling against the leaves. He shakes his hands out of his pockets before he anxiously shoves them back in—the gesture making me quicken my steps.

I lament the pro makeup job once more because I'd love nothing more than to press my face into my spot there, but I don't want to smear the maroon suit. I settle for sliding my hand in his and linking our fingers.

By the time he rotates around to face me, his eyes are already misty.

MEYER

"God, Fee." Something freezes my system like stage fright, except it's the exact opposite. It's that I have so much to say, so much I feel that I don't fucking know where to begin. "You really are my angel," I tell her, and I can't even bring myself to be embarrassed at how thick my voice is with emotion.

I've been staring at that goddamn tree for what felt like a century, dying to see her again. After seeing Hazel already an hour ago, I'm glad I had the time in between to gather a shred of my nerves, because Haze is already too grown for me to fathom. And Fee . . . *My Fee.* She takes my breath away more in this moment than she ever has. More than the first time she pushed me up against that tree, more than the first time she told me she loved me, even more than the time she blustered through the doors on the end of a storm and changed my and Hazel's lives forever.

I've always known she was made for autumn colors. The ambers and golds and reds around her sharpen the blush in her complexion, the copper in her hair and eyes.

Her dress is her. Simple ivory lace, the illusion of its having been tattooed onto her skin, hugging her small curves. She kicks a red boot out from the bottom and half-spins around to show me the back, where it's entirely open, only a few delicate buttons above the above the slope of her ass.

"You're—" I shake my head. I don't want to be a cliché and say she's glowing, even though she is. "You're incredible."

"So are you." My heart rolls over with a thud when she splays one palm against her lower belly, her smile so big it nearly forces her eyes shut.

"Dance with me?" I croak, because I only now feel the photographer's presence and need to hold her close, to stay focused on her, and this moment, and keeping her in my arms.

She nods and tucks herself under my chin, taking our laced fingers and pressing them against her, cocooned between us.

"How do you want to tell Haze?" she asks, and goddamn it that alone wriggles the first tear loose. By all accounts, today is her day, our day, and she's never stopped considering Hazel in all of it. She, who bore the brunt of Hazel's first hormonal changes hitting us, she, who was with Hazel when she broke her wrist last year.

I look down at her whiskey eyes. "Like this. Just us." She smiles up at me and nods.

THE CEREMONY CONSISTS OF ABOUT twenty-five of our closest and most treasured people, with Lance acting as officiant. He is hardly able to get through a sentence without bursting into tears—something I'm grateful for, since it ends up bringing some levity to the whole thing and helps Fee and me keep it together.

Our vows are simple.

We promise to love and cherish one another as we always have, to be partners in all things.

Clouds gather and tumble across the sky quickly as we walk to the reception—almost like one of those time-lapse videos. And before our first dance the thunder cracks overhead, the scent in the air changing.

I feel my face practically start to beam, because it couldn't be more perfect.

"Huh," my wife says with a grin. "Looks like rain."

ACKNOWLEDGMENTS

First and foremost, thank *you* for reading.

I'd be remiss not to jump right into it and start thanking everyone else, though. Because, for anyone not aware, the book community is so incredibly special. So many of you are the reason I felt confident enough to write this, and to want to continue. I know I'm supposed to say I'm doing it for me, and in a way that is the case. But you guys were the Meyer to my Fee; your support bolstered me until I found my voice and confidence. The fact that any of you takes even a moment out of your day to rate, review, or create something that cheers on my stories will never cease to amaze me.

Danielle, thank you for taking a chance on me sliding into your DMs in all my overly familiar and extremely casual glory. I'd love to claim professionalism, but self-deprecation and inappropriate content is more my speed, and you went for it. I'll never forget when you replied and told me you'd finished it and loved it. I'll never forget crying in my car in the Target parking lot when I saw that first aesthetic video.

Marisol, thanks for the therapy. What started as just fun

back-and-forth became friendship. I'm incredibly thankful for your support, for how you always remember the links to things when I forget, and for how many times I teased you with mere portions of this story. I promise to never do it again (haha).

Krysten, I still think we were separated at birth. So grateful to you for your constant time and just letting me bounce things off of you occasionally—as in, all day, every day. It's crazy to think that sharing an ACOTAR conversation on the internet turned into friendship. I'm sure there are weirder starts to relationships.

M'Kenzee, Genesis, Hannah, Leah, Krysten, Stephanie, Kelly, Kelly, Allie, Liz, Katie—thank you for beta reading and editing and supporting me even in my disorganized state. Thank you for how much you've already shared this story, promoted it and pumped me up about it. I'll never take for granted how you gave me and my books your time. I know what a precious commodity it is.

Sam, my goodness. You're a magician. Thank you for giving me a cover that is so beautiful it will inevitably lead more people into reading my words. I am amazed by your talent and your ability to translate "vibes" into art.

Ty, Emery, and Aven: thank you for loving me through the crazy. When I cried over imaginary people that lived in my brain and when I lost sleep and chose writing over free time, so often. I love you.

Grandma: if you read this one, too, I love you, but I'm begging you to please lie to me and tell me you didn't. Thank you.

ABOUT THE AUTHOR

Jessica Prangley

TARAH DEWITT is an author, wife, and mama. When she felt like she had devoured every romcom available in 2020, she indulged herself in writing bits and pieces of her own. Eventually, those ramblings from the Notes app turned into her debut novel. Tarah loves stories centered around perfectly imperfect characters, especially those with just enough trauma to keep them funny, without ever being forcefully cavalier. She believes laughter is an essential part of romance, friendship, parenting, and life. She is the author of *Rootbound, The Co-op,* and *Funny Feelings.*